Black Bat Mystery

AIRSHIP 27 PRODUCTIONS

Black Bat Mystery Vol. 1
An Airship 27 Production
Airship27Hangar.com

"Death Rides the Valkyrie" © 2010 Andrew Salmon
"A Deal with the Devil" © 2010 Aaron Smith
"The Beast of the Reich" ©2010 Mark Justice
"Claws of the Crimson Commissar" ©2010 Frank Schildiner

Cover illustration and logo design © 2010 Mark Maddox
Interior llustrations © 2010 Rob Davis
Back Cover Illustration: Rob Davis after Ver Curtiss

Editor: Ron Fortier
Associate Editor: Charles Saunders
Production and design: Rob Davis.

ISBN-13: 978-0692498002 (Airship 27)
ISBN-10: 0692498001

Second Edition 2015

Printed in the United States of America

10 9 8 7 6 5 4 3 2 1

Contents

Death Rides the Valkyrie

A Black Bat Adventure

by
Andrew Salmon

Chapter One

An Urgent Request

The sharp, muted rap on the stateroom door intruded upon the conversation Tony Quinn was having with his valet and confidante, Silk Kirby. Silk raised his tall, slender form up out of the club chair and strode to the door.

In the few seconds it took the man to cross the cramped quarters a strange transformation took place on the face of his employer. Until the knock had sounded, Tony Quinn's deep blue, keen eyes had been alive and vital. Now, swiftly, they changed. When Silk put his hand on the doorknob, Quinn's eyes were suddenly still, fixed and dead, staring straight ahead at nothing. In short, Quinn's eyes had become like those of a blind man.

Silk yanked open the door to reveal the inscrutable countenance of Hugo Vaeth, Captain of the *Valkyrie*.

"Who the devil is it?" Quinn demanded, his gaze seemingly rigid though he saw the airship captain plain as day.

Captain Vaeth, an emaciated-looking, tall man with hawk-like features strode in, his cap under his arm. His rubber-soled shoes squeaked slightly on the floor.

"Please excuse the intrusion, Mr. Quinn." Vaeth went on in clipped Austrian tones. "It is I, Captain Vaeth. I would have a word with you."

"My, my," Quinn grinned, beckoning Vaeth further into the room. "At this hour? Don't you Zeppeliners ever sleep?"

Vaeth frowned. "For this voyage, sleep is a luxury my Masters did not consider."

Quinn laughed easily, his gaze still fixed straight ahead. The two men had gotten to know each other in the ten hours since the airship had departed from Lakehurst, New Jersey on its journey west across the United States.

Deliberately baiting the captain, Quinn said, "Then again, what need have you of sleep? Or is it possible Chancellor Hitler neglected to appoint one of his Aryan supermen to command *Valkyrie*, the greatest technical marvel of the new Reich?"

"Bah!" Vaeth waved a hand dismissively though he was aware Quinn could not see the gesture. "My country is the deck beneath my feet and the metal, linen and gas around us. Hitler and his thugs... The less said about them, the better."

Quinn's acute hearing revealed to him the genuine ire in Vaeth's tone and he did not continue with his joke. "Captain Vaeth," he said, "your company is always appreciated. What can I do for you?"

Silk motioned the captain to the seat he'd been occupying when the knock had sounded. Vaeth lowered his ungainly form into it and regarded Quinn anxiously.

Quinn, for his part, kept his gaze slightly to the left of the man though he noticed the worry pinching his new friend's features.

"I do not have to impress upon you the importance of this tour my *Valkyrie* is making across your United States. There have been great changes back home in the three years since Hitler became Chancellor. Great unrest as well. And danger rises from that unrest. I have spoken out against these changes, mostly to deaf ears. For this reason, I feel a terrible storm is on the horizon and thus I was motivated to undertake this 'good will' tour – as your press so colorfully dubbed it. I do so in the hopes of fostering amity between Germany and your country."

"And we here in the US appreciate the gesture. When I lost my sight, my hearing became rather acute in compensation, but I don't need it to hear the war drums you speak of."

"The cretins ruining the Fatherland wish to use my *Valkyrie* as a symbol of National Socialist superiority. That is nonsense. However, we cannot escape the symbolic nature of our journey and it must proceed without incident. Factions in both our countries wish to sow distrust and fear for their own purposes."

Quinn leaned forward in his seat. "Has something happened to jeopardize this?"

Vaeth nodded.

"Captain?" Quinn prompted. "Has something happened?"

Vaeth recovered quickly. "Yes, forgive me. There has been an incident."

"Does this incident involve one of the dignitaries on board?"

"Yes and no. Allow me to explain. The eyes of the world are on my *Valkyrie*. The half-dozen diplomats and their wives know this and have stuffed the ship's safe with all of their finery."

Quinn saw where this was going. "There has been a theft."

Vaeth nodded again, but added. "Yes. A grievous one which may have harsh consequences on international affairs. The Heart of the Empire has been taken."

A reformed thief, Silk stepped forward at the mention of the heist. "What the deuce is that?"

Quinn replied to his friend's query. "It is a rather large ruby believed to have been originally atop the scepter Charlemagne was buried with. When the body was exhumed for reburial decades later, the scepter went missing. Only the ruby has been passed down to us by time. Christened the Heart of the Empire by Charles I, it is a priceless relic of a unified Europe."

"Hardly seems worth getting out of joint over."

"You do not understand," Vaeth interjected. "The Heart of the Empire is revered throughout Europe. At this time of uncertainty, its importance cannot be underestimated."

"You are correct, Captain," Quinn agreed. "As the ruby is the size of a softball and its value beyond calculation, it's possible the theft was purely for monetary gain. However, the state of affairs you speak of might also be the reason for the crime. Perhaps someone is sending a message."

"Bah! Someone? Rowland Ardai has taken it!"

"Ha!" Silk barked a laugh. "I'd love to see the look on McGrath's pan if that's true!"

"You are certain of this, Captain?"

"No. But who else could have taken it? A master thief like Ardai on my ship! I should never have allowed it."

"Reformed master thief. Or so Lieutenant McGrath and the papers say."

"He is a lifelong criminal. How do you reform such a man?"

Quinn's expression grew thoughtful.

Silk offered one possible explanation. "The press has hinted at some sort of 'crime college' possibly in upstate New York. Rumors. Load of hogwash if you ask me."

"And could such a place exist?" Vaeth demanded.

A slight smile tugged at one corner of Quinn's mouth. "I have my own theories. Which are best left alone for the moment. Have you any evidence of Ardai's guilt – beyond his past, I mean?"

"None. But the ruby was removed from the safe. No one saw or heard anything. Who else but someone practiced at such action could have done it?"

A tense silence grew. Then Quinn spoke, "I appreciate your dilemma, Captain Vaeth, but I don't know what you expect me to do about it. Ardai is in the care of Lieutenant McGrath for this trip – the police department's own good will tour of criminal reform – surely he can assist you in this matter."

"I have just come from seeing him!" Vaeth's manner took on a frosty tone. "He scoffed at the very idea. To him, Rowland Ardai is a symbol of all that is good in law enforcement."

Quinn smiled slyly. "So he sent you to me."

"Yes! How did you know? He told me you were the Black Bat – a costumed adventurer."

Quinn's smile became enigmatic. "McGrath has an overactive imagination."

Vaeth lowered his gaze to the floor. "Then you cannot assist me." He wrung his hands a moment, then smacked them down on his thighs. "If only the Alle-Männer were here!" Seeing the blank look this exclamation drew from Silk, he added. "They are a group of costumed adventurers similar, I suppose, to this Black Bat."

"I have heard of them," Quinn said. "Their name is derived from a Germanic tribe of the Third Century. The name means All-Men in English. They wage war on crime in the streets of Berlin."

Vaeth nodded, impressed that word of the All-Men's adventures had reached the United States. Then storm clouds seemed to form in his eyes. "When word gets out no one will care for the message this trip was meant to convey. Germany will be dubbed a gang of bunglers. The integrity of my crew will be questioned. I cannot allow this to happen."

"Captain Vaeth," Quinn said, his voice firm. "I may be blind but your concerns have not fallen on deaf ears. The presence of myself and my staff on board this airship is no coincidence. In the days leading up to this flight, I learned that Countess Wagenbach would be taking the ruby along on the journey and that McGrath intended to parade Ardai around the country like a prize steer. I booked passage on this flight in order to have my men keep an eye on things whereas I cannot. Therefore we will assist you in any way we can. And we shall do it quietly in the hopes the ruby can be recovered and returned with no one the wiser."

Vaeth's pinched features brightened slightly. "Thank you, Mr. Quinn. If you require anything from myself or my crew, consider both at your disposal."

"Very good. At first light, then?" Quinn offered.

The captain left them. After Silk had locked the door he turned and regarded his friend and employer expectantly.

Quinn's eyes and body seemed to spring to life simultaneously. He got up out of his chair and, with eyes flashing, moved about the room.

"What do you make of it?" Silk asked.

"I think we were right to tag along. It was a long shot that a hardened criminal like Ardai could go straight."

Silk cleared his throat harshly. He'd been a second story man until being caught red-handed by Quinn while trying to rob the man's home. Quinn had talked him out of the disastrous course Silk Kirby's life had taken and the two now fought for justice.

"You, my friend, are an exception," Quinn clarified.

"Should I clear away for the Black Bat?" Silk asked.

"Yes. He is needed," Quinn replied. "McGrath has already set the stage of suspicion thus the Bat will have to be one with the night. Hurry, Silk. There's work to be done!"

Chapter Two

A CALL TO ARMS

The path of justice had taken many turns for Tony Quinn. He began his journey as an up and coming young D.A. hounding crooks to the ends of the earth in the name of the Law. And it was in pursuit of this noble mission that fate dealt him a cruel blow.

While preparing to prosecute an important crime figure, he'd come into possession of certain documents vital to cement the man's guilt before a jury. However, in the midst of the trial, the crime boss's minions attempted to destroy the incriminating documents by hurling powerful acid upon them. Quinn had thrown himself in the path of the corrosive stream and it had struck him in the face. The acid had eaten into his features and he was blinded almost instantly.

Independently wealthy, Quinn had given up his position as D.A. and traveled the world in search of a cure for his blindness. The quest proved fruitless and his fortune useless in recovering that which had been taken from him. Resigned to the idea that he would never see again, Quinn settled into a hermit's existence, a virtual prisoner in his own vast estate. His only human contact was the reformed Silk Kirby.

It was when the future looked as black as the pall before Quinn's sightless eyes that Carol Baldwin appeared. She gained entry into his sanctum of sorrow by way of a strange offer. Her father, a police officer in a small mid-Western town, had fallen victim to a gangster's bullet and lay dying. Having followed Quinn's career as a junior D.A. and knowing his time upon this earth was waning, he wanted Quinn to have his eyes. Quinn, desperate and despondent, accepted the noble gesture and went West where a little known surgeon in Carol's hometown performed the operation, replacing Quinn's dead corneas with Sergeant Baldwin's healthy ones. The procedure was a success and Quinn regained his sight – a fact he kept secret from the rest of the world.

For in the months of his restless solitude he had long ruminated on the red tape that was strangling the legal system, allowing the guilty to stroll from the halls of justice with a contemptuous sneer on their lips.

During these dark moments of thought Quinn came to believe that a free and independent investigator would make more headway in the war on crime.

And thus the Black Bat was born.

Attired in a close-fitting black hood to conceal the deep scars around his eyes which would identify him to any who caught a glimpse of the Black Bat, somber clothing and crepe-soled shoes, the Black Bat began a one man war on crime. His knowledge of the law proved crucial to this pursuit and the abilities of the Black Bat were greatly augmented by certain physical changes he had acquired while sightless.

His sense of touch had become highly acute, his hearing uncanny. And he had retained these abilities even after his sight had been restored. Also the operation itself had produced some unexpected yet astounding results. Tony Quinn could see in total darkness as if it were broad day.

So armed to fight crime, Quinn had returned East in the company of Carol Baldwin and the ever faithful Kirby. Back home they joined with hulking Butch O'Leary and these four were the only ones who knew Tony Quinn could see. And only they knew of his double life as the Black Bat for they joined him in the fight for justice.

There was one more element fate had in store for Tony Quinn. Working in such close proximity to Carol Baldwin had stirred the embers of love in Quinn's heart. Carol felt likewise although neither would ever bring up the subject, knowing that married life was an impossible dream with the peril that came with the vocation the Black Bat had undertaken.

Now while the great airship slept, Tony Quinn began his transformation. Tight hood in place, covering everything but his eyes and crepe-soled shoes on his feet, he pulled on thin nylon gloves with rubber tips for gripping purposes. Two big automatics fit snug under each armpit and he clasped what appeared to be a large money-belt around his trim waist. In reality the belt held a number of tools and gadgets in hidden compartments. He slid a long, bat-ribbed cloak over his shoulders and the transformation was complete. Silk doused the lights and the room was swallowed by darkness.

The Black Bat crept to the door and his keen ears detected no sound from the corridor. An ebony gloved hand seized the door knob, turning it swiftly. As Silk's eyes adjusted to the gloom, he thought he detected a dim figure at the door. He blinked and the Black Bat was gone.

****

In the hallway, the sharp hearing of the Black Bat told him the way was clear and he sidled down the corridor to the stairs leading to B Deck. He was down them in an instant. Low voices coming closer echoed up the passageway. Darting his cowled head this way and that he spied a shadowed alcove and concealed himself there.

The voices came from two crewmen who passed bare inches from where the still form of the Black Bat hid and headed to a door leading deeper inside the vessel.

The Black Bat stepped from his hiding place and dashed up the narrow corridor. Soon he was in the ship's offices, cubicles really, from which the ship's officers could carry out their daily duties. The first one on the left was the Navigation Room. The Bat put his back to it for across from the office, on the right was the Purser's Office in which rested the safe the Heart of the Empire had been taken from.

The office was locked up for the night but the lock yielded in seconds to one of the various lock picks carried in the belt of the Black Bat. Stealthily he made his way inside, easing the door closed behind him. He relocked it.

The Black Bat did not turn on the light. His probing orbs scanned the room as though it were lit by a spotlight, taking in every detail. The safe revealed itself on the floor behind the aluminum desk.

He did not touch it however. Rather he withdrew a vial containing a chemical powder. With the use of the powder he set about obtaining fingerprints left by those who had touched the safe, including the prints of the thief! The stygian darkness was nothing to him as he worked and two sets of fingerprints appeared on the cool metal following his ministrations with the powder. These he lifted with the aid of special tape and the impressions so preserved disappeared into a pouch on his belt.

The Black Bat wiped the powder from the drawer handle and from around the safe. Satisfied, he crouched before the safe and, placing the rubber-tipped fingers of one hand on the dial, set about opening the thing. His ears caught the clicks of the tumblers as if they were thunderclaps. The safe door swung open.

Inside were files, some bundles of German reichmarks and many jewelry cases – an inspection of the latter revealed them to still have their contents. A large, ornately carved onyx box, larger than the other cases, sat on the bottom shelf. He picked it up and could tell by the weight of it that the case was empty. This was the case which had cradled the Heart of the Empire.

Footsteps approached. The Black Bat's uncanny hearing detected them long before they drew close to the office which gave him time to prepare. He returned the case and closed the safe door. Gingerly he spun the dial and straightened. An air duct high on the wall did not escape his notice and he was prepared to scramble into it should the approaching men try the office door.

The steady tread of the men and their relaxed conversation were all the indicators he needed that they suspected nothing. Sure enough they walked past the office without pause.

The Black Bat was free to take his leave.

The vent held his attention, though. He popped the screen loose and placed it on the desk. The shaft would be a close fit but it was manageable, leaving him free to return to his quarters totally unobserved. For the Black Bat had not forgotten that McGrath was aboard and if the Bat was spotted amongst so few passengers, McGrath would cast the light of suspicion on Tony Quinn.

Smooth as a gymnast, the Black Bat jumped and seized a pipe jutting from the wall in front of the vent. His sinewy arms hauled him up. He bent his knees and kicked up into the vent. Turning onto his stomach in the narrow confines, he reached down, took up the grill and replaced it.

Next began the painstaking process of inching through the vent back to his room. His progress was aided by the rubber gloves and soles which provided excellent purchase. The Black Bat snaked his way through the belly of the ship as silent as the grave.

Fifteen minutes later, Silk gave a slight start when a sudden knocking sounded from the vent grill in Quinn's room where the faithful servant awaited his master's return. Long accustomed to such nocturnal occurrences, Silk quickly recovered, removed the grill and helped the Black Bat descend from the vent.

While Silk replaced the grill, the Black Bat whipped the cowl off his head and strode to one of his suitcases. From this he extracted the court file on Rowland Ardai he'd packed for the trip and opened it to the last arrest report filed against the career thief. Withdrawing the sets of prints and scrutinizing them, he instantly identified those belonging to the Purser and set them aside. The next set, belonging, he was certain, to the thief who had taken the precious ruby he compared to the set of prints taken when Ardai was arrested. He compared the two and his suspicions were confirmed.

Silk rejoined his master who was shedding the costume of the Black Bat. "How did it go, sir?"

"We've made some headway on the matter," was all Tony Quinn would say. "There is much to do tomorrow. Let's turn in."

Silk headed to Quinn's bed to turn down the top sheet. He caught sight of the file with the print strips lying on top. Quinn was busy removing the garb of the Black Bat and did not see his servant seize up the file and compare the prints. The reformed thief studied the prints, holding them up to the feeble light.

"They are an exact match!" he exclaimed. He waved the fresh set. "Were these taken from the ship's safe."

Tony Quinn nodded.

"That clinches it, then. I knew it all along. Ardai stole the ruby!"

Chapter Three

THWARTED AT EVERY TURN

She may have been designated LZ-128 by her designers at the Zeppelin Works in Friedrichshafen, but she had been christened *Valkyrie* and the name was well suited to the majestic craft. Eight hundred and fifteen feet long and one hundred and thirty feet wide, she glided through the air like a great leviathan from the depths. The morning sun glinted from her silver hull, turning the ship into an eye-dazzling sight as *Valkyrie* continued her journey across the United States. The steady drone of her four 2,500 horsepower engines set the pace.

As Tony Quinn and Silk Kirby washed and dressed, Silk seemed anxious and pre-occupied. Quinn, guessing the reason, addressed his servant. "You must not say a word to anyone about Ardai's guilt or innocence."

"Innocence!" Silk bellowed. "We've got him dead to rights."

"Regardless, I want your personal word that you won't say anything to anyone."

Dumbfounded, Silk could only stand and stare at his master. But he trusted Quinn implicitly and gave his vow of silence concerning the breakthrough the Black Bat had made in the case.

The matter settled for the moment, Quinn and Silk proceeded to the Dining Room for a quick breakfast before getting an update on Ardai's night time activities from Butch O'Leary.

Their meal finished, the duo proceeded to the Smoking Room. As they had risen early, the Smoker was all but deserted. They found O'Leary sipping coffee at a corner table. Carol Baldwin was with him.

"What have you to report?" Quinn asked.

"Nothing. I told the both of you this was a waste of time. To think what I gave up to float around in this balloon!"

Silk shook his head. "Tickets to a ballgame are not worth squawking about."

"That's what you say. Only the Knights were in town and they've got a hitter name a Hobbs you gotta see to believe!"

"Baseball can wait, gentlemen," Quinn interrupted. He leaned in close to O'Leary and whispered. "A job was pulled last night. And Ardai is the most likely suspect."

"That's nonsense, Tony," Carol chastised.

Silk snorted but, sticking to his word, added nothing further.

"What!" O'Leary reared back. He slapped one broad palm down on the table so hard his cup rattled and upended. This drew the attention of what few smokers were present. Seeing the unwanted attention he'd garnered, O'Leary leaned forward and whispered hoarsely. "No way, Boss. He was never outta my sight. He ain't your pigeon."

Quinn settled in his seat, crossed his legs and then his hands over one thigh. "Why don't you fill us in."

O'Leary tugged at an ear. "It's like I said. Nothing happened all night. Ardai played a few hands with McGrath and them others. I sat in on a few until McGrath's line of talk about you being the Black Bat and how he'd prove it one day soured me on the game and I had a brandy and jawed with some of the crew and passengers who speak English. But I never took my eyes off Ardai."

Quinn's visage grew thoughtful. "Ardai played all night?" His tone was light, conversational, but O'Leary knew the man well enough to know there was burning curiosity behind the words.

"He went to the gents a time or two but that's it, I tell ya. He was never gone more than a couple of minutes. He turned in before midnight and I've got the cabin alongside his so I did likewise. I heard him moving around in there, then it was all quiet. I stayed up half the night, dozing, with my ear pressed to the wall and jumping at every creak this windbag made and didn't catch a peep out of the guy."

"What was stolen?" Carol asked.

"Countess Wagenbach's ruby. It is more than a priceless gem. Both historical and symbolic qualities have been attached to it. It must be found."

"How should we go about it?" Silk chided.

Before Quinn could respond, a loud booming voice sounded in their ears. The thump of a meaty paw on Quinn's shoulder announced the arrival of McGrath.

"Well, Quinn," the policeman began, good-naturedly, "how is the Black Bat this morning?"

Quinn, his eyes fixed dead ahead replied, "I wouldn't know. Have you seen him on board?"

"I'm looking right at him."

"You are mistaken."

"Am I?" McGrath lit a cigar from the electrical lighter provided for that purpose – all matches and lighters had to be surrendered by passengers when they boarded – puffed it hungrily until the tip flared. Suddenly he flicked the ashes directly at Quinn. They struck the lapel of Quinn's sport coat. Quinn did not react to this trick – typical of McGrath's efforts to catch Quinn unawares and trip him up.

"Oh, how clumsy of me," McGrath deadpanned.

"Throwing hot ash around is not the best thing to do on an airship, McGrath," Silk cautioned. "Chief, you've got ash on your lapel."

Quinn raised his right hand and deliberately brushed at his left lapel though the ash was on the opposite side.

Silk, catching the performance, added, "The right lapel, sir."

Quinn switched hands and swiped the ash from his clothes. He inclined

"Throwing hot ash around is not the best thing to do on an airship, McGrath," Silk cautioned.

his head towards McGrath. "I must agree with Silk. One shouldn't play with fire."

McGrath waved a hand dismissively. "Ah! Your act wouldn't cut it in Vaudeville!" He grinned like a cobra. "Besides we won't have need for clowns like the Black Bat much longer. Ardai is proof positive of that!"

"You sound certain," Quinn observed.

"You bet your bottom dollar. Our penal system can reform crumbs like Ardai. And he's just the beginning."

"The Captain appears to have some doubts."

McGrath moved in close to Quinn and hissed, "Trying to pin the theft on Ardai! Drop it! The Captain came to me with that line of bull and I shined him on. It's one of his crew with sticky fingers, if you ask me."

"Hey, McGrath" O'Leary announced. "Here comes your boy now."

All heads at the table turned to the door of the Smoker. Framed by the portal was Rowland Ardai. Of medium height with a spindly, slightly stooped frame, Ardai presented a most unassuming figure. Years of incarceration on the heels of a life hard lived seemed to have withered the man until he looked like a stiff breeze might blow him over. His large eyes darted this way and that and his haggard features were set in a permanent frown. His spidery hands spasmed with tremors.

McGrath extended a hand and beckoned the man to the table. "Park it right here, Ardai. Don't let these doubting Thomases throw you."

The ex-con jerked at the Lieutenant's loud tones but did as he was bade, shuffling to the table. "Good morning, Lieutenant," he uttered in a reedy voice. Ardai perched on the edge of a club chair as if poised to scurry at the first provocation.

"Good morning, Rowland," Quinn said, warmly. "I trust you slept soundly."

"That's sure, Mr. Quinn," Ardai replied tentatively yet with some gratitude. "The bed was like sleeping on a cloud after what I'm used to."

"Well, get used to it," McGrath said. "You've turned over a new leaf. The world's your oyster these days."

"I-I sure hope so," Ardai said, wringing his hands and staring down at the table. "Look, I know I done some bad things. I broke the law – I didn't give a fig for it! But I'm a changed man. I truly am. And I would no more return to that old life than I would sock you in the eye right now."

After a few minutes of general conversation, the group deposited their cigarette and cigar butts in the automatic clamshell-like ashtrays, which smothered the smoldering tips, rose out of their chairs and headed for the exit. There they were stopped by the room steward in a sentry-like box with adjoining doors that served not only as an airlock to the sealed smoking room but also as a bar. The smoking room was kept at slightly higher atmospheric pressure than the rest of the ship to prevent explosive hydrogen from leaking in. Once the steward was certain the passengers were smoke free, he pressed a button to open the door which gave access to the rest of the ship.

Quinn loitered about for a moment as Silk took O'Leary aside and whispered the directives their master had imparted before breakfast. O'Leary nodded and moved off with McGrath and Ardai. Silk rejoined Quinn and, taking him gently by the elbow, began leading him up the passageway en route to the control gondola.

"I did like you said," Kirby hissed at Quinn. "O'Leary's gonna keep an eye on Ardai as well as see what he can learn from the other passengers. On the quiet, mind you. We're gonna be over Chicago in an hour and things are going to start happening."

Quinn said. "We must see the Captain at once."

The two men took the starboard promenade. As they made their way forward they passed a handful of other passengers securing the best vantage points before the downward slanting windows so as to ensure the breathtaking spectacle of the Windy City sprawled beneath their gaze. There was much excitement in the air and the ship fairly hummed with anticipation.

Quinn, under the guise of being guided by Silk, threaded their way to the staircase leading down to B Deck which arched gracefully upwards along the keel of the great ship to the control gondola. At the base of the stairs stood one of the crew stationed to bar entry to any unauthorized personnel seeking to reach the control gondola. Seeing as Quinn was known aboard as being a friend to Captain Vaeth, the DA was granted entry and Silk helped him along with a quick nod of thanks to the stalwart crewman.

Upon reaching the control gondola they learned from the Watch Officer that Captain Vaeth was in his quarters, preparing letters before the ship reached Chicago.

The hull of the ship angled more steeply upwards as Quinn and Kirby moved past the control gondola to the Captain's cabin which lay roughly midway between the gondola and the nose of the ship.

Vaeth greeted them perfunctorily as he was pre-occupied with the papers on his desk. "Come in. Come in, gentlemen," he said. "This favorable wind will have us over Chicago earlier than predicted should the weather hold, and these dispatches will not wait." He secured a bundle of letters with a rubber band and added them to the pile by his elbow. "What can I do for you?"

Quinn got right to the point. "Has any headway been made?"

Vaeth's face fell. "None."

"I gather the airship will be dropping mail before we touch down," Quinn went on. "This is an ideal opportunity for the guilty party to rid themselves of the gem by concealing it in an outgoing parcel."

Vaeth managed a weak smile. "We think alike, Quinn. I've issued orders for all mail sacks to be inspected before they leave the ship. Every parcel opened and regulations regarding mail be damned! There is simply too much at stake!" He sighed. "I'm afraid our situation is about to become unmanageable should the search not turn up the ruby. We will be taking on passengers at Municipal Airport, including representatives from the German American Bund. Were it up to me, they would not set foot on my *Valkyrie*. The last thing this ship needs are more fools hypnotized by Adolf Hitler. Plus there have been threats against this ship out of Chicago! These concerns and the crowded conditions will make a discreet search all but impossible."

"Is he a good man, the officer supervising the search?" Quinn asked.

"Kessel is a devout believer in National Socialism. That is a mark against him. However I will say that, despite his political leanings, he is an exceptional officer. Combined with his unwavering belief in the Chancellor, I believe he would rather chop off his right arm than jeopardize the flight. If the gem is in those mail sacks, he will find it."

"Let us hope that he does," Quinn emphasized.

Chapter Four

PERILOUS LANDING

The city of Chicago sprawled beneath *Valkyrie*, majestic stone spires stabbing through the gloom. For despite Captain Vaeth's hopes, the weather had taken a turn for the worse and *Valkyrie* glided through the clouds in shrouds of fog. A light drizzle began as the ship reached the outskirts of the city and Vaeth was tempted to forgo the ceremonial flight over the city in favor of an attempt at a quick touch down at Municipal

Airport before the rain worsened. However Vaeth had strict orders not to miss an opportunity to parade the great ship before the masses. Thus he reluctantly ordered half-speed and spat 'up elevator' at the elevatorman who spun the wheel as the ship began her descent.

The swastika emblazoned on the port side tailfin, and the new government it represented in Germany, had dampened the world's enthusiasm for zeppelins and the promise of a golden age of air travel. Cries of 'see the famous fin!' and 'watch the zep come in!' had sounded in the heyday of *Graf Zeppelin's* journeys around the world just a few short years ago but now Vaeth could not help but wonder if those days were lost forever.

As the long cigar-shaped craft stretched out above the city, her motors droning, Vaeth could not hear the cheers ringing up from the street below. Then the clouds parted and a smile stretched the old aeronaut's hard lips. Crowds clustered on rooftops and on the street below all waved and cheered the passage of the great ship. Traffic halted as drivers leaned out windows and craned their necks. Others climbed atop the mired trolley cars for a better view.

Vaeth, caught up in the moment, ordered the ship lower – a dangerous maneuver in the rain but the airship was answering rudders and elevators and the 6-8 tons of water the ship was soaking in through the cotton outer skin was a load easily borne by the churning motors.

Valkyrie descended for all to see and Vaeth took pride in the reaction of the people below. And there was mutual admiration as well for the great city of Chicago for its impressive architecture was a marvel in itself and for a moment Vaeth forgot about thefts, propaganda, and the threat of war on the horizon.

The rain grew heavier, jeopardizing the landing they had to make and Vaeth was left no alternative but to order *Valkyrie* to the airport.

By the time the zeppelin reached Municipal Airport, the rain was a downpour thus, instead of landing, the airship spent four chilly hours hovering. It was six degrees above zero on the ground where 30,000 spectators crowded the airfield, faces turned up to the rain, watching the great ship slide and drift in the storm. A ground crew of 250 soldiers from Camp Whistler wearing white identification arm bands with '*Valkyrie 36*' stood ready to haul the ship to the ground. Khaki-clad National Guardsmen patrolled the fences while Cavalry units held back the crowd stamping their feet in the cold.

Security was an issue stemming from anti-Nazi sentiment and the threats against the airship Vaeth had mentioned to Quinn. In addition to this was the highly explosive hydrogen filling *Valkyrie's* gas cells as well as the equally volatile gaseous mixture, Blaugas, which kept her motors running. A strict no smoking policy was in place for the ground crew which chewed gum instead as they shivered in the rain.

The delay provided Tony Quinn and his aides time to compare notes on the crew and passengers aboard the zeppelin. Silk, secretly motivated by a personal conviction that Ardai was guilty of stealing the Heart of the Empire, volunteered to keep an eye on the ex-con while the others huddled together in a quiet corner of the lounge. The other passengers lingered at their prime viewing spots at the windows, loath to abandon them before landing.

"There ain't much to go on, Boss," O'Leary began. "That's the bottom line. We're in the midst of a handful of stuffed shirts who could buy baubles like that ruby without batting an eye. Ardai must be our man."

"Oh, Butch, I don't believe that for a second," Carol countered with some emotion. "Maybe there was a time he could have done it but now he's no more capable of such a thing as you or I."

Although staring straight ahead with the fixed expression of a blind man, Quinn watched the exchange, then added. "Leaving aside Ardai for the moment and presuming the innocence of the upper crust on board, we must turn our attention to the crew. They are the only remaining suspects if we eliminate the passengers."

"It's Ardai I tell ya," O'Leary blurted. "Though I'll be damned if I know how he pulled it off with me around his neck the whole night."

Quinn paused. "Have either of you noticed any of the crew behaving in a suspicious manner?"

"You mean aside from being blasted Nazis?"

Carol's face brightened at any hypothesis absolving Ardai being put forth. "Do you really think a crewmember stole the ruby?"

"It's the only alternative. How about it?"

Carol's face fell and she cast her eyes to the carpet. "It's like Butch says, the crew seems devoted to rubbing our noses in German ingenuity and that's about all."

"Butch?"

"There are some Nazi hardliners amongst the crew. But thieves... "

Quinn's frustration showed. "As far as the passengers go, none of them would have the expertise to pull the job."

"Ah, we're going in circles!" O'Leary grumbled. "It's Ardai. I've got nothing against the guy but that's how I see it."

"Oh, Tony," Carol groaned. "What are we going to do?"

Quinn lowered his voice to a whisper. "The Captain has Kessel checking the mail bags for the jewel. Perhaps he has discovered it." He rose up out of his seat. "Butch, keep an eye on things here. Carol, we need to get to the gondola."

Quinn and Carol were permitted to enter the control gondola where they found Captain Vaeth staring out the wrap-around, girder-studded windows, while grumbling at Kessel.

"Captain?" Quinn prompted.

Vaeth turned and regarded them. "Up elevator," he barked over his shoulder at the elevatorman. He glared at Quinn and shook his head slightly. "Kessel found nothing."

Kessel stared at them for a moment then returned to his duties.

A gust of wind tilted the ship sharply and Quinn and Carol had to grab the nearest girders for support until the ship settled back on an even keel.

"We are descending to Municipal Airport at last," Vaeth said for Quinn's benefit and without much enthusiasm because his statement announced their failure to solve the crime before matters worsened on board with the arrival of more passengers. "The weather is not ideal for our approach but it is safe enough for us to make the attempt. We should be on the ground in a few minutes."

Valkyrie descended through the heavy cloud cover over the airfield. Through the obscuring clouds the airfield suddenly appeared beneath them. The zeppelin headed downwind toward the airport, motors turning. A sea of upturned faces composed of spectators, and ground crew endured the diminishing precipitation as they gazed at the great ship circling the airdock apron clockwise.

"Shall I correct course?" Kessel asked.

"Keep her steady."

"Sir?"

"Keep her steady, I say! It is on my *Valkyrie* only because German law demands it."

Carol looked at both men, at a loss to fathom what had sparked the display. Quinn smiled inwardly. The Captain was deliberately approaching so as to not show the port side with the Nazi emblem painted on the tail fin. This bothered Kessel and his devotion to Nazi superiority.

Although the storm was weakening, the heavy cloud cover created a false twilight. The poor visibility had prompted hundreds of spectators, who had parked near the field, to turn on their automobile headlights to light the landing site. At first sight of the ship, car horns cut lose an ear-splitting racket and the thousands of spectators cheered lustily. *Valkyrie* now filled the sky over the airfield.

The 170-ton, wire-braced mooring mast, to which the ship would be fastened, was moved into position from the hangar. The wind slackened to almost nothing and *Valkyrie* sailed in. Captain Vaeth leaned out of the gondola window as he gently nosed the ship downward, guiding it towards the mooring mast. The motors roared smoothly and guide ropes were thrown out and seized by the anxious hands of the ground crew who pulled mightily upon them. In minutes the job of securing the nose of the ship to the mast was completed. Normally the task of hauling the ship inside the hangar would be the next step in the operation but it had been decided that *Valkyrie* would not linger in Illinois due to the threats against her. The zeppelin would drop off mail, pick up passengers and fuel, then be on her way.

Thus while the motors of the mooring mast chugged away, the gathered passengers stepped out into the gloomy air to await boarding. The ship was bathed in spotlights now and the roar of the crowd all but drowned out the steady thrum of the engines as they were powered down. When the ship finally came to a stop, a military guard deployed around the ship and the U.S. Customs Representative mounted the steps and boarded in order to examine the ship's papers.

"With the Captain's permission I shall see to the new passengers," Kessel growled.

Vaeth granted the request and Kessel exited hurriedly.

Flashbulbs erupted all around the gondola as the reporters fought to capture the boarding of the dignitaries once the Customs Agent had finished his work.

"The window," Quinn whispered, urging Carol's arm forward.

Carol guided them to the window overlooking the stairs and gazed out.

Quinn wanted very much to be able to watch the passengers boarding but of course could not betray his secret. Or maybe there was a way...

"Captain, do these windows open?" he asked.

"Of course."

"I wonder if Miss Baldwin might open one. I could do with a little fresh air."

"Certainly."

Carol cranked open one of the windows and Quinn leaned out and made a show of taking deep gulps of the chilly air. From his vantage point he observed Kessel shaking the hand of a tall, blonde-haired man in a uniform not unlike the ones Nazis currently sported all over Germany. *Ah, the German American Bund representative*, he mused. This man was a paragon of the Nazi ideal, which contrasted greatly with the tall, thin man at his back, standing to one side. The thinner man had two valises at his feet. The group was too far away for a normal pair of ears to detect what they said, but for Quinn he could eavesdrop easily and translation was not a problem for him as he spoke fluent German.

"Herr Faust, a pleasure," Kessel was saying, bowing slightly as he shook the man's hand. "It is a great honor that you chose to grace *Valkyrie* with your presence."

Konrad Faust smiled and pumped Kessel's hand once, then released it. "I would not miss it for the world. What a marvel! We here, I'm sorry to say, could never create such a wonder. But that could change, if we would only follow the exemplary example of the Fatherland."

Kessel and Faust disappeared up the ladder, the man behind picked up the bags and was lost from view.

For reasons known only to Quinn, he wanted to leave the gondola. He indicated this to Carol with further pressure on her dainty elbow. They paid their respects to Captain Vaeth and moved to the exit. Here they met Kessel and the man he'd been speaking with outside. Carol had to guide Quinn back so the men could enter.

Captain Vaeth came forward and introduced himself without much enthusiasm. For the sake of decorum and not from any personal motivation, Kessel introduced Tony Quinn and Carol Baldwin to the leader of the German American Bund who kissed Carol's hand and, thinking Quinn could not see him, grimaced at the scars around the D.A.'s eyes as he feigned a pleasant greeting.

Faust turned and introduced the man at his heels. "Mein offiziersbursche Ritter," he said, then smiled like a crocodile. "Forgive me, what is the word in English? Ah, my batman. Karl Ritter."

Quinn nodded in the general direction of the batman who made no move or uttered no sound in response to the introduction. Whereas Faust possessed the chiseled good looks and proportions of a matinee idol, Ritter was darker, with deep set green eyes and a hard slash of a mouth and his frame seemed hung haphazardly with lean muscle.

"It is fortuitous that I should meet you upon boarding, *blinder*," Faust said to Quinn. "For truly the United States and the rest of the world are blind to the might and ingenuity of the Fatherland and our glorious leader, Adolf Hitler."

Quinn kept his voice level. "If such are your true feelings, it's strange you should choose to live in the US rather than join your comrades in Germany."

Faust chuckled without mirth. "Oh, there is much work to be done here, *blinder. Valkyrie* is but the beginning. Soon the whole world shall be convinced of our superiority. My task is to educate the ignorant that a new order is upon us. Although I'm afraid such lessons will ultimately have to be taught on the battlefield."

"You speak of war," Quinn hissed.

"Should it come to that, you would have only yourselves to blame." Faust bowed slightly to Carol and, not acknowledging Captain Vaeth, took his leave with Ritter and Kessel at his heels.

Chapter Five

TRAGEDY BEFALLS VALKYRIE

The next two days were ones of anxious waiting for Tony Quinn and his associates. There were certain errands for which the Black Bat was needed but he dared not show himself until the routine aboard the airship had been re-established.

During this time, as *Valkyrie* once more cleaved gracefully through the sky under blazing sunshine, the new passengers insisted on inspecting the ship – the result of which was a tremendous amount of coming and going at all times of the day and night as the crew showed off the airship or passengers took it upon themselves to poke and prod every corner. Added to this somewhat chaotic action was McGrath, who felt compelled to show Ardai off to the new arrivals, sparking loud debate over convict reform. This fought for dominance over the endless cant Faust, always accompanied by his batman Ritter, spewed out about the greatness of Germany and how the Fatherland should, by right, rule the globe.

Quinn and crew were not idle during this settling in period however. He had instructed O'Leary to mingle with the crew, a suggestion the big bruiser gladly embraced because it got him away from the 'snobby muckety-mucks' as he put it. Carol, still consumed by worry over the plight of Ardai, was asked to see what she could glean from the female contingent of passengers. What these two hoped to learn, they had no indication from Quinn but they followed their instructions and had nothing new to report that first night when they gathered in Quinn's suite except the boasting of Countess Wagenbach who promised to display the Heart of the Empire once they reached Los Angeles.

Quinn and Silk took up station in the Lounge where the special D.A. hoped to put his sharp ears to the test and overhear intimate conversations that might shed some light on the matter. Kirby bristled at this inactivity. He squirmed in his seat and was half convinced his master had lost his mind.

It was in the wee hours of the second night that tragedy struck.

While the passengers slumbered and the night crew was at their stations, Carol Baldwin, unable to sleep, crept from her room to the Lounge and found a shadowed corner from which to sit and brood over poor, misjudged Ardai. As she sat woolgathering, the sound of someone entering the portside Promenade reached her.

It was Rowland Ardai.

The ex-con seemed in some distress and Carol's heart broke for the poor man she knew was innocent. Watching him approach the nearest observation window, something about Ardai struck her as queer. He moved as if drunk, head lolling, feet shuffling along and he held himself at an odd angle.

Then the slanted window before him shattered!

Carol put her fist to her mouth to stifle a scream.

What followed next dropped her in a dead faint.

Ardai thrust his upper body awkwardly through the open maw of the window. His feet left the ground. He tumbled disjointedly out into the night air high above the earth and was lost from view.

When Carol came to, she thought at first it had only been a nightmare, but the rush of icy night air through the shattered window revived her fully and the true horror of what she'd witnessed took possession of her.

With a shrill cry she bolted from the Lounge to Quinn's cabin where she pounded on the door.

Silk flung open the door and Carol fell into his arms, sobbing.

"What is it, Carol?!" Quinn called from inside the room. "What has happened?"

"R-R-Rowland just committed suicide!" she managed, then collapsed.

****

The next morning the broken window was discovered and caused a tremendous stir. Quinn reported the death of Rowland Ardai to the Captain who ordered an immediate investigation. Once news of Ardai's disappearance and, eventually, his fate, reached the other passengers, everyone clamored for answers.

Captain Vaeth addressed the passengers after an investigation had turned up a suicide note confessing his guilt, but not the gem. He told them that Ardai had taken his own life and that they had nothing to fear. He asked for a moment of silence for the lost man, then informed them that, since *Valkyrie* was over the Rocky Mountains at present, the airship would complete the journey to Los Angeles as there were no closer facilities capable of handling an emergency landing.

The passengers settled into an uneasy, anxious mood except for Faust who, of course, had to emphasize the overall weak character of the average American who cracked at the first sign of stress. Had Faust not been speaking to a mostly German audience, he might likely have been tossed out the same window Ardai had plunged through. Quinn took steps to make sure O'Leary was with the crew during Faust's pontificating. McGrath, meanwhile, seethed with silent humiliation after all his bold claims concerning Ardai.

"Well I guess that's that, sir," Silk concluded back in Quinn's suite. "Ardai took the ruby and couldn't live with what he'd done. I know the type."

"Ardai was innocent," Quinn said, simply.

"What?" Kirby replied, caught up in the implications of the sad turn of events. Then Quinn's statement registered. "Innocent? His prints matched those you lifted from the safe!"

"It is precisely because the prints match that he was innocent."

"That's crazy!"

"Silk, listen. We've been getting an earful of McGrath's crowing about prisoner reform ever since the papers got wind weeks ago that Ardai would be on this flight. It's all hogwash. The crime college rumors are true and Rowland Ardai was rehabilitated there. I happen to know that, during the process, patients are given new fingerprints to go with their new lives. If Ardai had stolen the ruby, the prints I obtained from the safe would not have matched his old ones on file."

Silk paused to consider this. "They were planted?"

"Exactly."

"By who?"

"That is the question which probes at the heart of the matter. The jewel was stolen by a member of the crew. I'm certain of that. But this is a German ship which came to this country directly from Europe. Thus the prints had to have been delivered to the guilty party by conspirators here in the US since Ardai was in custody prior to the ship's arrival. You'll recall she was several days at Lakehurst while preparations were being made for the voyage."

"You suspect Bund involvement?"

"Definitely. The German American Bund boasts tens of thousands of members all across the United States, drawn from all walks of life. I do not put obtaining Ardai's fingerprints beyond their abilities. They must have slipped them to a crewmember in New Jersey."

"It tracks. But then why did Ardai confess and kill himself?"

"I don't know."

Silk shook his head. "And which members of the crew are in league with the Bund?"

"This is what the Black Bat will determine… tonight!"

Chapter Six

UNSEEN TERROR

As darkness shrouded the narrow passageways of *Valkyrie*, and an uneasy quiet reigned aboard, Tony Quinn once again became the Black Bat. Forsaking the narrow hallway outside for the stealthy solitude of the air duct, he quit his suite and began snaking his way through the ship. He set his sights on the crew quarters.

Moving silently, the Black Bat soon arrived at the crew's quarters aft of the passenger area. He listened at the grate, heard rhythmic breathing, and eased into the room. Men slumbered and snored around him as he gingerly began his search of their belongings. Danger surrounded him as the men tossed, turned and snorted in their sleep. As both crew and passengers were only permitted 44 pounds of baggage each, searching the meager possessions of the crew took only minutes and did not reveal the gem.

Undismayed, he proceeded to the officers' quarters and continued the search in complete silence. In the baggage of elevator man Johann Lodel he uncovered a brass letter opener which bore a handled etched with the

Men slumbered and snored around him as he gingerly began his search of their belongings.

cube-like swastika jutting from the letters AV – the symbol of the German American Bund! He replaced the letter opener and eased the bag closed while the man slept inches away.

The Black Bat was poised to exit when a distant noise reached his sensitive ears. Hurrying silently, he crept to the door and opened it a crack.

Peering down the dark passageway, he spied a door at the far end. This gave on the vast interior of the zeppelin which was bisected by the axial walk – a triangular catwalk running the length of the ship. The sound, too low and distant for normal ears to register, issued from somewhere along the catwalk.

The Black Bat paused a moment to catalog the noises around him lest someone be approaching or stirring in their bunk. He assured himself the way was clear then glided out into the hallway, moving panther-like down it to the far door.

The door was ajar.

Trusting to the darkness, he passed through the doorway and merged with one of the angled girders that made up one side of the triangular walk. Cautiously, he gazed past the girder and up the corridor.

He could hear the noise quite distinctly now yet could see nothing. That was unusual and he moved towards the sound. The noise grew louder. Experience told him that he should be able to see the source of the noise but still he perceived nothing.

At over 800 feet in length and packed with 17 gas bags, 34 cargo areas, offices, fuel and oil tanks, ballast tanks, ladders to the outboard engine gondolas and access ways to the sides of the hull, there were literally hundreds of places in which one might conceal oneself. However the noise he heard, a sound like canvas on canvas, was being made by someone unaware they were not alone and thus had no reason to seek concealment.

The Black Bat eased closer. He identified the sound now: mail sacks being handled and wondered if his and Captain Vaeth's suspicions had proved correct. Was the thief attempting to get the Heart of the Empire off the ship by concealing it in the mail?

His first impulse was to leap upon the man and seize him. But there was still the matter of guiltless Ardai's sudden suicide and the reason the ex-con was being set up to take the fall for the crime to be fathomed first. *Valkyrie* would land tomorrow morning in Los Angeles, then all chance of getting at the truth would be lost. For the time being, the gem would be safe amidst the mail. If he could follow whoever had hidden it, he might learn something vital.

And so the Black Bat scaled up an access ladder into a pool of shadow and awaited the passage of the thief as there was only one way back to the populated section of the airship and it lay between his feet.

The sound up ahead ceased.

The Black Bat fixed his piercing gaze on the catwalk below him.

Footsteps rang softly on the metal, drawing closer.

The Black Bat tensed.

Then the footsteps receded behind him, fading fast.

The Black Bat had seen no one pass!

Perplexed, he slid down the ladder and gave chase. His quarry had stridden beneath him no more than fifteen feet from his hiding place and had done so undetected. This was impossible. The Black Bat sidled up the walkway on his rubber-soled shoes. Distant footfalls spurred him on.

Rushing, he was at the door in seconds. He peeked cautiously around the metal edge and saw a cloaked figure pass through the door to the passenger area. The Black Bat moved in, gaining ground with quick, silent strides. At the door to the suites, he paused, tilted his head so that one eye could gaze past the door up the hallway. The tall figure stood in the hallway, his back to the Black Bat.

The figure spoke – a whispered phrase in German: '*Ich rufe dunkel*.'

The Black Bat pulled back behind the door in case the phrase had been directed at someone facing the cloaked figure and might see the open door over the shoulder of the mysterious form.

Profound silence filled the hallway.

The Black Bat hazarded a glance up the hallway. It was empty.

Had he been a believer in spirits, the Black Bat would have been convinced that he'd been following a ghost for a man simply could not vanish into thin air. There had been no hurried footsteps, no sound of a door opening and closing. Just that whispered phrase, then silence.

Convinced the hallway was deserted, the Black Bat concluded that his foe must have somehow made it to the connecting door to the Promenade and rushed to catch up.

So fixated was he on the way ahead that he failed to register the faintest whisper of cloth behind him until it was too late. He caught a whispered phrase: *Es werde Licht!* Reacting with instincts honed in battle, the Black Bat attempted to fling himself to one side and avoid the blow he sensed was falling. But the flat, hard edge of a hand like granite rammed against his collar bone where his head and neck joined. Searing pain exploded in his brain.

The Black Bat collapsed, but strong hands kept the body from hitting the floor. The cloaked figure hoisted the Black Bat onto his shoulder and stepped gingerly onto the Promenade. Moving as though unburdened, the figure carried his prey to the very window from which Ardai had taken his fatal plunge. The glass had been replaced but the epoxy had not had time to set fully. Reaching out a gloved hand, the figure pushed the glass from the frame and cold air rushed in around him.

The figure shifted the unmoving form he carried and unceremoniously tossed the inert form of the Black Bat through the window and down to the frosted, jagged mountain peaks hundreds of feet below!

Chapter Seven

FALLING INTO PLACE

The morning dawned with great expectation amongst the passengers for their journey would be coming to an end. However that anticipation soon turned to fear when word of the window, broken out a second time, reached them.

It was O'Leary who had discovered the broken window. An early riser, he had come to watch the sunrise. Instead he had stopped dead in his tracks at sight of the window and the wind rushing across the Promenade. Upon further inspection he'd discovered a small section of the Black Bat's cape snared on a jagged shard of glass still in the frame. He'd hurriedly shoved the fragment into his pocket and rushed to find Silk who quickly confirmed that the Black Bat had gone out hours before but had failed to return.

Not wanting to alarm Carol over what they both silently hoped was nothing, they kept this news from her. O'Leary reported the window to a crewmember but omitted finding the scrap of cape.

At breakfast, Carol immediately noticed the absence of Tony Quinn as did McGrath who brooded alone two tables over. Silk and O'Leary dodged the matter as best they could, offering vague reasons but Carol grew suspicious.

"Where's Tony?" she insisted at last. "Tell me. Has something happen-ed?"

Silk and O'Leary exchanged glances and the big man reached into his pocket for the scrap of cape. Silk put his hand on Carol's arm and was about to speak.

"Why nothing has happened," Tony Quinn said, strolling into the Dining Room, his cane tapping out a route to their table.

Carol leapt to her feet and rushed to his side. "Oh, Tony! I was wor-ried."

"Whatever for? I'm fine. Let's eat."

She guided him to the empty chair at their table and he settled himself down, folding his cane and slipping it into the breast pocket of his jacket.

The other passengers were wolfing down their food. The airship's landing was only an hour away and they each sought a prime viewing spot for what was going to be an incredible event. All except for Faust and Ritter who ate quietly, their gazes fixed on nothing in particular.

Quinn and party made a show of lingering over their meals and thus were able to wait out the rest of the passengers who made their way to the Promenades still chewing the last morsels of their breakfast. Faust and Ritter remained behind but were at the opposite end of the room. McGrath stayed as well, wallowing in his misery, but he, too, was out of earshot.

"How did it go, Sir?" Silk asked, barely able to conceal his eagerness.

"I was tossed out the window," Quinn replied.

Carol gave a start but the restraining hand of Quinn on her arm quieted her down.

"Now it wasn't as bad as all that. I was cold cocked and out I went. The blow hurt like the devil, but my cowl took most of it and I was only stunned. I played dead to see what our quarry was up to. I didn't expect to have to make like a bird though. Luckily the landing railing was beneath the window and I took hold of that on the way down."

Carol leaned in close and gazed into Quinn's eyes. "Tony, you could have been killed!"

"Little chance of that. I clipped the grappling hook from my belt around the handle just to be sure. Good thing, too. I must have passed out for awhile. When I came to, I hauled myself back up. The day watch came on and the passengers were beginning to stir so I had to conceal myself in a closet until it was safe to return to my suite."

"Thank God you're all right," Carol said.

Quinn said, "We have much greater concerns."

"Like who tried to turn you into a bird," Silk elaborated. "When I get my hands on him, I'll…"

"You've hit the nail on the head," Quinn said, nodding. "We are faced with a diabolical enemy." He went on to explain the discovery of the incriminating letter opener and how he'd attempted to stalk and, in the end, been surprise by a figure he could not see. The others listened intently.

"You mean it was as if this man was invisible?" Carol asked.

"Incredible, I know, but that is what happened."

"And you have no idea who it was?" Silk asked.

"None." Quinn then added, "He is German, however. I heard him speak."

"A German who can turn invisible," mused O'Leary. He considered a moment before speaking. "This is crazy, but the guy sounds like one of the clowns from Biehn's adventure rags."

"What are you talking about?" Quinn asked.

"Well, when I was down with the crew, some of the boys had pulp magazines. One kid there, no more than seventeen, kept going on and on about one of the adventure magazines, a German one, called the Allie Manor or something."

"Alle-Männer," Quinn clarified. "The All Men. A group of German vigilantes."

"Yeah, yeah. The kid was nuts for the group. Anyway, his favorite was a guy who turned himself invisible with some kind of dopey cloak. Only the guy got killed in the issue Biehn has and he wants to bring the guy back." He nudged Silk. "Can you imagine a kid wanting to write that kind of stuff? I told him to concentrate on important literature like sports pages and *Ring*."

"Butch," Quinn interrupted. "I want you to find the boy and bring him to my quarters. Have him bring the magazine. Right away! Even if he is on duty. Tell him you have authority from Captain Vaeth. Just get him here."

"I'll have him up here in a jiff."

"Silk, I want you to get back to those mail sacks and find the ruby. I'm certain the man who attacked me stashed it there. We can't do anything about Ardai, but we might still prevent the theft of the jewel getting out. Off you go. But be cautious. We mustn't arouse suspicion."

Silk Kirby rose out of his chair and made as if he wanted to gaze out at the countryside below. He was quickly swallowed up by the crowd milling about the windows and was lost from view.

Tony and Carol got up and, arm in arm, strolled from the Dining Room towards the passenger suites for all intents and purposes like two young lovers. Carol held Quinn's arm a little more tightly than was necessary. She'd almost lost him the night before and the thought of it sent cold daggers into her heart. Quinn for his part, felt the same and did not object to the added closeness.

****

O'Leary joined them in Quinn's suite five minutes later. He ushered in a short, pudgy, uniformed youth with chubby cheeks and a shock of blonde hair.

Quinn addressed the boy in German, his tone friendly. "Good morning, Mr. Biehn. Butch here tells us you are a fan of adventure magazines."

"Ja!" He fumbled into his back pocket and withdrew a rolled up pulp. He handed it to Quinn but then caught himself and offered it to Carol sitting next to the Special D.A.

"We are interested in the Alle-Männer ourselves," Quinn went on.

Young Biehn's eyes flashed and a great smile split his moon face. He immediately launched into a rundown of each member of the German team, reciting from memory.

Quinn, mindful of the approaching touch down, held up a hand to halt the litany. "I believe one of them can even turn invisible…"

"*Ja! Ja! Herr Kobold.* He is my favorite!"

"How does he do it?"

"By utilizing the Cloak of Unseeing!"

"Really?"

"*Ja!* The Cloak of Unseeing came to him from the darkest reaches of the Black Forest where it had been used against the Roman invaders. Some say the garment was touched by Brunhilde herself and this is why it possesses such strange properties."

Quinn could not tell if the lad was mixing truth with the fictional inventions of the pulp writers. "And the real *Kobold* wears such a cloak?"

Biehn nodded enthusiastically. "It was this way: Our scientists attempted to learn the secrets of the cloak but they were attacked by scoundrels wanting it for themselves. Heydrich Stoller found the thieves lair and retrieved the cloak. He was permitted to keep it and became the adventurer *Kobold.*"

There was enough truth in the tale somewhere, Quinn decided, then continued his interrogation. "And what of the cloak itself?"

"It renders the wearer invisible for four minutes. But one must speak the incantation first."

"*Ich rufe dunkel,*" Quinn said. *I summon the dark.*

"Exactly! He can also cancel the spell by uttering… "

"*Es werde Licht,*" Quinn said. *Let There Be Light.*

Biehn's eyes bugged out of his head. "How did you know?"

During the exchange with Biehn, Carol, under the ruse of examining the magazine, had angled the book so that Quinn might see it with his peripheral vision. The cover depicted a bunch of crooks being bested by an invisible assailant whose presence was indicated by starbursts against the jaws and stomachs of the thugs. The title emblazoned across the bottom ran: *letzten Widerstand gegen Dr. Schicksal* – 'Last Stand Against Dr. Fate!' She had also shown him a frontispiece of the entire team with their names below the sketches. Kobold was shown as a tall, well-proportioned athlete type with chiseled features. Not unlike Konrad Faust in appearance.

In the brief silence which followed Biehn's question, he saw Carol examining the magazine and scowled. "They killed Kobold in that story!" he explained. "That's not the way it really happened!"

"Go on," Quinn urged.

Biehn removed his wallet and extracted a worn, faded newspaper clipping. He read it out to Quinn.

"'*The masked adventurer, known as Kobold, was expelled from the All-Men yesterday after a unanimous vote by the other team members. No reason was given for the dismissal but allegations of embezzlement had circulated. No evidence has come to light.*'"

He stopped reading and stared beseechingly at Quinn. "It is all lies of course! This was two years ago and no one has seen *Herr Kobold* since. The magazine could not print such lies so they killed *Kobold* in that story. But I am going to bring him back! I am going to clear his name!"

Quinn had all he needed from the boy so he urged Biehn to follow through on his literary ambitions, thanked him for his time and asked Carol to return the magazine. He sent the boy on his way.

When the three associates were alone, Quinn recounted his conversation with Biehn to his associates. O'Leary turned to Quinn asking, "You think it was this Kobold clown that tried to turn you into a bird?"

"Well not the version young Biehn is enamored of. That is the creation of hack writers. However the All Men do exist in the real world and I was attacked by someone who appeared invisible. A man, who spoke that exact phrase before he vanished. And it would explain what happened to Ardai."

Carol straightened in her seat. "What do you mean, Tony?"

"You stated that Ardai carried himself awkwardly before going out the window."

"Yes. It was very strange."

"Was it? Now think back, Carol. Imagine Ardai, groggy as you described, but being supported, carried by a murderer to the window."

"You're right, Tony! It did look that way. But he was alone. He – "

"Or was the man carrying him invisible?"

"Kobold murdered Ardai!" O'Leary hissed.

"It looks that way," Quinn concluded.

Carol spoke the thought they all had. "But why was he killed?"

"My guess is the conspirators did not want to take chances so close to the end," Quinn said. "With the theft pinned on Ardai, the man's death would remove any chance he might clear himself. Kobold did not count on a witness."

"All right. Kobold's our man. What's our next move?" O'Leary asked.

"The illustration in the magazine bore a striking resemblance to Faust," Carol observed. "Maybe he's Kobold. But the boy said Kobold's name was Stoller..."

"An invention of the magazine writers to protect the real man's identity," Quinn offered. "We need – "

Before Quinn could elaborate, Silk Kirby burst into the room. He was out of breath from running.

Quinn smiled. "Well, here at least is an end to one of the mystery plaguing this zeppelin. Silk you have the ruby?"

Silk shook his head. "No, sir! I went down to the mail sacks like you said. You should have heard Kessel kick up a fuss about that. But the Captain needed him and that put an end to his squawking. No sign of the gem. But, sir, I found these!"

He pulled a scrap of paper from his breast pocket and handed it to Quinn who took one look at it and leapt up out of his chair.

"Tony! What is it?" Carol asked.

"We don't have a moment to lose!" Quinn blurted, visibly shaken by the scrap in his fist. "To action, people!"

Chapter Eight

RACE AGAINST DOOM

Quinn leapt to the closet and withdrew the case that held the garments of the Black Bat. He spoke as he hauled the case out. "Carol and Silk, get to the control gondola! Quick as you can! Take your pistols and watch Kessel and Lodel. Be careful, use the guns only under extreme duress. We are surrounded by more than five million cubic feet of hydrogen."

"Boss," O'Leary came and stood next to Quinn. "What's the game?"

Quinn handed the scrap of paper to the man.

"It says: 'CAUTION! EXPLOSIVE. MADE IN U.S.A.' I don't get it?"

"That is the wrapper from a blasting cap. The German American Bund plan to blow up this ship," Quinn ejaculated. "It's all so clear now. With a policeman and a special District Attorney on board, they needed a distraction. The theft, Ardai… it was a feint to keep us occupied, while Kobold planted the explosives. Kessel must be in on it or else why would he try to prevent Silk from inspecting the mail sacks. We've been tricked. And time is running out!"

Carol gasped at the full implication of the threat they faced. "There will be thousands of people at the airport…"

"That is only the tip of the iceberg," Quinn said. "The destruction of *Valkyrie,* the devastation and loss of life will be blamed on the United States. Those caps, clearly printed 'Made in the U.S.A.' were planted in the mail because the bags will be dropped before we touch down. They will be found afterwards and the conclusion will be that the anti-Nazi sentiment here precipitated the disaster. Twisted by Hitler's propaganda machine, and our press, the incident could well be misconstrued as an act of war!"

"We have to stop them!" Silk insisted.

"We'll do our best. That's why I want you and Carol in the gondola. Kobold, Kessel, Lodel and whoever is with them will try to seize control after the mail bags, with their damning evidence, have been dropped. You and Carol must prevent that from happening."

"What about me?" O'Leary said his fists clenching and unclenching.

"Stay with Faust and Ritter. Don't let them out of your sight. Buy me the time I need to defuse the explosives." He pulled the cowl of the Black Bat over his head. "Silk, if you don't get a signal from me have the Captain take the ship as high as she'll go. We'll explode in the air and, perhaps, save some lives. Let's get at it!"

****

While Quinn and his team were rushing into action, Captain Vaeth gazed down on the spectacle awaiting Valkyrie at Los Angeles' Mines Field almost directly beneath them. The blazing sun overhead showed him the 60-foot mooring mast that had been trucked in from the Naval air station in San Diego. Stacked near the landing site were hydrogen cylinders brought in to top off the ship's gas bags. And he knew that the train with its tank car stopped on the nearby siding was carrying Pyrofax, a gaseous fuel, provided in place of Blaugas for the engines. The Officer-In-Charge of the ground crew set off a smoke bomb to show Vaeth the wind direction and the curling smoke momentarily obscured the 300 sailors and marines in place to handle the ship. 50 State Police, 1000 Deputy Sheriffs, 1200 members of the National Guard were all on hand, working the fences set up a minimum of 900 feet from the landing site to keep the crowd at bay.

And what a crowd it was! Almost 80,000 people had come out to see Valkyrie land. They stood, sat, and squatted, eating hot dogs and drinking Cokes, eyes turned upward to the glare of the sun for a glimpse of the massive airship rapidly descending. The cream of Hollywood stardom was also in attendance. From James Cagney, Errol Flynn and Douglas Fairbanks to Olivia de Havilland and Barbara Stanwyck, the stars had come to welcome Valkyrie to the City of Angels.

The Captain was barely aware of the hurried arrival of Silk and Carol who stopped in their tracks when they saw the sea of faces stretching out across the field.

However all was not glitz and glamour. In the bowels of the ship, the Black Bat scampered along the bisecting catwalk, eyes closed, his super sensitive ears strained to the maximum to sound out every corner of the vast interior.

Then he heard it.

A ticking noise.

He stopped in front of one of the massive gas bags taut with explosive hydrogen. The ticking noise was coming from above. Like a spider he scrabbled up a support girder. Finally he reached the top and there it was to the left of the venting valve. Three sticks of coiled dynamite with a small clock face on top. A time bomb.

With no time to lose, he whipped out the knife at his belt while he scrutinized the device. He located the trigger wire and severed it. The ticking ceased. The bomb had been rendered harmless.

It was then that a now familiar sound reached his ears.

A ticking noise.

Another bomb!

But where? Recalling the pile of blasting cap wrappers Silk had found concealed in the mail bags, he wondered how many bombs Kobold had planted. Bombs set to go off at any second!

****

Valkyrie swooped majestically out of the sky. The crowd roared its approval. In the control gondola, Silk and Carol were watching Kessel and Lodel warily. The men seemed nervous but steeled to action. Quinn's aids expected trouble at any moment. When the moment came, they were ready.

Kessel reached for his ceremonial sidearm and snapped open the holster flap.

Silk drew his gun and aimed it at the man.

"No so fast," he hissed.

Captain Vaeth turned to address Kessel and saw the gun Silk had pointed at the man. "What's the meaning of this!" he demanded. "Put that thing away! Do you have any idea where you are, man?"

"Captain," Silk began, his eyes fixed on Kessel. "This man and those Bund creeps are planning to blow up this airship."

Vaeth's eyes widened at this revelation.

"This is a lie!" Kessel spat and he moved toward Silk.

"Stay right where you are!"

"Mr. Kessel! Explain yourself!" Vaeth demanded.

And it was at this moment that the navigator, brandishing a pistol burst into the room and slammed into Silk knocking him off balance. Falling, Silk tore the wheel from Vaeth's hand.

Lodel left his post and stood beside Kessel, the navigator leapt upon the sprawled form of Silk while Carol dug in her purse for her weapon.

Vaeth stepped forward to take command of the situation but a gun flamed and he crumpled to the deck. Carol, gun in hand, fired at the navigator, taking him in the neck as he whirled to shoot her. Crimson splashed the windows and he fell headlong.

Then all hell broke loose.

****

Valkyrie swooped majestically out of the sky. The crowd roared its approval.

O'Leary sat with his eyes locked on Faust who chatted with his batman, Ritter. The two Bund men seemed uninterested in the awed gasps of the passengers crowded around the windows. The ship had just completed a turn and they were given a full view of the mass of people outside. One of the passengers, using binoculars, had spotted the wooden platform that had been erected for the Hollywood elite and this had brought about the biggest reaction.

Only O'Leary was missing the whole spectacle. All because of a couple of Bund jokers. He was just reveling in a particular notion of revenge when Faust spoke briefly to Ritter who got up and made for the door to the passenger suites. O'Leary was torn for a minute but he knew that Faust was the discredited Kobold he was to keep an eye on and let Ritter leave unchallenged.

****

The Black Bat had disabled two more bombs. The only thing working in his favor was that Kobold had planted all of the bombs in the same spot above every second of the 17 gas bags. This had meant a great deal of climbing, however, using the strong rope coiled in one of the pouches of his belt, the Black Bat had been able to swing from one bag to the next until the space grew too tight and he had to leap from the top of one to the other.

He stopped and listened intently.

There it was. Distant yet audible.

Ticking.

The Black Bat raced on.

****

Faust rose up out of his seat and joined the cheering, laughing group by the windows. O'Leary had no choice but to follow. At least he might get a look at the Hollywood big shots from this vantage point. That Cagney was his favorite.

He lost sight of Faust. The man had bent forward to peer down through the glass and a woman wearing a hat the size of a beach ball stepped back, blocking O'Leary's view. He threw his head this way and that but could see no sign of Faust. He stepped forward and entered the group, elbowing his way towards where he thought Faust was.

Then something hard and unyielding smashed against the side of his head and he fell senseless against the backs of the tight crowd pushing against the glass. With every eye fixed on the landing field. No one noticed as he slid to the floor and lay sprawled, unconscious.

McGrath, seeing O'Leary pitch forward, got up out of his seat and took at step towards the man. He received a sharp chop to the back of the neck and fell heavily against a table, upsetting it. He did not rise.

****

The control gondola was a scene of complete chaos. Silk was locked in deadly combat with Kessel. Both men had dropped their weapons. Vaeth crawled along the floor to where one of the pistols lay. Carol had ducked behind a girder and was exchanging shots with Lodel. Bullets ricocheted crazily against the steel walls and ceiling of the gondola. The front glass shattered, raining shards. A collective gasp from the people below reached them over the roar of gunfire.

Few on the ground were even aware of the shattered windows. What held them spellbound was the sight of the great ship swerving sharply to one side and stabbing downward, its huge nose aimed right at them.

The sharp tilt of the ship threw everyone on board forward. Carol held fast to the girder, but Lodel, his back to the forward windows, tumbled backwards. He hit the console, the breath driven from his lungs, lost his balance and pitched through the shattered glass and fell from the ship.

Kessel was able to throw off Silk and lunged for the wheel. From the floor Vaeth grabbed at his legs and received a kick to the temple for his efforts. He sprawled and lay unmoving beside the wheel.

Kessel seized the wheel and worked the lifters and stabilizers. The crew at their stations throughout the ship and in the engine gondolas were already fighting to correct the trim of the ship, oblivious to the disastrous use Kessel had in mind for it.

The ship stabilized and Kessel aimed it at the mass of people below. *Valkyrie* had a ground speed of 60 MPH. The zeppelin would reach the crowd in seconds.

****

The Black Bat straddled an aft gas bag and prepared to disarm the last bomb. But then the ship lurched, tilted crazily, and he was sent sledding down the gas bag. He struck a short gangway before the panel that gave on one of the engine gondolas jutting out the side of the ship.

As he stared at the door it opened and a middle aged man with a florid face and a goatee stood in the doorway.

"It's going to crash!" he blurted in German. "We must abandon ship!"

The Black Bat did not hesitate. He drew his .45 and aimed it right between the bulging eyes of the panicked crewman. "Return to your post or I'll kill you where you stand."

The Black Bat backed the man up by striding forward with the gun raised. They were both on the gangway now, the wind whipping their clothing. Cowed, the crewman returned to the engine gondola and climbed inside.

As the Black Bat was about to step through the door and back into the airship, the pile-driver thrust of an invisible boot drove into his stomach.

Kobold had struck!

The Black Bat staggered backwards. He lunged for one of the engine gondola supports to keep from falling. But before he could reach it a series of punches caused him to career off the short gangway and he tumbled into space.

Extending his arms desperately, the suction-like rubber fingertips adhered to the rough cotton outer skin of the ship, slowing his fall. The ground raced by beneath him as he slid down the circumference of the airship and slammed to the field below.

*****

Silk and Kessel fought for control of the ship. Carol could not fire at Kessel for fear of hitting Silk. Meanwhile Vaeth struggled to regain his feet. In the process he glanced out the window and saw the panicked, fleeing crowd in the path of the zeppelin. He lunged for the elevator controls and spun the wheel frantically before collapsing once more.

The nose of *Valkyrie* began to rise sharply.

*****

Dazed and winded, the Black Bat gazed up at the vast underbelly of the ship streaking by above his head. He was not out of danger, however. He had dropped under the keel of *Valkyrie* and saw the massive rear wheel of the zeppelin skim, then plow into the field as the nose of the airship rose. The huge wheel was now barreling towards him at 60 MPH! The Black Bat had only seconds before it crushed him!

Thrusting his hand into a pouch on his belt, he extracted the rope he'd used earlier. He shot a glance at the wheel churning a deep furrow in the grass as almost the full weight of the ship pressed down upon it. He could see the mud-caked tread as it whirled. The wheel was almost upon him.

He uncoiled the rope and flung himself to one side just as the wheel plowed the spot where he'd lain. With lightning reflexes, he flicked the grappling hook at the now receding tire and it wrapped around a stanchion. He was yanked along in the wake of the zeppelin, dragged by the great ship as it sluiced towards the crowd.

Pulling himself along, hand over hand, the Black Bat hauled himself up the rope as earth and grass splattered his face. He reached the wheel housing and clambered up. Crouching upon it, the base of the tailfin above his head, he withdrew a keen blade from a sheath at his waist and began sawing at *Valkyrie's* thick skin. Soon he had opened a hole large enough for him to pass through and he scrabbled into the ship.

He heaved himself up the side of the rigged gas bag in a desperate attempt to reach the bomb before it was too late. He made it, breathing heavily, every muscle taut from the exertion, and crawled to where the bomb had been positioned, knife in hand. He reached for the wires but an unseen foot crashed down on the hand of the Black Bat. Hot daggers of pain raced up his arm but somehow he held fast to the knife.

"Your attempt to save the ship has failed!" the invisible Kobold gloated. "We shall all die in a blaze of glory! The first casualties of a new war which will see the Fatherland rule the world!"

The Black Bat cradled his injured hand. No bones were broken and already the pain was fading. "You're mad, Kobold," he spat. "There is no glory in the slaughter of innocents."

Kobold cackled maniacally. "The world will pay for Versailles! In blood!"

The Black Bat moved with catlike reflexes and threw himself on the bomb. Using his muscled back as a shield he seized the trigger wire and slashed at it with the knife. Kobold kicked and stomped at his back and searing swords of pain stabbed into the spine of the Black Bat. But he sawed the wires apart.

The last bomb had been disarmed.

Kobold, sensing this, bellowed his rage and pummeled his foe mercilessly.

The Black Bat spun quickly and grabbed at the legs of his invisible adversary. The cabled muscles of his arms clenched around cloth and flesh his eyes could not see and he wrestled Kobold from his feet.

The two men slid down the side of the gas bag, flailing at one another.

****

Silk, bruised and bleeding from numerous cuts, drove a stout jab to the jaw of Kessel. The crewman staggered back against the console. Silk stepped in driving more blows into his weakened foe and Kessel withered under the attack as the nose of *Valkyrie* soared safely over the panicked crowd on the ground. The rear wheel had cleared the seething throng with scant inches to spare, the wind of its passing snatching the hats from the heads of those closest to it.

Valkyrie had cleared the crowd but with no hand on the wheel, the ship raced directly for the electrical wires bordering the field.

****

The Black Bat landed atop Kobold, pounding the air from the man's lungs. His fingers moved crab-like over the invisible form beneath him, seeking the man's throat. The strong hands of the Black Bat started to squeeze.

Kobold thrashed wildly and suddenly became visible. The Black Bat saw the hooded head of the man obscured by a cloak with ancient symbols stitched into every inch of the raiment. Kobold tried to speak the incantation but the vise-like grip of the Black Bat cut off the sound.

Kobold drove a knee up into the stomach of the Black Bat and the two men fell away from each other.

"I summon the dark," Kobold rasped in German and disappeared right before the eyes of the Black Bat.

****

In desperation, Kessel seized up his pistol and was about to fire when a bullet from Carol's gun cleaved into his breast and he crumpled to the deck, unmoving. The enemy dispatched, Silk dove for the wheel and, with the aid of Captain Vaeth, got the airship to rise as quickly as it could. But the power lines still loomed in their path.

With agonizing slowness, the nose of the ship rose and missed the wires by bare inches.

However they were far from clear. For the rear of the airship still floated close to the ground and the rate of ascent would not raise it high enough in time.

The ship was doomed.

Vaeth decided on a desperate, last gasp gamble and hurled the elevator wheel hard to one side. The result was an enormous groan from the ship as tremendous strain was placed on the rigid frame. It sounded as if the ship were about to break in two.

But the bold move paid off. The maneuver had set in motion a see-saw effect, plunging the nose downward while jerking the rear of the zeppelin into the air at an alarming angle. The rear wheel of the ship cleared the electrical wires with room to spare.

****

The maneuver sent everyone aboard sprawling. The Black Bat and Kobold tumbled head over heels. But the Bat recovered first and drawing his .45 with its muzzle flash suppressor, fired two rapid shots down into the ballast tanks beneath them. As these were full of the ship's waste water from cooking and bathing, it was a fetid brew that geysered up near the invisible form of Kobold, soaking the villain.

For a moment the Black Bat saw an outlined form as Kobold scrambled to his feet. He aimed his gun but the water soaking the cloak was rendered invisible. Kobold's boot lashed out and struck the gun, sending it whirling away. The Black Bat had other guns but dared not use them while surrounded by so much volatile hydrogen. The shots at the ballast tank had been a calculated risk.

Kobold was invisible once more. But the cloak could not mask the smell nor the water dripping from it, leaving a trail.

The Black Bat moved in.

Kobold dodged, thinking himself safely unreachable but he received a cross to the jaw followed by a blow to the solar plexus. He lashed out striking his enemy on the shoulder.

They separated and Kobold tried to flee but the Black Bat leapt and took the man down at the knees. They sprawled. The Black Bat rained blow after blow down on Kobold whose struggles grew weaker.

Suddenly Kobold appeared beneath the Black Bat as the cloak's power wore off. Seizing the hood of the cloak, the Black Bat ripped it from the man's face.

"Now, Faust – " he began, then the words died in his throat.

It was not Faust who lay beneath him but rather the man's batman, Ritter.

Karl Ritter was Kobold!

The former hero took advantage of the Black Bat's surprise and slithered free.

"You dare confuse me with that strutting blowhard Faust!" Kobold spat. "He, like you, Ardai and this ship, are but pawns in a much larger game."

They were near the hole the Black Bat had carved into the hull when he had climbed back aboard. Suddenly Kobold lunged for it.

"Ritter, wait!" the Black Bat warned.

Ritter turned and cautioned, "We will meet again, Bat! But not before Germany has won her final victory!"

Then he jumped down through the hole.

A shrill scream reached the ears of the Black Bat as he dove headlong and seized Kobold's cloak in a frantic, failed effort to prevent the leap. Clutching the Cloak of Unseeing, the Black Bat gazed down through the hole as Kobold tumbled, flailing helplessly. Captain Vaeth's see-saw maneuver had thrust the rear of *Valkyrie* more than two hundred feet into the air. Kobold, thinking the ship had been kept near ground level by his fellow conspirators in the control gondola, had leapt to his death.

Chapter Nine

OF HOPE AND SHADOWS

Back in the garb of Tony Quinn, the blind D.A. returned to the passenger area where chaos reigned. Bodies were strewn in heaps from the thrashing of the zeppelin, the passengers dazed from colliding with walls, tables, chairs and each other. Making sure he was not observed, Quinn threw himself under one of the lounge tables, rolling in the mess of spilled drinks and shattered flower vases, then, thoroughly camouflaged, he made a show of struggling to rise.

O'Leary, rubbing the back of his head savagely, stepped over the senseless form of McGrath and joined Quinn. He surveyed the damage Quinn had done to himself and nodded approvingly. "Good work, Boss," he whispered. "Now you'll fit right in with the rest of us mugs."

He helped Quinn to his feet and was instructed to head for the control gondola before the other passengers recovered their senses. There they found Captain Vaeth piloting the ship alone. He spied Kessel's lifeless body in one corner.

Carol shot a quick questioning glance at Quinn who nodded slightly.

She took the meaning that the threat had been neutralized and relaxed visibly. Quinn would recount what had happened in the aft section of the ship when he and his group were alone.

"It appears your ship is safe, Captain," Quinn said, keeping his tone light. "Although it was a ride none of us will ever forget."

Vaeth turned and glared at Quinn. "It is nothing compared to the ride the whole world may all have to go on soon!"

"Surely, it's not as bad as all that," Silk intoned.

"Your reporters will call all Germans insane after today's events. It will be said we have no regard for human life. And when they hear of the accursed traitors among us who sought to murder thousands!" He broke off.

Quinn raised a placating hand "I agree there will be a backlash over what happened today. However, the mad movement of the ship can be blamed on mechanical failure. As the mission of our enemies failed, it's safe to assume that the German American Bund will not want to shout their involvement from the rooftops. I believe the conspirators amongst the crew have been dispatched so no word of their involvement need leave this room."

"It might have been worse," Carol explained. "These Bund scoundrels hoped to bring about war between our two nations. If Tony's suggestions can prevent that…"

Vaeth shook his head, then squared his shoulders, saying, "It will be as you say. Matters could not be worse in the end. Perhaps the damage can be contained. We can pray that it works. I fought in the Great War and have no desire to be press-ganged into a second by the Chancellor and his thugs. I would do anything to avoid that though it seems inevitable at this point."

"We can only hope our governments will match your desire," Quinn offered. "It is only hate and distrust that will topple us over the edge. The conspirators here attempted to augment those feelings through mass murder and who can say if they succeeded or not. We can hope for the latter."

"And the ruby?" Vaeth asked.

"My people found no sign of it. Perhaps Kessel smuggled it off the ship. Perhaps it is still on board. We may never know."

"That is troubling to me," Vaeth admitted. "Have we lost the Heart of the Empire? What has become of the Pride of Germany?"

Quinn paused before saying, "Those are questions I'm afraid only time and history can answer."

+++

GOING BAT-Y

Writing a Black Bat tale was an undertaking I approached with a great deal of enthusiasm as he was to be my first costumed pulp hero. To date I'd had the good fortune to write Sherlock Holmes, Ghost Squad, Secret Agent X, Jim Anthony and Dan Fowler tales. Colorful heroes all, and immense fun to play around with but not quite so outlandish as a D.A. dressed like a bat!

Also, the invitation to try my hand at a Black Bat tale afforded me an opportunity to write a zeppelin story – something I've been itching to do for a few years. And what better place for such a tale than Airship 27? As our intrepid editor is an avid airship enthusiast, I knew I had to get my facts straight as far as these great airliners of the past are concerned. The fictional LZ-128 in my story fits nicely, I think, between the revered *Graf Zeppelin*, LZ-127 and the doomed *Hindenburg*, LZ-129. Given that LZ-128 was never constructed, I was free to do so in my tale by merging elements of both of these great ships.

The writing of the tale proved more of a challenge than I had originally anticipated. The process took over four months! Given that I usually take four *weeks* or less to complete a pulp yarn, you can see how this was cause for concern. However I feel the long process ultimately helped the story.

I began *Death Rides the Valkyrie* a week before heading to Chicago for the Windy City Pulp and Paper Convention. As this was my first chance to meet and speak with my fellow pulp fans face to face, I was delighted to attend and the con made a great impression on me. Plus I got to meet our editor extraordinaire Ron Fortier and art director Rob Davis as well as my fellow Holmes scribe, Van Allen Plexico among others. What a thrill! Of course, while travelling, my Black Bat tale was temporarily put on hold.

But I came back from that adventure with a new appreciation of how great pulp fans are and a burning desire to resume the flight of the *Valkyrie*.

Preis 20 Pfg

Alle-Männer

Nr. 31

Schrecken der Doktor Spinn

Including Chicago in the tale is a direct result of the amazing time I had at the con.

Back in business, I thought I was off and running and would have the tale wrapped up in no time. But then I found myself up against an unstoppable juggernaut: one Mr. Sherlock Holmes. The unparalleled interest in the greatest detective of them all soon consumed my time as I spent countless hours contacting hundreds of Holmes clubs in 20 countries to help spread the word about Volume One of Airship 27's ongoing Holmes anthology series in which I had a tale. The efforts of everyone involved helped to make the book a bestseller and a buzz about a second Holmes anthology began streaking across the ether. Well, after the fun I'd had writing my first Holmes tale, there was no way I was going to miss out on being a part of Volume Two.

At first I wrote the two tales simultaneously, using the left hand pages in my Black Bat notebook for the Bat and the right hand pages for Holmes, but sending Holmes and Watson to Portsmouth for my second tale soon involved too much research to go along with the writing and, alas, the Black Bat was forced back into limbo despite my interest and desire to finish my tale.

With my second Holmes tale finally done, I vowed to see the Black Bat through his adventure on the *Valkyrie* if it was the last thing I did! And this second delay also helped with the tale in the end.

For you see, right off the bat (pun intended) I had thought of a little fun to have with the real history of the character. It has been well documented that the Black Bat and Batman were essentially simultaneous, independent creations so similar that the matter almost went before the courts. For a number of years the two characters went head to head, or cowl to cowl, and we all know which caped crusader came out on top.

So, with tongue firmly planted in cheek, I thought it would be fun to make the Black Bat's nemesis in my story... batman! In this case a batman – an officer's butler. This little play on words was supposed to be as far as the gag went.

However, during those delays I mentioned, the idea of a batman villain percolated in my gray matter until I developed the idea that this batman had a secret identity. But who would this batman be?

The answer was a great opportunity to introduce the *Alle-Männer* or the All-Men, a group of original characters of my own invention, which I've been developing for some time.

So I hope you enjoyed this adventure of the Black Bat as well as the other tales in the book. If you did, please let Air Chief Ron know by dropping him a line to tell him you'd like to see more. There's no end of adventures for this caped crusader.

As an added bonus, we've included a mock *Alle-Männer* pulp cover for your enjoyment. Until next time, keep punching.

***

Ellis Award nominee Andrew Salmon lives and writes in Vancouver, BC. His work has appeared in numerous magazines, including Storyteller, Parsec, TBT and Thirteen Stories. He also writes reviews for The Comicshopper and is creating a superhero serial novel currently running in A Thousand Faces Magazine.

He has published or appeared in ten books: *The Forty Club* (which Midwest Book Reviews calls "a good solid little tale you will definitely carry with you for the rest of your life"), *The Dark Land,* the first of a series ("a straight out science-fiction thriller that fires on all cylinders" – Pulp Fiction Reviews), *The Light Of Men*, his first work for Airship 27/Cornerstone, which has been called "a book of such immense significance that it is not only meant to be read, but also to be experienced... a work of grim power" – C. Saunders. *Secret Agent X: Volume One* and *Three, Ghost Squad: Rise of the Black Legion* (with Ron Fortier), *Jim Anthony Super Detective Volume One, Black Bat Volume One* and *Sherlock Holmes Volumes One* and *Two* constitute his pulp fiction work at Airship27/Cornerstone to date.

Andrew's work will also appear in the upcoming *Mars McCoy* and *Sherlock Holmes Consulting Detective Volume Three* anthologies. Also a completely revised edition of *The Dark Land* will also be released through Airship 27/Cornerstone sometime in the near future.

To learn more about his work check out the Airship27/Cornerstone store (http://stores.lulu.com/airship27) and the following links: www.lulu.com/AndrewSalmon and www.lulu.com/thousand-faces.

A Deal with the Devil

A Black Bat Adventure

by
Aaron Smith

Detroit, Michigan, 1933:

Katherine Hardwick let out a bloodcurdling scream, expecting it to be the last sound she ever made. She was trapped, cornered, with nowhere to run to, no way to escape, and about to be murdered. In the dim light of the alley she could see the blade of the shadowy figure's knife. *Death is coming for me*, she thought as she let out that scream. They say that one's life flashes before one's eyes as the end nears, but Katherine Hardwick did not see her life, for she saw only that blade. It slashed once, but she tried her best to avoid it, moving more from instinct and desire for self-preservation than from any lucid thought. The blade found flesh, but not enough to slay, just slightly wounding her arm. The shadowy figure before her, looking like something from a nightmare, readied its arm to strike again. She knew that terrible blade would not miss its mark twice!

But a shot rang out! The wonderful crack of a gun's fire; Bang! The thing in front of her turned its back to look in the direction from which the shot had come, and Katherine Hardwick's life was spared for at least another moment. She took advantage of that gift and pushed her way past him, running like hell toward the light at the end of the alley. As she ran, she passed her savior. She saw a single man, his hat falling from his head as he ran towards the thing that had just tried to cut her to pieces. His trench coat, unbuttoned, was flapping behind him like two wings on a rumpled, all too human looking angel of mercy. She saw the gun in his hand, and she was grateful. She kept running, hoping that, whoever he was, he would use that gun to destroy the horror that had just tried to end her life.

Detective McGrath saw the girl run past him. She looked all right, almost. He could see that her arm was bleeding, but it didn't look serious. Maybe, he thought, he had arrived soon enough this time. Maybe tonight there would be no sudden death for an innocent woman. Maybe tomorrow's paper would be different; maybe it would not, once again, say "Midnight Maniac takes another victim."

Satisfied that the girl did not need his immediate aid, McGrath continued his pursuit. His footsteps pounded along the asphalt as he went running into the alley from whence the girl had come shrieking. He could see the figure, in its long black coat, still shrouded in shadow, at the back of the alley.

"Halt there! Halt! I said stop!" shouted the running detective, but he could see the black-cloaked killer start to climb up the fire escape ladder that hung from the side of one of the buildings that made the alley's walls.

McGrath fired! *Bang! Crack!*

"Dammit!" he cursed, as he heard the bullet strike brick without any detour through flesh or bone.

By the time the panting detective reached the end of the alley and looked up, he could see only the long tail of that jet black cloak as the killer clambered over the edge of the rooftop and escaped into the shadows. It would be the last that McGrath would see of the Midnight Maniac for a long time, at least in his waking life.

Six years later, New York City:

Detective Lieutenant McGrath of the New York Police Department sat up in bed. His white t-shirt was soaked with sweat and he was out of breath, although he had been asleep for hours. The same dream that seemed to come back every six weeks or so had come again and he knew that he would have no more sleep this night.

He switched on his bedside lamp, lit up one of his cheap cigars, and sat in bed thinking about the memories that kept bringing that damned dream back every time he thought he had seen the last of it.

That series of murders had been the last case he had worked on when he had served on the Detroit police force. It had been a particularly disturbing series of events, almost reminiscent of the Ripper murders of London in 1888. Four young women had been killed, cut to ribbons by some knife wielding assailant. Unlike the Ripper case, the victims had not been prostitutes, but wealthy or noteworthy young women, two the daughters of important political figures, one an actress on a visit home from Hollywood, and the fourth a nightclub singer who had just been signed to a recording contract and was to leave for Chicago the day after she was tragically and gruesomely slain. The would-be fifth victim, Katherine Hardwick, whom

McGrath had saved, had just been engaged to marry the city's district attorney. After her encounter with the killer, poor Miss Hardwick had suffered a nervous breakdown and the marriage plans had been called off. McGrath did not know what had ever become of her after that.

The "Midnight Maniac," as the press had called him, was never caught. The murders stopped after the failed attempt on Katherine Hardwick. McGrath assumed that he had either scared the killer into stopping, or the killer had moved on to another city. Still, he had read or heard of no reports of any murders anywhere in the United States that matched the details of the Maniac's work. Of course, McGrath could not possibly keep track of the crimes committed in every city or state, so it was possible that the Midnight Maniac was still at work somewhere, continuing his deadly career of murder.

The case, and all its horrid details, had taken a toll on McGrath, and his superiors had ordered him to take a leave of absence. That leave had been longer than he had expected. While he had been off-duty, he had grown depressed and started to drink too much. He decided that he needed a fresh start and had left Detroit for New York. With his resume, he had no problem getting onto New York's police department as a detective and it did not take long for him to be promoted to detective lieutenant.

Now, six years had passed and McGrath was more or less happy in Manhattan. The city certainly had its share of crime and there was never any shortage of interesting new cases to investigate. When things did get slow, there was always that damned Black Bat to look into.

McGrath took the law seriously and he hated the idea that any man could simply take the law into his own hands without answering to any higher authority like a commissioner or mayor. So what if the Bat's victims all seemed to be lowlifes, he had asked himself many times? It was still no excuse to let some black-garbed vigilante run wild with guns blazing! Sooner or later, an innocent was going to be caught in the crossfire of the Black Bat's personal war on the underworld, and McGrath intended to put a stop to it before that could happen.

So, Detective Lieutenant McGrath was pretty satisfied with life in the Big Apple, but always there in the background, ready to resurface at any moment and bring back memories that never seemed to completely fade away, was the Midnight Maniac…and those damned dreams.

The Next Evening:

"**O**uch! Darn it, Tony!" yelped Carol Baldwin for the thirteenth time that evening.

"Sorry, Carol," replied her escort, the young lawyer, Tony Quinn.

The couple was dancing, in attendance at a gala being held in support of one of the city's candidates in the upcoming city council elections. It was an elegant affair, with the men all dressed in tuxedoes and the women in evening gowns of all colors and designs, each trying their best to look more stunning than the next.

Carol's cry of pain had been faked, but she was getting to be quite good at making it sound real enough. Although Tony Quinn was, in reality, an excellent dancer, it was of the utmost importance that the general public believed him to be a blind man. This charade was assisted by his appearing to occasionally step on Carol's foot while they danced. Carol was one of the few people who knew that Tony's vision was even sharper than any other man's sight. She was also one of the few who knew of his other identity, as the mysterious crime-fighting Black Bat.

Despite the inconvenience of having to maintain the façade of blindness, Tony Quinn was having a good time at the party. The food had been excellent, the speeches by various political figures had been tolerable for the most part, and he always enjoyed an evening out with Carol. Besides all that, he was able to learn things. When a man is thought to be blind, people will often do things without stopping as they would if someone were watching. Tony was used to picking up on the subtle hints that people often dropped when they thought no one was watching. The way a married couple glanced at each other, for example, could tell more secrets than a thousand sleazy gossip columns. On top of the advantage of people not thinking that he was watching them, Tony Quinn also had the advantage of really having been blind once, although just for a matter of months. As often happens to blind people, his other senses became more acute during his months in the dark. Although his sight had been restored, he had kept the skills of his other heightened senses. When there was a conversation going on near him that he thought might hold some interest for him in either of his personas, as the lawyer or as the Black Bat, he was able to focus his hearing on that one exchange, intentionally shutting out the extraneous chatter of all the room's other conversations, the band's music, the clank and clatter of dishes and glasses, and the tapping of dancing feet.

When they were finished with their dance, the couple went back to their table and had a few drinks. Carol excused herself to go to the powder room and Tony Quinn sat alone for a few minutes, his sharp sense of hearing stretching outward to listen to the mass of sounds that floated about the room, listening for anything that might be of interest to him, in either of his identities.

He caught bits and pieces of various conversations. The mayor was slightly drunk and was beginning to slur his speech. The head of the city's fire department was enthusiastically flirting with a woman who was not his wife and must have been twenty years younger than he was. Two men were having an argument over whether Joe DiMaggio or Jimmie Foxx was a better hitter. Overall, Quinn simply heard a lot of useless chatter, with nothing of much importance or significance. He sat back in his chair, took another sip of his drink and awaited the return of his date.

In the hallway outside the powder room, Carol Baldwin thought she recognized the young woman who she saw walking in her direction, so she stopped the attractive young redhead.

"Excuse me, do I know you?" Carol asked her. Then it dawned on her. "Oh, no, I don't know you. I know *of* you. You're Barbara Sharpe, aren't you?"

"Yes. Hello," said the woman.

Barbara Sharpe was an actress, currently starring in a Broadway show, the first performance in which she had been given top billing. Carol had seen her performance only a week earlier and had been quite impressed.

"Hello," said Carol. "I just wanted to say that I think your new show is wonderful. I saw it last week and I intend to go again."

"Thank you very much," replied Miss Sharpe. "So many people have been saying things like that. It can be almost overwhelming at times."

The conversation between the two women was brief and polite but pleasant and then they went their separate ways. Barbara Sharpe went down the hallway and Carol Baldwin went back to her table to fetch Tony Quinn for another round of dancing and faking being stepped on.

The evening wore on and the party eventually faded into the past. Carol and Tony left the building and were met outside by Tony's car, driven by his chauffer, Silk Kirby, a former con man whom Tony had befriended and who now acted as an aide to the Black Bat in his ongoing war against the underworld.

Silk dropped Carol off at her place and then drove Tony Quinn back to the spacious, expensive house on the outskirts of the city, which served as both Quinn's residence and the Black Bat's lair. Kirby, along with the Bat's other helper, the hulking tough guy, Butch O'Leary, were quartered in rooms below the main house, where one would also find the Black Bat's laboratory, vehicles, armory, and other crime-fighting tools.

Tony Quinn slept well that night. He had had a good time at the social event and always enjoyed Carol's company. Had he lived a typical life, he could almost imagine himself settling down with Carol Baldwin, maybe even raising a family, but his life was a bit too complicated to try to squeeze in normalcy. Being a supposedly blind lawyer by day and a masked vigilante by night left little room or time for hearth and home and Tony Quinn knew that as long as his crusade against crime wore on, he had to remain a bachelor.

Early Morning:

Detective Lieutenant McGrath had only just arrived at the precinct house. He had sat down behind his desk with a cup of fresh, steaming coffee and picked up the early edition of the paper. He hadn't even made it to page two when a uniformed officer came rushing into the room, panting, almost breathless.

"Lt. McGrath, Lt. McGrath!" he shouted as he flew in.

"What is it, Sweeney?" the startled lieutenant asked. Officer Sweeney had an annoying habit of being too enthusiastic about police work at times, so McGrath was never surprised when he learned that Sweeney was all worked up over something so minor that it really meant nothing. Before Sweeney's answer came out, McGrath would have bet that it was nothing important. McGrath would have lost the bet.

"There's been a murder, Sir! The commissioner wants you on the case! He called the main phone line downstairs and I came up to get you."

McGrath put down his newspaper and jumped up from his chair. For a pudgy, sloppy-looking man, he could move quite quickly when he wanted to.

"Well then let's go, Sweeney!" he said as he pulled on his trench coat. McGrath felt truly alive when he was suddenly confronted with a new case to work on. He really loved being a police detective when things got busy.

The two policemen were down on Broadway within a few minutes. Sweeney's overenthusiastic manner affected his driving habits too and McGrath had to hold on for dear life as the patrol car swerved around corners and skidded and skipped between cabs and other cars, but they made it there quickly and unscathed. Sweeney led McGrath to the small lot behind one of the city's big theatres. There were three other officers and a coroner already there. They were crowded in one corner of the lot, their backs turned toward the direction from which McGrath and Sweeney were coming. McGrath knew what that meant. They were all staring at the body with such focus that it had to be a gruesome one.

"Sweeney, go keep an eye on the car," he said to his escort.

"But who would try to steal a police car, Lieutenant?" Sweeney asked, confused.

"It's for your own good, son, and it's an order," McGrath told him and the disappointed Sweeney went back to the car. McGrath was only sparing the weak-stomached young officer from the ordeal of being sick. He knew from previous experience that Sweeney just didn't do well around the sight of blood.

"Let me get in there, fellows!" bellowed McGrath as he approached the crowd of cops. "This is my case! Stand aside and let me have a look!"

The small sea of cops parted and McGrath walked through them to where the body of the victim lay. He was a hardened veteran of crime scenes, but this sight made him wince. The body was that of a young woman, slim and once lovely, but now a mangled mess of former humanity. There were knife wounds, slashes and deep rips, all over the body. The ground around the body was a pooled mess of blood and gore. The violence of the incident, now hours in the past, hung in the air like a phantom of the grisly deed.

McGrath knelt down for a closer look. He could tell that a large, razor-sharp knife had been the instrument of the poor girl's demise. It had been a brutal, savage attack, but also one of great precision. Of this, McGrath was certain. This had not been this killer's first victim. There was no sign of hesitation behind the blade strokes. Whoever the murderer had been, he was sure of himself. He had known how to place wounds, both those designed to inflict pain and suffering, and those meant to finish the job, to kill.

After a few minutes, McGrath stood and faced the onlooking police officers and the coroner. It was then that he noticed that it was not the coroner he was used to.

"Where's Doctor Sullivan?" he asked.

"Sullivan's been ill. I'm Martin Shaw, his temporary replacement. I just got in from New Orleans," said the unfamiliar coroner as he held out his hand in greeting.

McGrath knelt down for a closer look.

McGrath shook the offered hand and muttered a casual greeting.

"Have we identified the poor girl?" he asked.

Shaw replied, "Her name is...was Barbara Sharpe. She was an actress in this very theatre." He gestured at the back of the building behind which they were standing.

McGrath noted the girl's name and occupation. Then he walked around to the front of the building, intending to go inside and see if anyone who knew the victim might have an idea of why she might have been killed.

Several of the police officers assisted Dr. Shaw in getting the body into the waiting ambulance for transport to the morgue.

Noon:

Tony Quinn sat behind the desk of his Manhattan law office. He was reading the newspaper but, as always, was ready to discard it at a second's notice should anyone enter the office. It would not do, after all, to have anyone see a 'blind' man reading the morning edition. Since beginning to maintain the façade of being blind, Quinn had perfected his routine and was able to switch behaviors and personas instantly.

As he browsed the sports page, Tony heard approaching footsteps in the hallway. Normally, he would have quickly dropped the paper, but in this case he did not. During the brief time when he had been truly blind, he had taught himself to pick up on many auditory signals that sighted people usually missed. If it was a familiar person approaching, he could identify them by the specific pace of their walk. He knew who it was and he knew that his pretense of sightlessness was unnecessary around her.

Seconds later, Carol Baldwin opened the door and walked in. Tony looked up and smiled, but was met by the sight of a sad-faced Carol, looking shocked and distraught.

"What's the matter?" Tony asked.

She walked past him and went to the radio behind him. She turned the knob. There was a second of static and then the voice of a newsman was heard.

"The murdered body of Broadway starlet, Barbara Sharpe was found early this morning. Police have begun a full investigation of this tragic and brutal killing..."

"Barbara Sharpe...the girl who's been getting all those great reviews for the past week?" said Tony Quinn.

Carol nodded. She looked terribly upset and Tony couldn't figure out why the news was affecting her so much.

"It's tragic and terrible, but why has it upset you so much, Carol? People are killed everyday, but I've never seen it get you so shaken up."

Carol began to explain. "I met Barbara Sharpe last night at the party! We only talked for a few minutes…but she was so young, so beautiful, and so full of life and enthusiasm!"

Quinn came out from behind the desk and embraced Carol.

"What can I do to make you feel better?" he asked her.

She didn't even hesitate to respond.

"You can put on your black suit and go find the lunatic who did this!"

Tony Quinn had every intention of doing just what Carol Baldwin had just suggested.

Ten O'clock at Night:

McGrath was tired, very tired, but he did not want to go home just yet. He hadn't learned anything useful at the theatre. No one there seemed to have any idea why anyone might want to kill Barbara Sharpe. From every angle he had asked about, she seemed to have been well-liked by everyone she knew on the set of her show. Everyone described her as a cheerful, easy to get along with young lady. She had had no current romantic entanglements, as far as anyone who worked on the show knew, so McGrath decided that that was probably not a useful road to take the investigation down at that point in time.

After the questioning of the theatre staff and the cast of the play, McGrath had gone to see Dr. Shaw, the substitute coroner. Shaw, a thin, pale man of about forty-five, had gone into vivid, gruesome detail about the nature and variety of the awful wounds that had been inflicted upon Miss Sharpe. The specifics had been enough to make even a seasoned detective like McGrath cringe a bit at some of the nastier parts.

He had stopped for a quick dinner before returning to the precinct. It had grown dark and late as he sat there behind his desk, thinking. Now it was the middle of the night and McGrath was alone. All the other detectives had gone home for the night. There were still a few patrolmen in the building, but they were all downstairs, along with the desk sergeant. For all intents and purposes, McGrath was by himself, which was fine with him. There were dark thoughts and ideas on his mind and he liked to ponder such things in solitude.

As McGrath had listened to the coroner's report and its grisly details of the injuries that had killed Barbara Sharpe, he couldn't help but think of the similarities to the Midnight Maniac murders of six years before, in Detroit. He couldn't help but wonder.

It can't be; he kept telling himself! These are similarities…and that's all, he repeated in his mind, over and over again. "It's just your mind and memories playing tricks on you!" he muttered out loud to himself. "But those wounds…the way the cutting was done; it's the same style, the same method!"

McGrath's mind was racing. *What if it was the same killer, now doing his horrid deeds in New York City? Perhaps,* thought McGrath, *this is my second chance, an opportunity to finally catch the one killer who's managed to elude me for all these years! Maybe now I can finally put an end to the slayings of those poor women! Maybe now I can make the nightmares stop!*

The weary investigator got up and walked across the office. He poured himself a cup of coffee and went back to his desk. He stared down at the desktop, at the steam slowly rising from the piping hot black coffee and it reminded him of the steam that would often rise from the sewer grates on cold mornings. He got lost in the memories of the bloody scenes from Detroit, where he had first been confronted by the terrible deeds of the Midnight Maniac.

Nearly an hour passed. The coffee slowly and steadily grew cold, but McGrath didn't notice. Had he been a religious man, he would have been praying, but he was just thinking, remembering, and swearing a silent oath that this time would be different. He would find the beast who had carved up poor Barbara Sharpe…and he would put the animal down!

"Good evening, Lieutenant," whispered a low, raspy voice that seemed to come from nowhere.

McGrath instinctively reached for his gun. When he had grabbed it, he pointed it out in front of him in a quick blur of motion and then looked up at the source of the voice.

"You!" he shouted. "Don't move a muscle!"

It was too late though. Before McGrath had finished his sentence, The Black Bat had both of his .45 automatics out of their holsters and aimed at the startled detective.

"I'm not here to play cowboys and Indians, McGrath," the Black Bat snarled. "I just want to talk. I know you'd love to lock me up, but I think you know as well as I do that there might be someone far more dangerous than me stalking the streets of our city tonight."

McGrath put his gun down on the desk.

"You've never shot a cop, as far as I know. All right, we'll talk…but don't try anything. One shot and all the boys downstairs will come running up here. You can't outshoot a whole roomful of cops, can you?"

The Black Bat responded to the detective. "No, I can't outshoot a room full of cops, but we're not going to let it come to that, McGrath. I know you don't approve of my methods, but I also know that you've been assigned to this Sharpe murder, and I think you know that I'm the lesser of two evils here by far. Tell me what you know so far…and maybe I can help you. It's obviously weighing heavily on your mind, or you wouldn't still be here at this hour."

McGrath leaned back in his chair and lit one of his obnoxious, foul-smelling cheap cigars. "I've been remembering things, and they're not pleasant memories. There was a case years ago, back when I worked in Detroit. There was a series of murders; the victims were all young women, and all in the public spotlight in one way or another. There were a few daughters of prominent city figures, an actress, a singer, the fiancée of the city's DA, although that last one managed to get away when I finally caught up to the killer. I shot at the son of a bitch, but he ran off into the shadows. I never did get a look at his face. He wore a cloak and used the darkness of night to his advantage. Now I'm not saying there's a connection here…but the method of this murder is too damn similar for it to not cross my mind."

"So you think this killer may have resurfaced here and now, in this city?" asked the Black Bat.

"We'll see soon enough," said McGrath. "He never waited too long between victims. If it is him, poor Miss Sharpe won't be the last to die."

"Thanks," said the Bat. "I'll try to see what the underworld flunkies are saying. Do us both a favor, McGrath; try not to shoot at me until we put this creep away…or six feet under."

With that last statement, the Black Bat swirled his raven cloak around him and moved in a quick blur of motion out the nearest window and was gone before McGrath could make a move.

The tired detective sat behind his desk feeling like he had just struck a deal with the devil. He just hoped this devil was less of a Lucifer than the man he suspected had come to New York City.

The Next Morning:

At eight-fifteen, Silk Kirby dropped Tony Quinn off at his law office. The young attorney walked in the front door with his white cane in hand. Quinn entered his office and was surprised to see a package, addressed to him, sitting on his desk. It was a fairly large and thick envelope.

He tore it open. The first sheet of paper inside was a handwritten note.

'Sorry it's not in Braille, but I'm sure you'll find a way to read it. Pass it on to your masked friend when you're done, McGrath'

Under the handwritten note was a pile of old police reports from Detroit, and a collection of newspaper clippings, all relating to the Midnight Maniac murders of six years previous. McGrath obviously wanted to share the information with the Black Bat. He occasionally left messages for the Bat with Quinn. Tony knew that McGrath suspected him of being the Bat, but the detective lieutenant, despite his efforts, had not been able to prove anything. Now, at least temporarily it seemed, McGrath and the Black Bat were on the same side, trying to find out who killed the unfortunate Miss Barbara Sharpe. That was fine with Tony Quinn. McGrath might have been an annoyance at times, but he was no bumbler. He was a competent, experienced detective. Quinn was glad they would be helping each other out this time.

He sat down behind his desk, took off the dark glasses that were part of his charade of blindness, and began to read through the contents of the package. As he sat there for the next hour, digesting the grisly details of those long ago crimes, he grew angrier and angrier. If this was indeed the same disturbed individual and he was loose in Manhattan, then the Black Bat would make certain that he paid for his evil acts!

As he read the newspaper clippings, he heard the footsteps of Carol Baldwin coming down the hall. She entered the office.

"So what did you learn last night?" she asked him.

Tony put down his reading material and looked up at Carol. Without his dark glasses on, his unique features were visible; the strange color of his eyes with their lost and restored vision, and the jagged, tiger-claw type scars that ran down the sides of his face.

"I had a little talk with McGrath, the police lieutenant," Tony told her. "He's convinced that this Sharpe murder was committed by a man who killed a series of young women in Detroit six years ago. McGrath just narrowly missed catching him then. He sent me these old reports and articles. Judging by these documents, McGrath may very well be right. I think this Midnight Maniac, as they called him, has come to New York!"

"How do you intend to catch him?" Carol asked.

"I'm not sure yet," Tony Quinn replied. "There doesn't seem to be any way to predict who his next victim will be. The only criterion seems to be that they were all young women who were in society's spotlight; heiresses, actresses, singers, and other prominent women. There are a lot of those in New York. He probably picks his victims from the news and just goes after them when the opportunity arises."

Carol thought for a moment. Tony could always tell when she was getting an idea because of the way she pouted slightly and tilted her head to one side. After a minute or two, she spoke.

"I'll be the bait!"

Tony almost fell out of his chair.

"You can't be serious!" he blurted out. "You will absolutely not be the bait for any murdering maniac stalking the streets of this city! It's far too dangerous!"

"Tony, please just hear me out!" she protested. "We can just have them put something in the paper. You have friends at the Times from when you worked for the DA's office, don't you? They can make up some fictitious award or something; say I'm receiving it for some charity work or something, and print a nice picture with it. That might get this killer's attention. You'd never have to let me out of your sight. As the Black Bat, you can just melt into the shadows and follow me anywhere I go. I'll feel perfectly safe knowing that you're out there in the darkness watching out for me."

Tony thought for a moment.

"Are you sure you'd want to do that?" he asked her, amazed by her courage. "There's no guarantee he'd even fall for the bait?"

"Mister Quinn, are you implying that I'm not pretty enough to attract that psychotic maniac?" she teasingly said.

Tony stood up from the desk, walked over to where Carol was standing, and kissed her.

That Night:

Detective Lieutenant McGrath puffed on his cigar as he waited on the rooftop of the precinct house. He was glad it was a warm evening, as he had been waiting for nearly an hour. Late that afternoon, he had received a message from the Black Bat, asking him to meet him on the roof.

The detective jumped, startled, as the raspy voice of the masked vigilante came from behind him.

"Good evening, McGrath," he snarled, in the voice that he only used when in costume, in order to set his voice apart from that of Tony Quinn. "We need to talk. A very courageous young woman had volunteered to help us catch this Midnight Maniac, if that is truly who has committed this new murder."

"Young woman; what young woman?" asked McGrath.

The Bat explained. "Carol Baldwin, the daughter of a late policeman. Her father's interest in justice must have rubbed off on her. It seems she knew Barbara Sharpe, although not very well, and wants to help track down her killer. She was warned that it might be dangerous, but she insisted."

"Baldwin? That's Quinn's lady friend. It figures," McGrath mumbled under his breath.

"What was that, Lieutenant?" asked the Bat, who had actually heard the remark, but was being rheotorical.

"Nothing, nothing," answered McGrath. "What's this big plan of yours?"

The Black Bat related the idea that he had come up with earlier.

"In tomorrow's paper, you'll find an article about Miss Baldwin being given a trophy for her time spent volunteering for certain charity organizations. It will be accompanied by a photograph. The story is a complete fabrication. It is our hope that this article will draw our suspect's attention to Miss Baldwin. From the moment that the article appears, she will be in close proximity to one of us; you during the day and me after nightfall. That is, of course, if you agree with all of this. Should you refuse to help us, I will not put the woman at risk by proceeding without you. Tell me now and I can still stop the presses."

"Let's try it," said McGrath. "Any chance to catch this killer is worth the risk. Believe me; I wouldn't be standing up on this roof with you if I didn't want him caught. This Sharpe murder is only the beginning if this is the same guy. You didn't see what I saw in Detroit."

The Bat handed a scrap of paper to the detective.

"This is Miss Baldwin's address. By the time that morning paper hits the stands, you'll be watching her. She'll know you're following her, but she won't react to you. She'll go about her normal business during the course of the day. Don't lose track of her whereabouts for even a second. Is that understood?"

McGrath shoved the address into his trench coat pocket. His face took on an expression of annoyance.

"Are you giving me orders, you masked lunatic?" he snapped, but he looked up to find that the Black Bat had vanished into the shadows.

McGrath decided that he had better head home and get some sleep if he was to be at Carol Baldwin's place at the crack of dawn.

The Black Bat returned to his large manor on the outskirts of the city. He had no pressing business as Tony Quinn the next day, so he decided to try to sleep through the morning and some of the afternoon if he could. He didn't think the killer, if he tried at all, would go near Carol Baldwin until night. McGrath would be near her during the day. If the Black Bat was going to be guarding her at night, he wanted to be fully rested and ready. He arrived home, gave orders to Silk Kirby to wake him no later than two in the afternoon, and went to bed.

Mid-Morning:

Detective Lieutenant McGrath had been trailing Carol Baldwin since just past eight that morning. He had been outside her apartment at six, but had not actually seen her for the first two hours. At fifteen minutes after eight, Carol had finally emerged from her front door. She had begun to walk down the street and McGrath, keeping a modest distance, but never letting her out of his sight, had started to follow her. For the next two hours, he had watched her go about her business; banking, a bit of shopping, a short stop for a cup of coffee in a little diner on the corner of the avenue, a pause at the post office, and a few moments at a newsstand, where she made small talk with the proprietor and read the article about her that graced the day's paper.

As he watched her, McGrath couldn't help but admire the courage of a young woman who would intentionally risk being the target of a demented killer to see that justice would be done. What a dame, he thought to himself!

At eleven, McGrath called in, as he had promised the Black Bat he would do. He had been given a number to call, but had no idea who it would call. On the other end of the line, a voice answered. It was male, but sounded like the speaker was talking through a handkerchief to disguise his voice.

"Yes?" asked the voice.

"This is McGrath. All is well. She's shopping."

On the other end of the telephone line, deep in the hidden tunnels beneath Tony Quinn's mansion, in the lair of the Black Bat, Silk Kirby was relieved to hear that the morning had been uneventful and that Carol Baldwin was safe so far. Soon, Kirby would wake his boss and the nocturnal avenger, the Black Bat, would wake, go through his daily exercise routine, scan the papers for any news that might be relevant to his continuing war on crime, and eventually head out into the streets of the city, when it grew dark, to take up the watch when McGrath's daylight shift reached an end.

After calling the mystery number and checking in, McGrath hung up the telephone and continued his surveillance of Carol Baldwin. His attention was so focused on his task of watching Carol that he failed to notice that he himself was being followed.

A block behind McGrath, Dr. Martin Shaw was keeping an eye on the detective's movements. He was getting frustrated. It had always been his habit to spend the day watching his next victim, before moving in for the kill when the night arrived.

Shaw cursed the detective under his breath as he continued to follow him as he followed Carol Baldwin. *Dammit,* he said to himself; *that persistent little bulldog of a cop ruined things in Detroit, and now he's getting in my way here! Why was McGrath watching Carol,* Shaw asked himself? *Had they somehow figured out that she was on the list? How had this happened?* It didn't matter, Shaw decided; Carol Baldwin was just like all the others…and she would have to be used as yet another example. Only when the world finally learned its lesson could the task of Shaw's blade of justice end! He was tired of it; tired of seeing those silly women get all the attention, all the adoration of the public, just because they were pretty and young and smiled and made nice remarks when the reporters asked them about their acting or their singing voices or their stupid charity work or whatever millionaire or politician happened to be their father or their fiancé! *Enough was enough,* Shaw thought! Doctors were the real heroes, as far as he was concerned; men of skill and intellect, saving lives and curing disease! They deserved to be on the front page of those newspapers, not the silly socialites and their painted lips and dainty smiles!

As the morning went into afternoon and the day grew later, Carol Baldwin kept moving. She ran more errands, had her hair done, did a bit more shopping, and kept busy. McGrath never lost track of where she was or what she was doing. Shaw never lost track of either of them. When he found a woman who needed to be used as an example, he would see the job through to its finish. Only once had he failed, with that Hardwick woman in Detroit. He had vowed never to allow that to happen again. The world needed to be taught a lesson about certain things, and Dr. Martin Shaw considered himself to be just the man to do the teaching. It was grisly, dirty work, but someone had to step up and deliver that message.

Evening:

Tony Quinn woke up just past noon. He immediately went down to the tunnels and chambers beneath his large house and got to work. Being the Black Bat and surviving the experience night after night was not an easy thing. He had to keep his body and mind in prime condition. He spent an hour in rigorous exercise, honing every muscle. Then he ate a big meal and sat down with all of the day's papers, looking for any article that concerned crime. In a city as big as New York, there were always plenty of such stories to be found. He concerned himself with crime of all types. Whether it was the standard mob types, or petty muggers and purse snatchers, or Nazi spies, or serial murderers like the Midnight Maniac, all criminals had to be careful to not cross the path of the Black Bat. Many had tried to put an end to his crime-fighting career. All had failed, and many had died doing so. The Black Bat was ruthless and relentless in his one man crusade against crime. He was willing and able to do the things that the police could not do from within the boundaries of the law. The Black Bat respected the law, but chose to work outside of it.

After his daily routines were over, he waited. At six o'clock, Silk Kirby answered the ringing telephone which was connected to a secret number which could not be traced to the main house. It was McGrath calling in to report that Carol had returned to her home, at least for the time being. Kirby told McGrath to wait there until the Black Bat arrived and signaled that he was ready to take over the watch.

Upon hearing the results of the telephone call, Quinn began to ready himself for the night ahead of him. He tossed aside his regular clothes, and his identity along with them. Then he began to don the distinctive costume of the Black Bat. He donned his black suit, black shoes, black gloves, and black mask. There was no variation in color to the costume; it was all black. He fastened his long cloak around his shoulders. Last, but far from least, he put on his belt and inserted into the holsters the two .45 caliber automatic pistols that were his primary weapon against the underworld. The costume had been designed that way for two reasons. First, the all black ensemble served to let him conceal himself in the shadows, to move unseen when he wanted to. It gave him the ability to seem to appear from out of nowhere... and disappear at will as well. Second, when he did choose to allow himself to be seen clearly, his appearance was dramatic and very, very effective in scaring the sense and clear thinking right out of his enemies' heads. Fighting a war against crime in civilian clothes would simply not be anywhere near as effective.

His transformation complete, the Black Bat got into his black car and shot off down the road, into the darkening city of New York, where he hoped to take one more deadly threat from the streets that he was sworn to protect.

McGrath was crouched in an alley across the street from Carol Baldwin's building, trying to not look conspicuous as he watched her window. He could see her silhouette in the lamplight and he was glad to see that she seemed to simply be going about her business. He waited for the signal that the Black Bat was on the scene, though he knew not what the signal would be.

After some time had passed and the nightfall had come to completion and the streets were fully cloaked in shadow, punctuated only by the evenly spaced streetlights, McGrath felt a light touch on his shoulder. He jumped slightly, startled a bit, and found a folded note, suspended from a thin strand of thread, hanging down to the level of his shoulders. He took the note from its thread and opened it.

'Thanks. Go get some rest, Lieutenant. I'll take it from here.'

The note was signed with a small scribble, in black ink, that was obviously meant to represent a bat. Above his head, McGrath heard a soft scraping sound. He looked up and saw a thin rope fly across the street, many feet up in the air. One end of the rope hooked onto the rooftop of Carol Baldwin's building. The other seemed to be attached to the roof of the structure against which McGrath was leaning. Then, swiftly and with very little noise, he could see a large, man-sized cloaked shape, clad all in black, sliding across the sky, along the rope, moving from one rooftop to the other. The Black Bat was on the scene!

McGrath was starving. He had to eat, having not done so all day. He knew a little greasy spoon diner down the block. He decided to make his way there for a quick hamburger. After he calmed his appetite, he would come back and keep watching, he decided; the Bat might be there now, but two sets of eyes were always better than one. So, the hungry detective left the scene.

The Black Bat made his way across the rooftop of the apartment building. He slid almost silently down the rear fire escape and located the proper window. He tapped on the window, seven times, in a pre-arranged rhythmic code.

Carol Baldwin walked over and opened the window to admit the masked vigilante. They did not converse. They both knew that the Bat would have to conceal himself as quickly and efficiently as possible in case the Midnight Maniac was observing from some hidden vantage point. The Black Bat went into a closet and shut the door behind him. He might not be able to see with the door shut, but his extra sensitive hearing would be able to pick up any sound that might indicate danger.

He sat on a packing crate that was on the closet floor…and he waited. Outside in the apartment's main room, he could hear Carol moving about. His skill at listening was so sharp that he could identify most of the sounds of her actions. He heard the sound of her slipping off her shoes and dropping them to the floor. He heard her sit down on the couch, although her slim body made very little noise. He could hear her pick up a magazine from the table and begin to turn the pages.

A block and a half away, McGrath was polishing off his dinner. He took a last bite, chugged down the final few drops of his coffee, and paid his bill, leaving a nice tip for his waitress, a pretty blonde who he would have tried to chat up if he had the time to spare. Someday, he had told himself many times, he would get up the nerve to ask that waitress out to dinner with him, but not tonight. Tonight he had to keep an eye on another beautiful woman, one who just might be in the deadliest of danger! He left the diner and made his way back to his little hiding spot between the buildings across from Carol's place. If anything was going to happen that night, McGrath hoped it would happen soon. The quicker this whole thing was over with, the better it would be, for all parties involved.

Midnight:

McGrath was trying his hardest to not fall asleep right there in that alleyway. It had been hours since he had resumed his watch. He wanted a cigar, but did not want the billowing smoke to give away his position. The light was still on in Carol Baldwin's apartment. McGrath had seen no further sign of the Black Bat, but he had not expected any. The Bat was too good at being stealthy for that.

Inside the apartment, Carol Baldwin couldn't help giggling out loud despite the danger in which she had placed herself. She had been trying to act normally, but not fall asleep for hours now. She had sat there and read every magazine and newspaper that she had lying around the place. She was on her last bit of reading material and it was something that she found very amusing, in a ridiculous sort of way. Some writer had gotten the bright idea to turn the real-life vigilante, the Black Bat, into a character in one of those lurid pulp magazines! Carol figured that it had probably helped the magazine's circulation, but she had to laugh at the overdramatic prose and the way the poor defenseless women who the busy Bat had to keep saving were depicted. *Oh well,* Carol thought as she read and laughed, *if they didn't make it so overdramatic and poetic, nobody would read it and the poor writer would be out of a job!*

Inside the closet, the Black Bat was still fully awake and alert. He was used to keeping late hours, so the fact that it was midnight did not faze him in the least. At one point, Carol had slipped a glass of water in the door for him, but other than that he had just been sitting there, listening, for the entire night. He didn't mind at all. It was what he did, and as tough as it sometimes got, he wouldn't trade being the Black Bat for anything in the world, so long as there were crimes to be stopped or prevented.

In the staircase that led from floor to floor of the apartment building, Dr. Martin Shaw stood, halfway between the fourth and fifth floors. Gaining access to the building had been a cinch! He had simply lied to the doorman and said he was a new tenant. Carrying his medical bag didn't hurt the situation for Shaw. The very appearance that he was a physician helped his efforts to make people trust him. It was amazing what a medical license and a smile could accomplish. It was late at night and the staircase was deserted, so Shaw had the perfect place to make his preparations. He opened his bag, which didn't really contain many medical implements at all. He pulled out the black, hooded cloak that he always wore when doing his nocturnal job and put it on. The hood went up around his head in a way that produced a mask of shadows around his face. this way, no one could clearly see his thin, pale face and definitively identify him should anything ever be found to connect him to his actions as the man the Detroit press had labeled as the Midnight Maniac! He took the long, sharp surgeon's knife from the bag and secured it in his belt. He took his lock-picking tools as well, confident in his ability to use them. The dexterity of a surgeon's hands could easily be utilized for breaking and entering too. He hid the bag behind a garbage can that stood on one of the landings between flights of stairs and continued on his way up. He reached the fifth floor and ventured into the hallway. There was no one around to see him there.

He made his way to the door that he knew belonged to Carol Baldwin's apartment. He slid the lock-pick into the keyhole and rooted around until the mechanism caught. There was a faint clicking noise and he knew that the door's bolt had moved. He swung the door open quickly and entered the apartment.

Inside, Carol had nearly dozed off on the couch, but she snapped to full alertness when the door burst open and a tall, thin figure in a black cloak entered her home. As the intruder drew open his cape and took a long, lethal-looking blade from his belt, Carol let out a scream.

Crack-crash! The door of her closet split in the middle and splintered into a multitude of pieces as the Black Bat burst forth from the little room where he had concealed himself for the past several hours!

Carol jumped up from the couch. The Midnight Maniac stepped forward, further into the room, his terrible knife glaring like a shard of broken mirror. The Black Bat strode forward, towards the demon he had been waiting for.

"Carol, go in the bedroom! Lock yourself in!" he commanded.

The woman ran into her room and slammed the door behind her. Once inside, she put her ear to the door to listen to what was happening in the outer room.

The Midnight Maniac was faster and more agile than the Black Bat had anticipated. Before the Bat could draw his guns, the Maniac had crossed the room via two long strides and a sudden leap. He came crashing into the Bat, surgical knife flailing forward! The knife narrowly missed piercing the Bat's costume-shirt and flesh, but sliced harmlessly through his cape. The Bat's fist slammed forward, connecting with the Maniac's side. The murderer let out a grunt, then tried to take another swipe with the knife. He missed again. The Black Bat shoved him away with both hands. As the Maniac fell backwards, nearly tumbling to the floor, but regaining his balance, the Bat drew his guns. As he prepared to pull the triggers and blow the Maniac away, the cloaked killer threw the knife towards the Bat! It skimmed against his wrist, slicing into flesh, not deeply, but enough to make the Bat let go of one of his guns. The other gun went off, but missed its intended target, shattering a window instead.

Outside and across the street, McGrath heard the sudden sound of a gunshot and the shattering of glass. He looked across the street and up as Carol Baldwin's window explode outward, sending shards of glass to the

The door splintered into a multitude of pieces

street below. McGrath was across the street in seconds, shoving his way past the doorman while waving his badge in the air and shouting, "Police! Let me pass!"

He ran inside and up the stairs, panting as he went, unused to such physical exertion. He cursed himself for getting older and fatter. He made his way to Carol's apartment and found the door wide open, with two black-clad men wrestling on the floor. There was a large knife lying in one spot, and two guns elsewhere. McGrath drew his own gun. He was tempted to shoot them both, but for this one night, he was on the same side as the Black Bat.

"Stop, both of you!" he shouted. "I'll shoot! Black Bat, get away from him and I'll put a bullet in him!"

McGrath could see the Bat trying to roll away from the Midnight Maniac, but the two wrestling bodies were too entangled. McGrath swore.

Carol Baldwin heard the shouts of a third voice in the room and ventured out of the bedroom. "Shoot that killer!" she shouted at McGrath.

"I would if the damn Bat would get out of the way!" he barked back.

The two cloaked rivals kept wrestling on the floor. The Black Bat's leg shot out and kicked over the small table that held the lamp. The lamp crashed to the floor; the bulb shattered; the room was plunged into darkness! The Bat had done it on purpose, hoping to use his unique night-vision to subdue the Midnight Maniac more quickly and easily. Before he could take advantage of the darkness though, the Black Bat felt a sudden stinging feeling, a short burst of slight pain, which he recognized as the sensation of a syringe needle being plunged into his arm! He felt himself suddenly growing weak.

The Midnight Maniac stood and bolted for the door. McGrath couldn't see well enough to tell exactly what was happening.

"McGrath, go after him!" the Black Bat said, his strength fading fast. McGrath ran out the door and followed his adversary down the hall, hoping and praying that he would be fast enough.

In the apartment, Carol Baldwin had the sense to light a candle and shed some light on the room again. She found the Black Bat almost unconscious.

"Call Kirby..." was the last thing he said before he faded into a deep sleep. Carol checked his pulse and breathing. He seemed to be all right, just unconscious. She went to the phone and dialed the direct number to the Black Bat's lair. Silk Kirby answered and said he'd be on his way immediately.

Outside, the other police summoned by McGrath had arrived. The

Midnight Maniac had slipped away into the darkness of the Manhattan night and now McGrath was barking orders at all the gathered detectives and officers to search every place within walking distance for any sign of the murderous madman, though he now had little hope that the killer would be caught that night. As insane as the Midnight Maniac might be, McGrath knew he was not stupid. He had evaded capture for too long to be a simpleton.

When Silk Kirby arrived in the area, with Butch O' Leary along to help if he could, they managed to sneak into Carol's apartment building amid the chaos of too many police tripping over each other, as well as all the onlookers who had been awakened by the gunshot and breaking glass. They made their way to Carol's apartment. Butch lifted the unconscious Black Bat and snuck him down the rear fire escape. Silk scooped up the Bat's guns and the knife that the Maniac had left behind. Soon, they were on their way back to the Quinn residence in the sedan used by Quinn (and always driven by Kirby) during the day. The Black Bat's car would have to wait in that area until later.

Carol Baldwin, shaken but unhurt, waited in her apartment for the inevitable return of Detective Lieutenant McGrath. He came back, ascertained that Carol was all right, grew angry when she told him that the Black Bat had left and taken the evidentiary surgical knife with him, and offered to put Carol up in a hotel for the night in case the Maniac came back. Carol Baldwin was brave, but not dumb, so she accepted and packed a small bag with what she would need for one night away from home.

Knowing that the area was now swarming with police, unlikely as they were to find anything, McGrath went home, knowing he would be more effective the next day if he got some rest.

Noon, the next day:

Tony Quinn coughed once as he woke up. He opened his eyes and was glad to see the ceiling of the Black Bat's lair looking down at him. He sat up, his head aching a little. He saw that he was still in his Black Bat costume, except for the hat and mask.

"Mornin' Boss!" said Butch O'Leary, as he handed Quinn a cup of coffee.

Quinn took a sip. "What happened?" he asked the towering strongman. "Is Carol all right?"

Silk Kirby stepped into the room and answered the question before O'Leary could get another sentence out of his mouth. Of the two assistants to the Black Bat, Kirby was most definitely the faster talker. In fact, talking was his primary talent. O'Leary's strong suit was pounding skulls into brick walls, at least when he wasn't working on Quinn's cars.

"Miss Baldwin's just fine, Boss," said Silk Kirby. "The police put her up in a room last night for safe keeping. She called a little while ago. She's bringing your car back here. She had the good sense to take the keys from your cloak last night when you passed out. Me and Butch went and got you and brought you back here, but we left the Bat-Car around the corner from her place. Oh, and that police lieutenant called the secret line a few hours ago. He wanted to talk to you, but I told him you were busy. He said he had some information for you...and he said you shouldn't have kicked that lamp over!"

Carol Baldwin arrived at Quinn's house a short time later. She and Tony ate lunch together. As he ate, Tony felt his strength return to him. Whatever the Midnight Maniac had injected him with; it had only weakened him temporarily.

When he had finished eating, he excused himself for a few minutes and went to telephone McGrath.

"Homicide department, Lieutenant McGrath here," answered the gruff voice of the detective.

"It's me," growled the Black Bat in his 'professional' voice.

"Are you all right?" asked the cigar-chomping cop, probably more concerned for the good of the case than for the health of his temporary ally.

"Back to full strength," the Bat assured him. "Did your men find anything last night?"

"As a matter of fact, they did," McGrath said. "Can you meet me on the precinct roof tonight?"

"I'll be there at ten. By the way, don't worry about Miss Baldwin. She's staying at Quinn's place tonight. She'll be safe." Then the Black Bat hung up the phone.

Tony Quinn spent a few hours with Carol, and then pushed himself through his daily workout to assure himself that there no lingering effects from the drug. He felt fine. At nine o'clock, he donned the Black Bat costume, complete with a new cape to replace the one that had been torn by the Midnight Maniac's knife, and headed back into the thick of the city.

Ten O'clock:

The Black Bat was punctual. McGrath was, for once, glad to see him.

The detective tossed a black doctor's bag to the masked avenger as he arrived on the roof.

"We found that stashed in the staircase of Miss Baldwin's building," McGrath explained. "It seems our suspect is a doctor!"

"I'm not too surprised by that," replied the Black Bat. "The old police reports said the victims were killed with surgical precision…and that was definitely a surgeon's knife that he was wielding last night."

"Speaking of which…you do realize that stealing evidence is a crime, don't you?" McGrath grumbled.

"Add it to the list, Lieutenant," the Black Bat sarcastically shot back.

"There's more," McGrath continued. "I think I might know who the Midnight Maniac is under that cloak and hood!"

"Then spit it out!" barked the Bat.

McGrath began to explain.

"Once I realized that our suspect might be a doctor, I started thinking. I made a few calls to my old friends in Detroit and I looked for any doctors who were living in Detroit around the time of the first murders and who had recently moved to New York. There were actually a few, but not too many to do a bit more research on in a pretty short time. As it turns out, there were also three murders similar to the Detroit cases and this recent Barbara Sharpe thing during the intervening years. Those deaths took place in New Orleans. Guess what? There was only one doctor who lived in all three cities during the right time frames! I actually know him!"

"Well who is he? What's his name?" demanded the Black Bat.

"The name is Dr. Martin Shaw," said McGrath. "He was a renowned surgeon in Detroit, but got on the bad side of his hospital administrators when he kept complaining about not getting enough recognition. It seems he thought doctors deserved more press and praise than actors or sports figures. After Detroit, shortly after the night I shot at the bastard, he moved to New Orleans and worked in a hospital there. Now he's been here, in New York, for a few weeks, filling in for one of our coroners."

"Why haven't you arrested him yet?" asked the Bat.

"I tried," said McGrath. "He never showed up for work this morning, and he's already cleaned out his apartment. He must have realized I'd find the bag he left and figure it out. He could be on a train out of town by now for all I know!"

The Black Bat left McGrath and headed back to the Quinn manor. He had no intention of randomly searching the city for this man. There had to be a logical way to figure out his whereabouts. He intended to go home and think about it until he found a solution.

He drove back to his house, frustrated, but confident in his ability to eventually track down this killer. He just hoped he would be able to do it before any more innocent women were killed.

He parked his car in the underground garage and got out. Silk Kirby suddenly came running out of the hallway.

"Boss, thank God you're back!" Kirby was shouting. "He came and he took her!"

"What? Slow down, Silk. Tell me what happened!" the Bat said, hoping Kirby didn't mean what he feared he meant.

"I was down here smoking a cigar. I didn't want to smoke upstairs because Miss Baldwin said the smell bothered her. I left her up there with Butch. I heard a scream and a loud thump, so I dropped the stogie and went back up. I found Butch lying on the floor. I think that crazy maniac guy stuck him with a needle like he did to you…and he took Miss Baldwin with him! I got to the window just in time to see a little red car speeding away. I wrote the plate number down. Here," said Kirby, handing a scrap of paper to the Bat.

"Dammit! He must have known that Carol was a friend of Tony Quinn. It's not exactly a secret. He took a chance on her being here, assuming a blind man wouldn't put up much of a fight. He must have dodged Butch and stuck that needle in him before he could put up too much of a fight. Where is Butch anyway?" asked the Bat.

"I dragged him to his bed. He's all right, just weak. The stuff didn't knock him all the way out, I guess because he's such a big ox, but he won't be moving around much for a while," Kirby answered.

"All right, thanks for the plate number, Silk. You did well. I'll be back later."

The Black Bat raced down to his lair and grabbed the telephone. Would McGrath be at the stationhouse or had he gone home, he wondered?

He called the precinct. McGrath was there. The Black Bat gave the detective the plate number and the car's description. He told McGrath to have the police keep a look out for that car, but not to do anything if they found it. The Black Bat would meet McGrath at the precinct in thirty minutes.

The Black Bat's black car raced down the roads. He had to make this trip as quick as possible. The life of Carol Baldwin was at stake, so he didn't give a damn about risking a speeding ticket, as if the police would be able to catch him if they wanted to! Butch O'Leary had made some unique adjustments to the Black Bat's car and it was able to outrun almost any other vehicle on the road. As he drove, he prayed he would not be too late.

He reached the police precinct and found McGrath waiting out in front. The detective jumped in and the Bat resumed driving. It was an odd situation for them both. At any other time, McGrath would have been first in line to either arrest or shoot the Black Bat, but their mutual contempt for twisted, homicidal maniacs had made them, at least temporarily, into partners in crime-fighting. They were both acting out of necessity and they both knew that as soon as this case came to an end, assuming they both survived it, their old game of cat-and-mouse would resume.

"They found the car," McGrath said as the Black Bat drove. "It's parked outside an old, empty medical practice about a mile from here. Make the next left!"

The Black Bat drove swiftly and confidently. Soon they were at the reported location. There it was – a small red sports car with plates matching those from Kirby's little scrap of paper! The Bat could see that several plainclothes cops were seated in cars along the street, trying to not look like cops, with varying degrees of success. McGrath must have told them to wait until he arrived, the Bat knew.

The Black Bat's car whizzed by and parked in a lot a few buildings away from the abandoned doctor's office. McGrath went to join his men.

"If you don't see any sign of anything happening in five minutes, break the door down and storm the place!" the Bat shouted to McGrath as he ran into the spaces between the buildings.

The Black Bat intended to find a rear entrance to the place. If he made a direct entrance, any chance of sneaking in and rescuing Carol, assuming she was still alive, might be blown. It wasn't only that either; he didn't want all those cops seeing him and opening fire despite McGrath's orders! It wouldn't do anyone any good for him to race to the scene and try to help, only to be shot by the police he was trying to help.

He made his way to the rear of the building. The rear windows were boarded up. The door was covered by a large sheet of plywood. The Black Bat tore the boards from one window and climbed through the opening.

The glass had long before been shattered. He made his way into the building. It had apparently been unoccupied for quite some time, as it looked dirty and dingy inside.

He walked down the hallway. He finally found a door that had light coming from under it, as if there was a lamp switched on inside. He put an ear to the door and listened with his super-sharp hearing. The voice inside chilled him to the bone.

"Ah, my dear Miss Baldwin, you're awake! You managed to get away from me last night. Only one other woman has ever done that. I don't like girls who run away from me; hence the fact that you are now strapped to this table! You know, Carol, a few quick, precise cuts usually do the job quite nicely, but you have been a bad, bad girl...so I'm going to do this more slowly."

"You are out of your mind!" the voice of Carol Baldwin said.

"Perhaps I am," the Black Bat could hear the Midnight Maniac say through the door. "But I do not like to be reminded of that fact, Carol. Perhaps I'll remove your tongue first. That would certainly shut you up, now wouldn't it?"

That was it. The Black Bat had heard enough. He kicked the door in!

Wood splintered and shattered. The Bat drew his guns, ready to riddle the Midnight Maniac with every piece of hot lead his chambers could hold...but he stopped. The Maniac had a scalpel pressed against Carol's neck, right at the jugular, as she was strapped down to a surgical table. There was no way he could be sure the bullets would stop the blade from making that one deadly incision before death claimed the murderer.

"Let her go and fight me like a man!" the Bat hissed at the demented doctor.

"No, I'll do this my way!" the Midnight Maniac retorted. "I had no reason to want to kill you, masked man, until you came after me last night! This little creature is the one who needs to die! There are lessons to be taught to the world! The prettiest one is not the most important. The man who hits fifty home runs is not the real hero! Do you know how many lives I've saved? Do you have any idea?"

The Black Bat laughed.

"You're an idiot," he said to the Midnight Maniac, who looked truly shocked that anyone would make such a comment at a moment like that.

"You're trying to prove a point about the heroism of doctors...by slicing up innocent women? That has got to be the single stupidest idea I've ever heard. Don't you remember the Hippocratic Oath? No, apparently you don't. You're no Hippocrates…you're a damned hypocrite!"

"How dare you?" the Maniac snarled. "I've saved countless lives!"

The Black Bat stared hard at him, glaring with every ounce of menace he could muster shining in his eerily colored eyes.

"Step away from the girl…or I'll kill you where you stand," the Black Bat hissed at him, but he still dared not take a shot without risk of that gleaming scalpel cutting into Carol.

Then, in a perfectly timed act of selflessness, Carol Baldwin wrenched her neck an inch away from the madman's blade, struggling against her restraints…and bit the Maniac on the wrist!

The scalpel fell from his hand and clattered to the floor! The Black Bat pounced, tackling the Maniac and pinning him to the wall. Face to face with the Midnight Maniac, the Black Bat snarled at him.

"I could have shot you just now, but I want to make you feel just a little bit of the pain you've given out…in Detroit," the Bat said as he punched the Maniac in the abdomen.

"…in New Orleans," and he hit him a bit higher, cracking ribs.

"…and here, in my city!" and the Black Bat's powerful fist connected with the Midnight Maniac's jaw, breaking teeth and sending blood spitting out.

The doctor of death crumbled to a heap in the corner of the room.

The Black Bat picked up the Maniac's discarded scalpel and sliced away the leather straps that held Carol to the table. He hugged her once.

"Go outside and tell McGrath that everything is fine, but tell him to give me a few minutes with this monster," the Bat said, relieved that Carol would be all right. He had two reasons for sending her outside. He wanted her to delay McGrath from coming in too soon, and he didn't want Carol to witness the rest of the horrific scene that was unfolding inside the building.

When Carol was gone, the Black Bat turned back to his fallen foe. The Midnight Maniac was still on the floor, staring up at the man who had just beaten him to a pulp.

"How does it feel, Martin?" the Bat asked him. He hoped that calling the psychotic surgeon by his first name would unnerve him enough to drop his defenses even more, giving the Black Bat a further advantage.

Dr. Shaw struggled to stand. The Bat let him rise. He saw no reason to knock him down again. In fact, he found himself hoping that he would make another attempt to attack. That would give him an excuse to fill him with bullets.

"It doesn't hurt as much as seeing my contributions go unnoticed," complained the doctor.

"I have no sympathy for you, you animal. You're not even a human being," the Bat told him. "I've saved a few lives too, you know. I saved Carol's life twice now in two days, and you know what? All I need is to see her smile at me to know that I've done the right thing. I've saved many lives…and taken lives away from a lot of men who would have murdered innocents, and do you know what I have to show for it? The police hunt me, the press paints me as a lunatic, and as many people are afraid of me as root for me, but none of that matters. I do what I do because I know its right, not for any reward. That's the mindset a real doctor would have, not an egotistical monster like you. You disgust me, and you will never kill another innocent girl! This will end here, tonight!"

The Black Bat stepped forward and grabbed the Midnight Maniac by the front of his cloak and pulled him forward. He tore the cloak away, revealing the regular shirt and pants underneath. Dr. Martin Shaw didn't look so threatening without his gaudy cape and hood. He just looked like a pale, thin middle aged man with a disturbed mind and a talent for victimizing innocent women. The very sight of him repulsed the raven-cloaked avenger of the New York night. The Black Bat was about to drag him out the door by his collar and hand deliver him to McGrath when he saw a quick flash of silver. Another knife! The Bat tried to dodge, but the Maniac's hand was a quick one and the blade struck a glancing blow, wounding him, though not deeply, along the ribs!

The murderous doctor pushed past the Bat and ran into the hallway of the building. The Bat, momentarily hunched over in pain, lifted his shirt to look at his injury. He was relived to see that it was only a minor, if painful, flesh wound. Luckily, this was an old medical building. He quickly found an old roll of bandages and did a rough and sloppy but adequate job of stopping his own bleeding. It will have to be good enough for now, the Bat said to himself, and he prepared to continue the fight.

Now, the Black Bat would have to hunt his prey. The place was surrounded by police, so Shaw could not get out of the building. That certainly worked to the Bat's advantage. The fact that the building was old and decrepit also helped, as it was unlikely that all the lights would work. That might present a problem to the Midnight Maniac, but the Black Bat could see in the dark as well as he could see in the light of the brightest day.

Hands ready to draw his twin .45s at the slightest provocation, the Black Bat ventured into the corridors of the building. Good, it's dark, he noticed.

He had that thought too soon, he realized, as the hallway was suddenly flooded with light. Shaw must have found the main electrical box!

The demented demon-doctor suddenly ran into the hallway, blade held high, and charged straight at his black-caped adversary. *The fool is suicidal*, the Black Bat thought! *Fine! If that's how he wants to end this game, I'll give him what he wants!* There was no hesitation. The black-gloved hands squeezed the twin triggers.

Spak-spak-spak! The guns of the Black Bat fired again and again! Hot, blazing bullets flew and the body of the Midnight Maniac, the body that had slain far too many innocent young women, jerked and twisted with the impact of the projectiles, and then fell backwards, to land in a bloody, lifeless heap upon the cold, hard floor of the old abandoned medical building. The Black Bat holstered his two smoking guns and walked over to the place where the corpse had fallen. He picked up the knife and put it in his belt, and then took something out of that same belt. He had produced one of his small bat-shaped symbols, his calling card, and he placed it on the dead man's forehead.

He muttered one word, "Idiot," and turned away from the dead body of the one who had been the Midnight Maniac and had brought fear and horror to three cities. That reign of terror was over now…and the Black Bat smiled, just enough to show that he felt a grim satisfaction at what he had just done.

He walked down that hallway and went to the front door. He knew he was taking a chance by doing so, but he opened the door and walked out onto the front steps. As he exited the building, he heard the sound of a dozen detectives drawing their guns.

"Don't even think about it, boys," said Detective Lieutenant McGrath. "Any man who opens fire on the Black Bat will answer to me!"

The Black Bat stopped and looked at the assembled crowd of police officers.

"Thanks, Lieutenant," he said. "Do me a favor and give Miss Baldwin a ride home." He waved at Carol, who was sitting in the curb across the street, draped in a blanket that had been provided by one of the policemen.

"Sure. No problem," McGrath shouted back. "Where's the killer?"

"I'd send in the real coroner if I were you, McGrath," answered the Black Bat. "And here's a piece of evidence for you." He tossed the Midnight Maniac's knife, the last weapon that the murderer would ever wield, onto the sidewalk in front of him. Then the Black Bat turned and quickened his pace to a brisk jog and was off into the shadows where he belonged. The

The demented demon-doctor suddenly charged straight at his black-caped adversary

police stood where they were, not a single man moving the intercept the departing vigilante.

The Next Day:

The morning papers declared the death of the Midnight Maniac. They reported that the grisly end of the mysterious killer marked the closing of cases in Detroit and New Orleans as well as New York City. Much mention was made of the heroism of Detective Lieutenant McGrath and the bravery of Carol Baldwin, who had nearly been another victim of the terrible criminal. Only some of the articles mentioned the involvement of the Black Bat, which was typical, since the mayor and police commissioner usually discouraged any press members from making appreciative comments about vigilantes.

Tony Quinn spent most of the day at home. The wound on his side was not very serious, but he decided to take a few days off from his exercise routine and any of his dangerous nocturnal escapades as the Black Bat. Butch O'Leary was soon his old self again, as the weakness brought on by the Midnight Maniac's syringe was only a short term obstacle. Within a week he would be complaining about the wear and tear that the Black Bat put on his car, and happily whistling as he made the needed repairs.

In the evening, Tony had Silk Kirby drive him into the city to pick up Carol Baldwin for dinner. Carol had spent the day resting after her ordeal of the previous night. Her landlord had already had her shattered closet door and damaged front door lock replaced, as well as the window that had been destroyed by the bullet from the Black Bat's gun. She was happy to be back in her own place again. She had even had the store send over a new lamp to replace the one that had been broken in the fight between the Bat and the Maniac. Tony and Silk picked her up at seven and they went to Francini's, their favorite Italian restaurant. Tony and Carol went inside, while Silk Kirby took the car to find his own place to eat, as Francini's was a bit too upscale for Silk's liking.

The young couple talked about everything except the affair of the Midnight Maniac. That ordeal was the last thing they wanted to discuss over dinner. The evening was a good one for them both. The appetizers, main course, and dessert were perfect. They both smiled a lot, which was something they had not done often enough over the past few days.

At one point in the evening, Tony was amused to overhear a passing man comment to his friend that it was a shame that a woman as attractive as Carol Baldwin should be wasted on a blind man. Tony knew the man would be quite envious to know that Tony could see Carol much better than he could…even in the dark.

Detective Lieutenant McGrath had been up since the night before. What people who only see police procedures in the movies don't know is that the paperwork and other mundane duties take far more time than the dramatic moments. For every time a cop draws his gun, there are thousands of times he sits watching the clock tick slowly as he files report after report, wishing it was the end of his long shift. The end of the Midnight Maniac had only been the start of McGrath's work. The crime scene had to be gone over, the coroner had to come – the real coroner, Dr. Sullivan, this time. The body had to be photographed as it lay, and then taken to the morgue and autopsied. Then the case's lead detective, in this case McGrath, had to go back to his desk and write out a very thorough full report, accounting for every detail. When all that drudgery was over with, he had been summoned to the office of the police commissioner, Jerome Warner, and been thoroughly scolded for involving the Black Bat in this business without official permission. He argued that there would most likely have been more murders if not for the Black Bat's involvement, but it did little good. Still, he could not be officially reprimanded, as he was, after all, the hero of the day, at least in the papers! Warner had simply wanted to have the personal satisfaction of chewing out poor McGrath. McGrath chalked it up to jealousy and quickly forgot about it.

When Warner was done with him, McGrath went back to his desk to pack up and get ready to leave for the day. He found a note sitting on top of his heap of paperwork. 'There's something for you on the roof,' it said.

He made his way to the rooftop and found, bound in twine, a bundle of papers. It was the police reports and newspaper clippings that he had passed on to the Black Bat, via Tony Quinn's office. He took out a book of matches and burned the damn things where he stood, watching the smoke billowing up into the Manhattan sky. He felt like the departing smoke was carrying a great weight away with it; a weight that had been a burden on his shoulders for far too long.

Many miles away from Manhattan, it was a rainy evening in Detroit, Michigan. The hallways of the city's biggest mental hospital rang out with the usual sounds of patients having fits of discomfort and sickness, doctors, nurses and orderlies trying, often in vain, to maintain order, and the other noises that one is likely to find in such a place. In one small room, however, the world seemed like a much better, much safer place than it had been only a few hours before. The newspapers, when the staff had finished with them, were often tossed into some of the rooms, to give the patients something to look at. Katherine Hardwick had found one tossed on her floor and had picked it up. Her frequent bouts of panic and depression often kept her from reading for long, but this time she couldn't take her eyes off the article on page three.

'Midnight Maniac Slain by New York Police'

For the first time in six years, the woman who had just narrowly escaped the deadly blade of the Midnight Maniac smiled. In a few days, her own 'miraculous' return to sanity would make the papers itself.

Back in New York City, McGrath finally managed to get away from that desk and that rooftop and that whole precinct house. He told the desk sergeant to tell the captain that he would be taking the next day off. He was exhausted from the whole case and, now that it was over, the tiredness was very noticeable. He left the station, made his way to his favorite diner, the one not too far from Carol Baldwin's apartment, and ordered a nice thick steak. When he finished his meal, he finally, after what must have been a dozen dinners in that place, got up the nerve to ask that pretty blonde-haired waitress to go out with him sometime. She agreed.

He paid his bill and headed home. He usually took a cab, but he elected to walk. He figured he was already tired, so he might as well go all the way to complete exhaustion. A little exercise might not be a bad idea, he thought, and he had certainly felt his age running up all those stairs in Carol's building.

He was home thirty minutes later, back in his shabby and small, but comfortable, apartment. He smoked his last cigar of the day and went to bed. He fell asleep more easily than he had in more than half a decade. There were no more nightmares for Detective Lieutenant McGrath.

"Blessed Are the Frightened Children"

by Aaron Smith

In the essays that accompanied my stories of *Sherlock Holmes* and *Ki-Gor: Jungle Lord*, I made mention of the contributions that my grandfather made to the development of my imagination. In having to write an essay to go with this, my second *Black Bat* tale, "*A Deal with the Devil*," I find myself thinking that it is now time to give credit to my grandmother for her role in shaping my imagination, which is, after all, the source of the stories I write.

When I was a very small boy, my grandmother would sometimes tell me bedtime stories about Jack the Ripper! Ha! I can almost hear the screams of the child psychologists, if there happen to be any reading this. "How terrible," some of you might be thinking, "That's the way to scar a poor child's mind for life!"

To anyone who might be tempted to make such comments, I'd like to assure you all that I am very, very grateful to Grandma for telling me those tales (and in case anyone is wondering, yes, they were quite gruesome and dramatic, although she did leave out the fact that the Ripper's victims were prostitutes). If I'm sure of one thing, it is this; that woman has a definite talent for scaring the wits out of a little kid, and I think that's a wonderful talent to have. It's good for kids to be scared sometimes. Sheltering children from any little thing that might frighten them is a terrible idea, no matter what might be politically correct to think these days.

It wasn't just Jack the Ripper either. Grandma terrified me with tales of vampires, witches that stole and ate little children, and the ever intriguing cursed tombs of dead pharaohs! Years later, when I read of the fact that Bram Stoker's mother used to relate old Irish ghost stories to him when he was in bed, it made me realize how important a little fright could be in developing the imagination. Look where it got old Bram!

As for me, I didn't turn out to be a serial killer or a psychopath or any such monster. The only real lingering effect of those dark nights and tales of terror was that I grew up to be a (gasp!) writer.

The interesting thing is that I had forgotten about Grandma's storytelling talents for years and years. When I started to write my second Black Bat story and wrote the opening scene with the Midnight Maniac trying to kill that poor woman in the alleyway, those old memories came rushing back to me. I could recall exactly how it felt to be a little kid, blankets wrapped tightly around me in bed, eyes closed, visualizing those foggy London streets, the flash of a blade coming from the shadows, followed by a sharp scream, and the rest of the lurid spectacle.

Yes, fright is a healthy thing for a young mind to experience. It is at the root of all suspense fiction and I wouldn't trade those early terrors, or even the nightmares that sometimes resulted from them, for anything. Like all early experiences, the impressions left by those stories contributed to who I am today. Anyone who reads this Black Bat story and enjoys it should feel as grateful as I do to Grandma, for without her scaring the willies out of me in that dark bedroom in Paterson, New Jersey; it is very unlikely that this tale would ever have been written.

Several months had passed since I wrote my first Black Bat story, *Unholy Terror*, and I was very happy to be revisiting the New York of the 1930s, which is home to the Black Bat. It felt good to be writing, once again, about the Bat, his alter ego Tony Quinn, his girlfriend Carol Baldwin, his buddies Silk Kirby and Butch O'Leary, and especially Detective Lieutenant McGrath, who was part of the main focus of the story. I was also happy to bring back one of the supporting characters that I created for that first story, the overly enthusiastic Police Officer Sweeney.

I love pulp-style stories of the 30s, I love noir elements, I love ruthless murderers (at least fictional ones) and I love masked vigilantes. The Black Bat stories give me an opportunity to combine all of these things to come up with a whole that is as much fun as any of its parts. I hope my second Black Bat story is just one of many to come.

So, thanks to those who originally created the Black Bat, and thanks to Grandma for showing me how creatively stimulating a little fear can really be!

THE BEAST
OF THE
REICH

A Black Bat Adventure

by
Mark Justice

Chapter One
THE DEMON IN BLACK

The gates of Hell had opened before Archie Brenner.

Archie wasn't a brave man or a reckless one, which had certainly not aided his criminal career. He hated violence, was a terrible shot and got nervous in strange places. Still, a guy had to make a living, and Archie was a good wheelman. So when somebody was putting a job together and needed a driver, Archie's was usually the first name on the list.

Stinky Lombardi had called Archie two nights ago and told him about the score. One night's work, maybe a couple of hours sitting down at the docks while the other fellas were in the warehouse, then back home to the wife and kid. It paid two hundred bucks.

"Yeah?" Archie had said, trying to hide his interest. "And who am I working for?"

"Me," Stinky said.

"And who are you working for?"

"You don't need to know, pal."

"I got my standards," Archie said. "I like to know who I'm getting involved with."

"Hey, if it's a problem, I can call Vito Piccirilli."

Archie thought about the rent, the gas bill, and the doctor's bill for little Archie Junior. Then he thought about what Madge would say if she found out he turned down two bills.

"I'm in," he said.

As it turned out, two hundred bucks wasn't worth it.

The night had started out all right. Archie stole the big sedan up on the east side and picked up Lombardi and his crew on schedule. They made good time to the docks, where Archie parked behind the big warehouse.

Lombardi made Archie turn on the radio shortly before nine o'clock. Lombardi listened intently for a time, then told Archie to shut it off.

One of the other men said, "No change?"

"Nope," Lombardi answered.

Archie hadn't been paying much attention. He studied the dock area. He'd worked down here for a few months, before he realized that he was allergic to labor. Still, it was familiar turf, and he thought the evening was going to go well. But when Archie met the man Lombardi answered to, he felt a chill from his scalp to his feet.

The boss man was thin and very tall, slouching slightly like a praying mantis. Archie had a thing about bugs. A scar ran down the left cheek of the stranger. A small black mustache decorated his upper lip. He was dressed in a dark overcoat and a fedora.

"This way. Quickly," he said. The accent was thick, foreign.

When Archie didn't follow the crew, the foreigner turned and gave him a nasty look.

"I stay here," Archie said. "I'm the driver."

The stranger stared for another few seconds before he hurriedly walked away with Lombardi and the others trailing behind him. They rounded the corner of the large building and disappeared

Archie climbed back in the sedan and tried to read the racing form he'd brought with him, but he had parked too far from the streetlight. He had been on enough jobs to know you didn't turn on the car's interior light and draw attention to yourself, even if the street seemed empty.

As if his thoughts had been broadcast aloud, the night erupted into chaos.

Archie heard the shouts of Lombardi and his men, followed by the sharp crack of gunfire. The shots sounded smaller than they did on radio and in pictures, and this convinced Archie they were real.

He was torn. Did he stick, and wait for the others to return? Or did he save his own skin and get out of there?

Archie thought of his axe-faced wife and how she would react if he returned home without the money. Then he wondered what damage he'd do to his reputation and future employment if he fled because Lombardi's boys had run into an overeager night watchman or something.

He got out of the car and crept to the corner of the building.

He heard more shots and at least one scream. Archie wanted to run, but he forced himself to peer past the brick corner of the warehouse. In the darkness he could make out the three men who lay motionless on the gravel parking lot, including Stinky Lombardi. Another gunshot exploded nearby. In the muzzle flash, Archie saw the impossible: a leathery form that looked like oily smoke brought to life.

He wanted to move. His legs would not obey.

He didn't know how it had happened, but the black, monstrous figure had suddenly appeared before him.

A squeak of fear escaped from Archie's lungs. It was the only sound he could make.

What stood before him had come directly from the horrible Bible stories his grandma had told him when he was a child, about how the devil would walk the earth and bring along his army of demons to torture and kill every man, woman and child. The nightmare was black and shiny from head to toe, with great wings that fluttered behind it like an evil banner.

In each clawed hand, the demon clutched a big automatic. The tiny part of Archie's brain that wasn't consumed by panic wondered why a supernatural creature from the deepest pits of Hades would carry guns.

"Who do you work for?" the demon whispered. Its voice was full of rage and fire. Archie never considered lying.

"I don't know nothin'. I'm just the driver."

One of the creature's claws disappeared beneath its wings and reappeared without the .45.

"Don't kill me, okay?" Archie whined. I gotta wife and a kid and I don't like her much. The wife, that is. But I'm all she's got and –"

There was a swift motion in the darkness, black moving against black, then Archie felt a blinding pain and his consciousness became a part of the night.

The Black Bat kneeled next to the unconscious man. He hadn't struck him that hard, and he suspected the smaller man had passed out from fear as much as the blow. Obviously a low level thug, the diminutive man wasn't worth the waste of a bullet.

The Black Bat stepped to the shadows of the warehouse, where he instantly blended into the surrounding darkness. Dressed entirely in black clothing, the masked avenger appeared to be a living piece of the evening gloom. Only his eyes were visible, peering from the hood that concealed his features, two bright orbs that burned with a hunger for justice.

He surveyed the big lot in front of the warehouse. Though it was dark, the preternatural vision of the Black Bat pierced the night as easily as if the clock said Noon. His sensitive ears detected no sound, save for the soft moans of the unconscious man and the distant hum of traffic.

There was at least one more man here. The Black Bat had observed him standing apart from the others, issuing orders like a military commander. When one of the hoods had spotted the Black Bat and opened fire, the leader had slipped away.

There.

It was a soft sound, the crunch of gravel beneath the foot of someone who was trying to walk with stealth.

Beneath his hood, The Black Bat smiled. He released his second automatic from its holster beneath his armpit.

Another crunch. This one was louder. The man was gaining confidence. Perhaps he believed the Black Bat had fled.

The steps grew closer.

The Black Bat stepped away from the wall. The tall man in the overcoat started. He uttered an oath in another language and aimed a gun in the direction of the Black Bat.

The shot dug a furrow from the brick wall behind the masked man. Thankful for the darkness that threw off the shooter's aim, the Black Bat dove to the ground, squeezing off shots from both big automatics.

The tall man grunted in shock and fell back, clasping his hand. His gun – the Black Bat saw it was a German Luger – skittered across the graveled lot.

"Ungeheuer!" the man cried. "Schnell!"

The Black Bat took a step toward the prone German, intending to scoop up the gun and render the man unconscious.

Instead, he found himself flying through the air. The suddenness of it made his head spin and left him momentarily confused. Then the Black Bat realized that his head was spinning because he had been struck with a powerful blow. He landed on one shoulder and skidded across the gravel parking. On impact, he felt a sharp pain in his shoulder that filled his vision with bright points of light.

The Black Bat pushed up with his uninjured arm. His ears rang and the back of his head throbbed. The blow had come so fast, even his extraordinary senses had been unable to prepare him for it. And the strength of the attack had been fearsome. His vision swam before him, rendering useless his unique ability to see in the dark. The parking lot and the large building were gray shadows in the greater darkness. He could see no better than any man.

Loud, heavy footsteps approached the Black Bat. He couldn't see who approached, save for a large shadow. A huge silhouette, larger than any man could possibly be.

The Black Bat reached for his gun, and then realized that he had been holding both weapons when he was struck. The automatic in his left hand was gone. It must have fallen from his hand. He still gripped the other gun, but he was unable to lift his arm.

The Black Bat was helpless.

He heard his unearthly enemy grow closer. The Black Bat forced his battered body to sit as upright as he could, desperate to face his foe with what little strength remained.

The footsteps stopped inches from his body and the enormous shape that now stood before him blocked whatever faint light existed.

The Black Bat smiled grimly. He prepared to lash out with his legs. Perhaps he could topple the behemoth. Regardless, the masked avenger would not surrender quietly. He would battle his enemy with his last breath.

The warehouse parking lot was suddenly flooded with light. The Black Bat heard the roar of a powerful engine, one he knew quite well. A car door slammed and a man shouted.

"Police! Stop where you are."

The Black Bat lost sight of both men – if, indeed, the larger one was a man. He heard whispered words in German and rapid footsteps on the gravel.

Faster footsteps approached and strong hands pulled him to his feet.

"Sir, are you all right?"

Silk Kirby was the Black Bat's valet and personal assistant, a slight man whose appearance belied his speed and strength.

"I'm okay, Silk. Just a little shook up."

"I saw two shapes, but one of them…sir, one of them was enormous. What was it?"

The Black Bat stood on unsteady legs. His ears still rang with the force of blow he'd taken. His right shoulder throbbed. The arm hung limply at his side, the automatic still gripped in his hand. "I don't know." He spotted the other gun several feet away, near the building. He pointed with his good arm. "Silk, my automatic."

While Silk Kirby scrambled to retrieve the .45, the Black Bat managed to get his other gun holstered. He surveyed the scene. Several dead men were sprawled across the gravel lot. The small man who had claimed to be the driver lay near the corner of the warehouse.

The Black Bat didn't need his keen hearing to recognize the distant sound of sirens.

"Here, Sir." Silk handed the gun to his friend and employer.

"I need your assistance with something else," the Black Bat said.

"Yes sir." Knowing his boss's intention, Kirby produced a gold cigarette lighter from the pocket of his trousers. It had been a gift from his employer the previous Christmas.

The Black Bat used his good arm to remove an odd object from a pocket in his unusual belt. It was a thin metal rod with an oddly-shaped base. The Black Bat held the object toward Silk. The smaller man ignited the lighter and held the flame against the base of the rod. In the flickering light, Silk could see the pain in the Black Bat's eyes, the only part of the avenger's face visible through his mask. The Black Bat had been injured, though he would never complain.

After a moment, the Black Bat knelt next to one of the dead bodies and pressed the base of the metal rod against the corpse's forehead.

When he removed the object, a shape had been seared into the dead man's forehead, a winged silhouette.

The brand of the Black Bat.

The police – and anyone else who heard of tonight's violence – would know who was responsible. The Black Bat was well aware how rumors and gossip spread, both through law enforcement and the darkened watering holes of the underworld. All would know the Black Bat had been here this night to dispense vengeance.

The Black Bat had Silk heat the brand again, then he returned to his grisly task until all the corpses had been marked.

"Sir, the police will be here any second," Silk said.

"I know," the Black Bat said as he stood. "I need your help one more time."

Silk nodded toward the unconscious man. "He's coming with us?"

"Yes," the Black Bat said. "To the house."

Despite his slight appearance, Silk Kirby was quite strong. He hefted the unconscious man over one shoulder and carried him to the sedan. He deposited the man in the back seat. He returned to help the Black Bat into the car, but the dark-clad crimefighter waved him away. Once they were in the vehicle, Silk turned off the lights and drove away, sticking to alleys and side roads until he was sure they had evaded the police.

He then guided the powerful automobile to a very special structure at the edge of the city.

Chapter Two
FRANK'S HEADACHE

"**...AS** the fighting in Warsaw appears to be over with the surrender of the final units to the German and Russian invaders." Frank Cavendish let the final page of his news copy fall silently to the studio floor, as he concentrated on the sponsor message.

"That's the Ten O'clock report of WNWY News, made possible by the generous sponsorship of Bishop Diamonds, Manhattan's finest jeweler. Friends, when the urge for beauty *strikes*, and romance *consumes*, why not feed the fire of *passion*, with a beautiful gem that will forever *elevate* you in the eyes of that special paramour? Why wait *one* year, *three* years, even *5*? Tell her *tomorrow*. Let her know how you feel with a *night* she will never forget, thanks to Bishop Diamonds, West 47th Street, in the heart of the diamond district. And now, from the Paradise Ballroom, the swinging sounds of Terry Wright and his Players in the Night."

The sound of a clarinet blared from the speakers in the small announcer's booth, the opening to Wright's theme song "Rumrunner's Rag". Cavendish hated it.

Through the control room window, Bill Salyers, the engineer gave him an "okay" sign with his thumb and forefinger. Behind Salyers, Vic Castellini glared at him. The young copywriter probably wanted to criticize Cavendsih's reading of the commercial. Damned fool. Didn't he realize Cavendish made his lousy copy sing? Frank had been doing this a long time. You'd think some people would respect that.

Cavendish left the studio and headed for the back stairs.

"Cavendish…" Castellini called after him.

"In a minute." Cavendish threw open the door and climbed to the roof.

When he reached the top of the building, he stepped out onto the pebbled surface and lit a cigarette. For early October, it was a fairly warm night. He stood at the edge of the roof and studied the city.

"Look at all those lights," he muttered. The sight never failed to inspire Cavendish.

That's where he was meant to be. Out there. At the clubs and the theaters, with beautiful women on his arm and the applause of an enraptured audience ringing in his ears. Frank Cavendish had always known that his destiny lay in show business. He had always figured radio would be a pathway to theater and the pictures. After all, he was a good-looking man with a nice voice.

He had it all planned out. Get a juicy role on a good drama or comedy. He would even take a part of those ridiculously dull morning soap operas if he had to. At least it would get him in front of women. That's who Frank saw as his audience. Once his photo appeared in the fan magazines, the mothers and daughters of America would demand to see him in motion pictures. Look out, Hollywoodland, here comes Frank Cavendish.

Only it wasn't working. He'd been in this burg for six years and the farthest he'd come was reading depressing news and shilling for two-bit businesses on the lowest.

Well, all that was about to change.

Cavendish smiled as he took a long drag on his cigarette. Something had been bothering him for a while and last night he'd figured it out. It was a brilliant plan, and Cavendish wanted in. So earlier this evening he approached the one person who had to be in on it.

His demands were simple. For all the trouble that someone had gone to, some big money had to be involved. Frank wanted in on it. He wasn't greedy, so he named a figure that was respectable but not piggish. He made it very clear. The Powers That Be had to put Cavendish on the payroll, or he would rat them out to the authorities.

Soon Frank would be able to afford the lifestyle of a star, even if the career was still a dream. He shrugged. He could live with that.

He had his eye on a newer place over near the park, where a bunch of the theater stars lived. He'd need a new car, too, along with someone to drive it.

He flicked the cigarette butt over the edge of the building. Life was about to get very good for Frank Cavendish.

He heard the roof door slam open, and he sighed.

Never a moment's peace. Was it too much to ask that he be allowed a brief respite before his next arduous reading? Besides, he didn't have to be back on until Eleven.

"Castellini," Cavendish said through clenched teeth, putting the full force of his powerful voice behind it. "I said not now."

Cavendish heard the scrape of a shoe on the roof's surface. It was a thick noise, heavier than a runt like Castellini could make. Maybe it was Salyers, the engineer. That fellow ever missed a meal.

If it were Salyers, Cavendish needed to be charming. An engineer could make the most gifted announcer sound horrible.

Cavendish turned to greet the portly engineer only to stop and emit a tiny squeak of fear, a feeble little sound for a man with such a rugged voice.

It wasn't Slayers who stood before Cavendish.

In the flashing light from the beer sign across the street Cavendish saw the largest human being he had ever encountered.

If it *were* human.

Cavendish took an involuntary step back.

The man-monster continued to approach.

It was three men wide and two men tall, or so it seemed to the terrified announcer. The beast was completely bald. Its eyes were shadowed beneath a massive brow ridge and its mouth was far too large. The creature smiled as it came closer. Drool ran from a corner of its mouth.

Cavendish took another step backwards, aware of the roof's edge waiting just behind him. Despite his fear, he wondered about the tailor who had made the suit uniform the creature wore. It was military, that was certain, encompassing enough material to cover a mid-size circus.

As the hulking form grew near, Cavendish saw an insignia on the sleeve of the uniform.

A swastika.

This was a Nazi? The Germans had soldiers like this behemoth?

Cavendish stuck his hands out in front of him, like his pale appendages had a chance of stopping the inhuman brute.

"Slow down, old boy," Cavendish said. He tried to keep his voice calm, but he detected a slight quaver. "The – the war's across the ocean in Europe. This is America. We're at peace. Do you understand?"

The man-monster didn't answer. Its smile grew wider and Cavendish was nauseated by the stench of its breath.

The large hands grabbed the announcer's head.

They squeezed.

An incredible blast of pain cut off Cavendish's scream before it began. He could actually hear the bone of his skull creak and begin to crack.

No, he thought, *this can't happen. I'm going to be rich. I'm going to be a star.*

The pain grew to a white-hot eruption of agony. The world was consumed first by a piercing white light before everything collapsed into darkness.

The monstrosity held the cadaver that had been Frank Cavendish over its massive body. The announcer's crushed head dangled limply.

The beast tossed the body over the side of the roof. Before the corpse

The creature smiled as it came closer. Drool ran from a corner of its mouth.

crunched to the pavement below, the monster left the roof's edge and returned to the stairs.

Chapter Three
ARCHIE IN THE AFTERLIFE

Archie Brenner was dead. He knew there could be no other explanation. Just before he died he had seen the demon from Hell. Now he was on a table in an unfamiliar room, unable to move.

This had to be a morgue. That made sense. What Archie didn't understand was why he was still here, inside his body. Why wasn't he in Heaven or…that other place? Or even floating around as a ghost?

Nobody had even hinted at the idea that you were stuck in your body after you died, able to observe but not act, especially if someone were about to make you the star attraction at an autopsy.

The way Archie saw it, that just wasn't fair. If someone -- a priest, say, or his grandmother -- had told him that he would be chained to his dead body he'd have chosen a safer profession, like an accountant or a librarian.

As for the autopsy, Archie had a bad feeling that it was about to begin. He saw shadows on the wall. There were at least two people in the room with him, only these new arrivals were alive. At least he hoped they were. Their shadows were certainly active.

He felt a tiny jab in his arm.

Oh, *swell*. Not only was he dead, Archie could still feel.

This wasn't going to be very pleasant.

But, oddly enough, Archie's mood swiftly became rosier. He felt light and happy. Being dead no longer seemed like something he should be upset over.

Time passed. Archie wasn't sure how much. He thought he might have dozed off. Now he could hear voices.

A man said, "How long has it been?"

"Nearly thirty minutes," a woman answered.

"That should be enough time for it to work."

The shadows returned. Archie was happy. The shadows were his friends and he was glad they were back.

One of the shadows separated from the wall and hovered close to his face. Two bright eyes smoldered in the center of the dark shape.

"What is your name?" the shadow's voice rasped.

"Archie." He was surprised he could speak. Apparently the spirits of the dead could talk to shadows.

"Your last name?"

"Brenner. Who are you?"

The shadowy head drew closer.

"I am called the Black Bat."

"Oh, I heard of you," Archie said. "Back when I was alive."

The shadow head looked at someone Archie couldn't see. Probably another shadow.

"When you were…alive," the Black Bat said, "why were you with those men at the warehouse?"

"Just driving. That's what I do. Did. The best driver. Ask anybody." Archie was getting sleepy again.

"Who were you driving?"

"Stinky Lombardi and his crew."

"What were they doing at the warehouse?"

"Robbing it, I guess," Archie said. "I mean, did you know Stinky? He wasn't there to paint the place." Archie giggled. It was nice to know the dead had a sense of humor.

"Why did they pick that place?" the raspy voice asked.

"The guy told them to."

"What guy?"

"Foreign man," Archie said. "Might have been German."

"Did you see him?"

"Oh, yeah. Brother, he was a piece of work. Scar on his face. Little mustache. Strange accent."

"What was his name?" the Black Bat said.

"I don't know."

There was silence for a moment as the eyes of the silhouette studied him. After a bit, the whispered voice said, "Did any of the men discuss their plans or do anything unusual?"

Archie thought about that. "Not really. Oh. Stinky made me turn on the radio. He listened real close for a minute, then he told me to turn it off. He said nothing had changed."

Again, there was silence from the Black Bat. The shadowy head nodded to someone else. In a few second Archie got another poke in the arm.

"Hey," he said. "When does my autopsy start?"

"Go to sleep," the Black Bat said.

So Archie did.

The Black Bat and a beautiful young woman stepped through the hidden laboratory door into a hallway that led to a spacious library. In the room were Silk Kirby and another person, a large fellow.

The Black Bat peeled off his dark mask, unveiling the face of a young man, a face that might have been described as handsome were it not for the deep scars around his eyes. The scars were the result of a savage attack that had cost district attorney Tony Quinn his sight.

"How's the prisoner?" Silk asked.

"He thinks he's dead," the young woman said. Carol Baldwin had served as nurse during Quinn's interrogation of Archie Brenner. Though the prisoner had been in no condition to appreciate the sight, Carol was a beauty: petite, blonde with blue eyes that could nail a man to the spot.

She was also responsible for Tony Quinn's career as the Black Bat.

After he had been blinded during his career as a young, crusading district attorney, Carol had donated the eyes of her father, a murdered police officer, so Tony could undergo an experimental and risky surgery.

With his vision restored – and improved; he could now see perfectly in the dark – Tony Quinn had adopted the guise of the Black Bat to fight criminals where the law could not reach.

Something else extraordinary had happened. Tony and Carol fell in love.

It was a relationship that they both understood could never be consummated until the Black Bat's war on crime ended.

"You never told me what led you to that warehouse," Carol said.

Quinn nodded at the large man standing in the middle of the room. "It was Butch."

Butch O'Leary blushed, belying his tough exterior. He had a big head and huge hands. He had been known to punch through solid oak doors and, once, a cinder block wall. He appeared to have no neck, so massive were his shoulders. Despite his slow-witted appearance, Butch was an important and loyal member of the Black Bat's team.

"I just saw some stuff, that's all," he mumbled.

"Nonsense," Quinn said. "Butch saw suspicious characters casing the warehouse."

"I used to work down at the docks," Butch said. "Between fights. I still know some of the guys, and I drop by to visit. A couple of times this week I saw some guys sitting in a car outside that warehouse acting real funny."

"After he told me, I decided the Black Bat needed to investigate." Quinn smiled at the big man.

"What was in that building?" Carol said.

"Nothing. At least not after I used my contacts to discover that the Army had leased the building. Some sort of secret research was going on there. I managed to convince a skeptical major that he needed a new address."

The four chose seats among the library's comfortable furnishings. Silk had already prepared a tray with coffee, cups and saucers.

"Who is this Stinky fellow the little man mentioned?" Carol asked.

"Stinky Lombardi?" Silk said.

"You've heard of him?" Quinn said.

"I worked with him once. And only once. Lombardi would sell out his own sister for the price of a good bottle." Silk Kirby had been one of the best confidence men in the field until he broke into the home of Tony Quinn. Soon the sharp dressed Kirby found himself working on the right side of the law, thanks to the persuasive arguments of the former district attorney. In his brief career, the Black Bat had found Silk's unique skill to be invaluable. "I didn't realize he was one of the men killed tonight. I can't say he'll be missed."

Tony Quinn sipped his coffee with his left hand. His right arm was cradled across his chest.

"How's the arm, sir?"

"Never mind that, Silk. Did you get a good look at that goon who knocked me around?"

"No, sir," Silk said. "I only saw his silhouette when I threw on the lights. He was huge. The biggest man I've ever seen."

Butch growled softly.

"Do you think he was wearing some sort of armor?" Silk said.

Quinn shook his head. "From what little I could see, he was flesh and bone. He was unlike anything I have ever encountered, but there was nothing mechanical about him."

"Tony," Carol said, "that prisoner said he thought the man Lombardi was working for might be German. Do you think this has anything to do with the war in Europe?"

"I can't say for certain. Yet the tall man *was* German, and he called that creature '*Ungeheuer*'."

The color drained from Carol's lovely face. "That's the German word for monster."

"Yes. An apt description, in this case," Quinn said. He winced as he readjusted his right arm.

Butch could stay silent no longer. "Give me a shot at that guy, boss. We'll see if he can handle a good American right hook!"

"Simmer down, you big ape," Silk said. "You didn't see this thing. It would cream you."

Butch muttered under his breath. Quinn could clearly hear the cracking of the big man's knuckles as he clenched his fists.

"It's going to take more than fists to bring down this creature, Butch," Quinn said. "In fact, I'm going to work in the lab."

"Anything we can do?" Carol stole a glance at Quinn's injured arm.

"Yes. Get some rest. You, too, Butch. You'll need your strength very soon, I'm certain. Silk?"

"Yes sir?"

"I'll need you to assist me in the lab tonight."

"Yes sir."

"But first you and Butch take our guest and drop him off near his home. The sedative should wear off in an hour or so. His address is in his wallet."

Butch was alarmed. "Boss, you're gonna let him go?"

"He's harmless," Quinn said. "He's the bottom of the rung. Besides, he'll do more good spreading the myth of the Black Bat than he would rotting away in a cell."

The next time Archie awoke, his first thought was that Heaven smelled a lot like Brooklyn. He blinked away the drowsiness and realized where he was. It was the alley next to his own building.

He was alive.

He was unclear of what happened after the job at the warehouse. He had a vague memory of being in a hospital room and of fearing he was dead. That last thought stuck a chord with Archie. He pulled open his shirt, ripping three buttons off in the process. He reached his hand inside and felt around. His hand throbbed in pain, but he didn't find what he feared was there.

There was no autopsy incision. He sighed in relief.

Archie stood up and made his way to a rotting crate stacked against the wall. Its contents had either decomposed or, more likely in this neighborhood, been stolen. Archie dug around inside the dark interior of the box and came out with a half pint of whiskey. His wife wouldn't allow booze in the apartment, but a man occasionally needed a little snort, so Archie kept a bottle or two squirreled away.

He took a long draw from the bottle and savored the warmth that spread through his gut. He began to feel like himself again. Even the throbbing pain in his hand had started to fade.

Archie still wasn't sure what had happened at the warehouse. Most likely he had been hit accidentally in the struggle. He was still fuzzy on the details. Maybe the cops had been tipped. The important thing was that Archie had escaped and made his way home. Somehow. That crazy dream – the hospital or morgue, the shadows, the Black Bat – had been a result of the blow he had suffered. The best thing he could do now was to lay low and wait to see what had happened to Lombardi and his crew. It didn't look like he was going to get that two hundred bucks but it beat getting thrown in the joint or a bullet in the head.

Another drink, then he'd slip inside and hope that shrill creature he was married to didn't wake up.

Damn, his hand hurt. Had he gotten in a good punch during the dust up at the warehouse?

Archie took a step toward the sidewalk, into the soft glow from the streetlight.

He examined his hand. The back of it and the knuckles looked fine. He turned it over. The pain was centered in the palm.

He held his upturned hand to the light.

In the center of his palm, a brand had been seared.

It was the shape of a bat.

Archie's bottle fell from his other hand and smashed against the pavement. That sound was drowned out by Archie's scream.

Chapter Four
THE SCENE OF THE CRIME

The sun was barely up when Lt. McGrath of Homicide stood in the alley behind a downtown building and stared at the unusual corpse splayed on the bricks.

"This town is gonna be the death of me," he grumbled. "Either that or the Black Bat." The short but stout man pulled a cigar from an inner pocket. He removed the wrapper and stuck the stogie in his mouth. He worked it with his teeth without lighting it.

A police photographer snapped pictures of the dead man. An ambulance was parked around the corner, waiting to haul their payload to the morgue.

"Lieutenant?" A beat cop who looked like he could barely shave stood near McGrath, fearful of his superior's legendary temper.

"Yeah?"

"I got the station manager here. A Mr. Devlin."

The kid smiled expectantly.

"Whaddya want? A medal?" McGrath said around the cigar. The young cop flinched. These kids always wanted a pat on the head. Since when did you get extra points for just doing your job? "Did you make that call?"

"Y-yes sir. He should be here any time."

"Good. Now make yourself useful. Find me some coffee."

"Lieutenant?" The kid wasn't sure he'd heard McGrath right. "You want me to fetch coffee?"

"Yeah, junior we got other people to gather clues and solve cases. Two sugars. Now beat it."

The young cop beat it.

The photographer said, "Finished here, sir. I'll get these back to the precinct."

He left McGrath alone with the corpse and a tall thin man in a dark suit. Mr. Devlin looked like an undertaker with his thin, sallow face and deep-set eyes. The only thing that spoiled the illusion was the obvious discomfort the tall man felt in the presence of the body.

"So this is the man who used to be – " McGrath flipped through a small notebook. " – Frank Cavendish."

Devlin was staring at the body and its oddly crushed head with a look of fascination.

"Mr. Devlin?"

"What? Oh. Sorry." He straightened his lapels and met McGrath's gaze. "Yes. Cavendish worked for me. He was an evening announcer."

"What did that mean exactly?"

"He would read the news headlines. Introduce programs. Make sponsorship announcements." Devlin's color was improved now that he was in familiar territory. "He was a competent employee, if a bit more egotistical than most."

"Was there anybody he didn't get along with?" McGrath asked.

Devlin giggled, a child-like sound that clashed with his dour appearance.

"Why don't you ask me to list those he did get along with? It would take much less time."

McGrath didn't like the radio station manager. He found his thoughts turning toward some charge he could use to drag the man down to the precinct. But that wouldn't help him find out what happened to this Cavendish fellow.

"Did Cavendish have a disagreement with anyone recently, say last night?"

"Not to my knowledge," Devlin said. "Of course, I wasn't in the office last night."

"Who was?"

"There was an engineer. And one of our writers."

McGrath flipped to a new page in his notebook. "I'll need – "

Devlin raised a thin, pale hand. "They're here. Upstairs."

McGrath raised an eyebrow. "They work all night?"

"No, no," Devlin said. "The search for Cavendish took some time and when I heard what had happened, I knew someone from the police department would wish to speak with them, so I asked them both to stay."

Devlin was so pleased with himself he almost smiled.

"Great," McGrath said.

"Oh, and I don't think he left a note."

"Pardon?"

"A note," Devlin said slowly, as though the veteran cop was on his first case. "A suicide note."

Now it was McGrath's turn to smile. "Mr. Devlin, have you looked at the, ah, late Mr. Cavendish?"

"Why, yes. Certainly." Devlin stole another brief glance at the dead man, before he returned his gaze to McGrath.

"Notice anything odd about the body? I'll give you hint. Start at the neck and look up."

Devlin swallowed. "Well, there's a lot of blood."

"Yes…"

"Isn't that normal for…this sort of thing?"

"Somebody takes a fall from that distance, there will be some blood, yes sir. I'm referring to the condition of his skull."

Devlin studied the cadaver again. "It appears to be, ah, crushed."

"Right." McGrath said.

"Lieutenant, this man flung himself off the roof. I would think his head would be damaged." Devlin sniffed and straightened his jacket lapels again.

"Not like that. I've seen quite a few jumpers in my day. None of them had a head that looked like it had been caught in a vise. So there wouldn't be a suicide note, you see? Your man there was murdered."

Devlin turned white. "But – but – "

McGrath took the cigar from his mouth and jabbed it at the taller man. "I think it's time we went inside and talked to your other employees, don't you?"

The stammering of the radio man was interrupted by the young beat cop. "Lieutenant McGrath?"

McGrath sighed and rubbed the back of a hand across his close-cropped mustache. Without looking at the kid, he said, "You better not have forgotten the two sugars."

The beat cop cleared his throat. McGrath turned. The young cop wasn't alone. "Sir, here are the – "

"Yeah. Got it." He waved the younger cop away. "Counselor. Beautiful morning, isn't it?"

Tony Quinn, the former district attorney stood next to the cop. Quinn wore dark glasses and carried a white cane in his left hand. His right arm was in a sling. Quinn's valet, Kirby, stood a step behind his employer. "I really wouldn't know, Lieutenant."

McGrath chuckled. What seemed to be a bit of cruel humor on his part was actually the tough cop's firm belief that the lawyer was not, in fact, blind. McGrath was certain that Tony Quinn was the man behind the mask of the criminal known as the Black Bat. Though he had never been able to prove it, McGrath would never falter in his conviction that Quinn led a double life, and only pretended to be blind. The Black Bat regularly made a mockery of the laws of the city. Though he sometimes seemed to be on the same side of the cops, the Black Bat was, at best, a ruthless vigilante. McGrath would never tolerate that. Not in his city.

"What happened to your arm, Quinn? Did the Black Bat bite off more than you could chew?"

Quinn smiled. "Your delusions never end, McGrath. In fact, I tripped getting out of my tub and wrenched my shoulder. It is a bit uncomfortable, so you can imagine how thrilled I was to be summoned down here at this ungodly hour."

"The city of New York appreciates your help," McGrath said.

"What do you need?"

McGrath quickly and efficiently laid out the facts about Frank Cavendish and his gruesome death. In a hushed tone, Quinn's man Kirby described to his boss the condition of Cavendish's skull. During the conversation, Devlin, the radio station's manager, stood silently, looking for all the world as though he wanted to be anywhere but that alleyway.

After McGrath finished his summary, Quinn said, "What do you expect I can do?"

"I know you always had an interest in unusual crimes, counselor."

"McGrath, you know I'm in private practice now."

"Uh-huh," McGrath said. "Let's go upstairs and speak to the last people to see Cavendish alive."

Devlin hurried to the building's entrance, anxious to get away from the corpse. McGrath signaled the boys from the morgue to take the body away.

Quinn took the arm of his valet and followed Devlin. McGrath brought up the rear. He watched Quinn's blind man act with amusement. Many times in the past he had attempted to trick the lawyer into admitting he can see as well as anybody. He wouldn't be trying again this day. If McGrath could prove Tony Quinn was the Black Bat he would have no choice but to arrest the man.

No, McGrath didn't want to reveal Quinn's secret, at least not today. His instincts had served the cop well for many years, and when he saw the condition of Frank Cavendish's body, with the skull crushed like a soup can, he realized that this might be something too big for a cop.

As much as he hated to admit it, McGrath might need the assistance of the Black Bat. The black-garbed criminal had proven useful to law enforcement in the past, enough that even McGrath could admit the vigilante had his uses.

That didn't for one second diminish McGrath's determination to one day bring in Tony Quinn and his alter-ego.

But someone in the city could murder a man as easily as a child would squeeze a grape. If the Black Bat could help, then Lieutenant McGrath was a big enough man to accept the assistance.

All this required getting the Black Bat to the scene of the crime.

McGrath was certain the vigilante had just arrived.

It was hot in the manager's office and the temperature did nothing to improve Tony Quinn's mood.

The pain in his shoulder wasn't unbearable, but it constantly throbbed like a bad tooth, which proved distracting. Add to that the fact that he had worked all night in his lab without a break, and Quinn was understandably impatient.

And intrigued.

If McGrath called him down here, there had to be something of interest to Quinn...and the Black Bat.

The grizzled police veteran was probably the most dedicated cop in the city. He saw it as his mission to lock up every criminal in New York, the Black Bat included.

Of course, McGrath's suspicions about Quinn were correct, though he would never let the man know that. Quinn often found McGrath's attempt to expose him to be amusing. However, today was different.

As Quinn stood in the alley, pretending to be blind, he studied the condition of the dead man's body, particularly the pulverized skull.

Seeing the violent destruction to the head of the radio announcer made Quinn think of the monster he had faced at the warehouse the previous night. The creature's immense hands could have done the damage to Cavendish.

But what was the connection between the raid on the warehouse and the murder of Frank Cavendish?

Quinn grimaced. It was difficult for him to play the part of the helpless blind man when that monster was free to kill. Quinn's blood burned for vengeance, longed for the feel of the Black Bat's guns in his hands and for the familiar shadows of the night.

McGrath questioned the engineer, Salyers and Castellini, the writer. The two men appeared exhausted. The chubby engineer glared at the cop, while the younger copywriter tapped his foot relentlessly, like a man who was living on coffee alone. Both had said that Cavendish had been his usual arrogant self the previous night, He'd done the ten o'clock news as usual, then was seen going to the stairwell that led to the roof.

"We checked the roof," McGrath said to Quinn. "It's pretty dirty up there, and we got two clear sets of prints. One was medium size, matching Cavendish. The other..." McGrath shook his head. "The other was a big boy, I'll give you that. Biggest damn boots I've ever seen."

Quinn felt a twinge of pain in his damaged shoulder. He clenched his hands into fists.

"Oh, and we found this, but it's probably nothing." He withdrew a folded handkerchief from a jacket pocket. He unfolded it to display the contents. Quinn forced himself not to look.

"What is it?" he asked, just as a blind man would.

"It looks like gravel, sir," Silk said.

"Yeah," McGrath said. We found it nowhere else on the roof, except in the middle of those giant footprints."

Quinn chanced a glance at the evidence. Even through the filter of his dark glasses he recognized the type of gravel that had covered the parking lot at the warehouse where he'd foiled the robbery the previous night.

The parking lot where the Black Bat had encountered that monstrosity of a man.

There was no doubt now in Quinn's mind: Frank Cavendish had been murdered by the same creature that had nearly finished the Black Bat.

Unless there were more than one of them.

No. Quinn wouldn't allow such a dark seed to take root in his mind.

That possibility was too horrible to contemplate. He'd only seen one of the man-monsters. That's what he would deal with for now.

"Can we go?" The skinny young writer stood up. He bounced a clenched fist against one leg. "I'd like to get at least an hour's sleep before I have to write tonight's material."

"You got all their contact information?" McGrath spoke to an older uniformed cop who stood silently against the back wall of the office. The cop nodded.

"Okay. You two can take off." Slayers stood, too, and the men started for the door. "We may need to talk to you again, so don't plan any vacation for now." Both men agreed before departing.

"Is that all, Lieutenant?" Devlin, the manager also stood from behind his small desk. He was anxious for the ordeal to be over. A murder investigation was apparently not as thrilling as he may have hoped.

"Unless my esteemed colleague has anything else," McGrath said, with a gesture toward Quinn.

"If the Lieutenant is referring to me, then, yes, I have one small request," Quinn said. "I'd like to visit the studio where Cavendish last worked."

McGrath chuckled. "Something you'd like to 'see', counselor?"

Devlin blanched at the presumed insensitive comment. "Lieutenant! My word!"

The veteran lawman man reddened slightly, but his voice was firm. "It's okay, Mr. Devlin. Quinn and me, we got an understanding."

"Mr. Devlin?" Quinn said.

"Certainly." The manager came from behind his desk. "This way."

He led the others upstairs to a suite of studios. "We have two large auditoriums, with seating for the public. We can host symphony orchestras," he said proudly.

The view Quinn had through the open door of the empty room leant the impression that it had been some time since the studio had been used.

"On either side of the big studios are two smaller announcer booths. This is the one where Cavendish worked last night."

Quinn took Silk's arm and was led into a room scarcely larger than a closet. It held two microphones on stands, a stool and a lectern. Several sheets of paper were scattered in a pile on the floor.

"Is this what you wanted, Quinn?" McGrath said from the doorway. The booth was too small for all of them to enter.

"Silk, please describe it for me," Quinn said.

Silk complied with the request, as though his employer was actually sightless. When Silk finished detailing the room's contents, Quinn took a tentative step forward and touched one of the microphones. He tapped the floor with his white cane until he reached the glass window of the control room. His apparent curiosity was merely a ruse, designed to get him into position.

"I believe that's all," he said. "Thanks you, Mr. Devlin."

McGrath looked at him strangely, shook his head and left the doorway.

Quinn stepped forward, and nudged a microphone cord with the tip of his shoe. He toppled to the floor, breaking his fall with his good arm. Still, the impact on his wounded shoulder jarred his teeth.

"Oh!" Devlin exclaimed. He moved forward to assist Quinn, but Silk stepped between the two, blocking Quinn from Devlin's sight. When that happened, Quinn scooped up as many of the loose papers as he could and shoved them into his coat. Silk helped him to stand.

"Are you okay?" Devlin asked.

"He's fine," McGrath said. He had returned to the doorway in time to see Quinn gain his feet. "Mr. Quinn is very spry."

Silk shot the cop an angry look, but said nothing.

Devlin had regained his composure. "Well, if there's nothing else..."

"That's it for now," McGrath said. "I'll see these gentlemen out."

On the elevator down, McGrath said, "Do I have your interest, Quinn?"

"It's a fascinating case, McGrath. Who's your suspect – King Kong?"

McGrath practically bit his cigar in two. "Listen, you two-bit faker –"

Silk stepped between Quinn and the angry cop.

"Outta my way, shrimp," McGrath barked. Silk wasn't much shorter than McGrath, but the Lieutenant was twice as wide, all of it muscle.

"Easy, Silk," Quinn said. "Honestly, McGrath, I still don't see why you called me down here. I'm just an attorney now. What help did you expect?"

"Why, your insight and experience, of course. And maybe, just maybe, you could have our friend look into this mess."

"What friend?"

McGrath placed one hand across his forehead and the other over his nose and mouth, until only his eyes were exposed.

"He's miming a mask sir," Silk said. "As in the Black Bat, I believe."

Quinn laughed. "Really, McGrath, you should see some sort of specialist over this obsession you have with the Black Bat and me."

McGrath glowered at the pair of them while chewing on his cigar.

When the elevator reached the lobby, McGrath exited first and headed through the doors to the street. Silk Kirby led his boss to the large sedan parked at the curb.

Quinn tapped the floor with his white cane until he reached the glass window of the control room.

When they were underway and safe from prying eyes, Quinn removed his dark glasses.

"How do you feel, sir?" Silk asked.

"I'll be fine," Quinn said.

"What were those papers, if I may ask?"

Quinn reached in his jacket and brought out the papers he had retrieved from the floor of Frank Cavendish's booth.

"Cavendish's script from last night, I believe."

"You think they'll help?"

"I'm beginning to believe they might."

Quinn thought about the flattened skull of Cavendish and of the beast that he had fought the night before, and he could feel the heat rising upon his skin. He needed his guns in hand and his enemy before him.

"Where to, sir?" Silk said in his calm, even tones.

"Home," Quinn said. "We have some more work to do, then a little rest. Tonight the Black Bat hunts."

Chapter Five

THE BLACK BAT STRIKES

Walther Olbricht, a proud *schutze* – or private – in the German *Wehrmacht*, paced restlessly in the dark, trying to get his land legs beneath him once more.

He was, in equal parts, fascinated and frightened at being in New York City. Fascinated because of all the lights and all the people. Olbricht had never seen one place that was so large, even though what small bit of sightseeing he did was late at night. He was frightened because of the tales he had heard – mostly from other soldiers – about the lawlessness in New York and a creature of the night who murdered men and drank their blood. He was called *Schwarze Fledermaus*, and Schutze Olbricht feared meeting him.

Olbricht didn't even know why he and the others were here, other than, again, the rumors he heard. The Americans had something the Nazis needed. It was a secret and one that was closely guarded.

When he had asked a question about it, Herr von Kleist told him to keep his own counsel or risk being turned over to the *ungeheuer* as a plaything.

Olbricht shivered. He feared Herr von Kleist even more than *Schwarze Fledermaus*. The *ungeheuer* was a terrifying creature, true but it was as mindless as a brain-damaged child. It was von Kleist who controlled it, ordered it do many evil things.

Olbricht was a good soldier, loyal to the Fatherland, but he hated serving under von Kleist, an evil man without honor. Yet von Kleist, who wasn't even part of the military, had been given free reign on this mission to America, thanks to his position as an advisor to the fuehrer. To cross Von Kleist was to betray his nation And Walther Krieger could never do that.

He shivered again, this time from the breeze that came off the nearby river. Olbricht's fellow soldiers – seven men he had served with for a year – stood with him several blocks from the warehouse. Each of them wore non-descript civilian clothes, at von Kleist's orders. All of the men were anxious to complete their task and return home. Herr von Kleist told them the next time they returned to America it would be as conquerors.

Walther Olbricht would rather return to Braunfels, where he had grown up and where his sweetheart still lived. Olbricht had to admit that this didn't seem likely to happen soon.

A rumble of a truck engine drew Olbricht's thoughts back to the present. He swallowed hard, since he knew who – and what – was in that vehicle.

The truck parked near their position and Herr von Kleist climbed down from the cab. The soldiers saluted him.

"Heil Hitler," von Kleist said. As always, he was dressed in a long coat and a fedora. A long scar crossed one cheek. Legend said von Kleist had gained it in a duel.

"What you are about to do will honor the Fatherland for centuries to come."

The men waited impatiently for their instructions. They had learned that von Kleist could be rather long-winded.

After many platitudes concerning the destiny of Germany and the Nazi party, von Kleist finally got down to brass tacks. "When you get inside, quickly move to find any chemicals in the open or hidden away. Also any papers. I know you don't read English. Just look for papers with numerals. Bring it all back."

"How will we carry it?" It was another soldier, Erich, who spoke up.

Von Kleist opened the door to the truck's cab and produced seven canvas bags with leather handles.

"Are you armed?"

The men nodded. Olbricht patted the Luger pistol in the leather holster on his hip.

"Here." Von Kleist handed each of them a small flashlight. "Now go. Work swiftly, for your country and your fuehrer."

Something large shifted in the back of the truck. Olbricht was glad to put distance between himself and the vehicle's cargo. He led the others to the side door of the warehouse. It was locked, as expected Olbricht drew his Luger and pointed it at the door handle. He squeezed the trigger. The explosion nearly deafened Olbricht. Sparks flew from a bullet's impact on the metal door.

But Olbricht hadn't fired.

He turned. A figure shrouded in black stood twenty feet away. A dark cloak flapped behind the figure, gently swaying with the wind. One hand gripped a huge American handgun.

A terror stronger than any he had ever experienced froze Olbricht to the spot. He wanted to cry out to his companions, shout the name of the legendary enemy he had recognized. Instead, throat constricted by fear, he could only whisper.

"*Schwarze Fledermaus*".

The man with the gun appeared to be paralyzed with fright. His companions, unfortunately, didn't feel the same way. German guns were drawn, but the Black Bat fired first. He struck down two of the men with his first three shots, then dived for cover around the east corner of the building. When the remaining men scurried after him, Silk Kirby and Carol Baldwin emerged form their hiding spot around the warehouse's western corner with guns blazing.

He knew the warehouse was empty, thanks to his tip to his military source, a high-ranking man who owed the Black Bat a large favor.

Despite his disapproval of her participation, The Black Bat's heart swelled with love and admiration for Carol. She had insisted on coming, and he had learned long ago that once her mind was made up, dynamite couldn't move her. Despite looking like a fresh-faced debutante, Carol was tough as nails, and she had eagerly signed on as a soldier in the Black Bat's war on crime.

The guns of Carol and Silk dropped two more of the gang, leaving three scrambling for cover behind two large, rusting flatbed trucks in the center of the parking area. It would be difficult to surprise the hidden men; this lot was lit much brighter than the last warehouse. The Black Bat holstered the automatic, an effort that painfully jostled his damaged shoulder. He ignored the pain. There would be time to care for his injury later or not at all.

He reached in the unusual belt around his waist. It resembled a money belt crafted from black leather. However, the pouches carried items far more useful than currency. The Black Bat produced a small black globe roughly twice the size of a golf ball. He flicked a switch built into the surface of the ball, counted to three and tossed it at the truck. A cloud of thick, black smoke poured from the blackout bomb. It was a concoction developed by Tony Quinn some months ago. Not only did it provide instant darkness, a chemical in the smoke irritated the eyes, nose and throat of whoever breathed in the fumes. It wasn't lethal, but it would take the fight out of a man.

From another pouch on his belt, the Black Bat retrieved a compact breathing device that fit over his nose and mouth, and a thin pair of goggles to protect his eyes.

He waded into the smoke.

Though his vision was superior to that of normal men, even the Black Bat couldn't see through black smoke. He trusted his sensitive hearing to lead him to his prey.

The three men were coughing, and swearing in German. He grabbed the thug closet to him and silenced the man with one blow of a gloved fist. The German fellow dropped like a stone.

By pure chance another one of the gang backed into the Black Bat. Before Quinn could react, the German blindly landed a powerful blow on his injured shoulder.

Quinn's vision exploded into white comet trails of pain. His head swam and his knees buckled. The Black Bat rolled onto the parking lot, curling his body to protect his shoulder. As he struck, he kicked out his legs and swept the gunman to the ground. The man's head smashed onto the surface of the parking lot with a loud thump.

The Black Bat staggered to his feet, even as he heard the running steps of his remaining adversary. The man was trying to find a way out of the smoke. The Black Bat heard a shot and the sound of a falling body.

He walked through the smoke until it thinned out enough for him to see Carol and Silk crouched over the body of a blond man, the same one who had been ready to shoot the lock off the door.

The man was barely out of his teen years. Tears ran down his cheeks, an effect of the stinging chemicals in the black smoke and, perhaps, the bleeding hole in his side.

The Black Bat tore the goggles and air filter from his face. Ignoring the screaming pain in his shoulder, he knelt next to the fallen man.

"Where is your leader," he said in German.

The wounded man coughed. He locked eyes with the Black Bat. His features softened and he said, "You are but a man."

"Yes," the Black Bat said. "We'll get help for you. Just tell me where I can find the man with the scar."

"V-von Kleist. He…he is nearby."

The Black Bat's fine hearing detected the sound of heavy footsteps approaching. The young soldier heard them, too.

"*Ungeheuer*," he said, just before he died.

Carol Baldwin screamed. The massive creature, larger than any man, was hurtling at them far faster than the Black Bat believed possible. It was dressed in the uniform of a Nazi officer. With lightning speed of his own, the Black Bat drew an automatic and fired. The monster staggered from the first few shots, before it straightened and continued toward them. The dark avenger emptied his clip into the creature, to no avail.

Bullets didn't stop the beast.

The Black Bat stepped in front of Carol, to shield her from the freakish brute. But, as the *ugeheuer* drew near, Silk Kirby jumped between the rampaging monstrosity and his employer. Silk possessed a strength that belied his slight frame. It didn't matter. The misshapen monster slapped Silk with the back of one hand and the smaller man went flying through the night.

The Black Bat didn't have time to worry about his aide. He raised his good arm and tied to position himself to get one swing at the thing's head.

Suddenly, with a roar that would have made a grizzly bear proud, Butch O'Leary hurtled from out of the shadows and collided with the beast. The giant of a man was dwarfed by the Nazi monster, yet he managed to knock the creature off its feet. Butch landed with his knees in the center of the brute's chest. He began to pummel the face of the monstrosity while swearing a thunderous stream of oaths. Butch, kept in reserve by the Black Bat for this very occasion, had seen what the ogre had done to Silk, and he aimed to get revenge.

The Black Bat used the delay to dig another weapon from his belt. It was a glass vial filled with liquid of a deep purple color. It was what he and Silk had spent the night concocting in the hidden laboratory.

"Butch, roll away!"

But Butch couldn't move. The Nazi beast had clamped on to the Butch's wrists. The creature rose to its feet, dangling Butch in front of him like a puppet. In one swift move, the monster lifted Butch over its head, then slammed him to the ground with bone shattering force.

Butch moaned once, then was silent.

Behind the Black Bat, Carol Baldwin cried out.

"*Ungeheuer!*" The Black Bat held the glass vial in the air. The purple liquid sloshed about.

The monster seemed surprised to hear its name spoken by someone other than its master. It paused for a second, head cocked to one side like a dog listening to the sound of distant thunder.

Then the beast growled. It charged toward the Black Bat and Carol.

The Black Bat threw the vial. It stuck the pavement a few feet in front of the monster and shattered. A purple mist swirled upwards to envelop the creature.

The Nazi brute continued on for a few more steps, until it was less than a foot from the Black Bat.

It fell forward until its wide misshapen face struck the parking lot.

The Black Bat turned to Carol. "Run." he said. "I had to make the gas strong enough to drop this thing. It can kill most anyone else."

"But Butch…" Carol said.

"Go!" Without waiting to see if Carol obeyed, the Black Bat held his breath and ran to Butch's side. The body of his loyal aide was sprawled in a way that indicated severe injury, but the Black Bat had no time to be cautious. If he hesitated, Butch would be dead for certain. He knelt, grabbed Butch's wrists and, with his good arm, dragged the large man as far from the gas as he could. Fifty feet away, he collapsed, praying that he had made it to safety. He drew in a large breath. Butch was motionless beside him.

In the distance, several sirens were coming closer to this spot.

He heard a scream, a voice as familiar as his own heart.

Carol.

He heard the slam of a car door and the rev of an engine. With a squeal of tires, the car pulled away.

It had to be the man with the scar, the one called von Kleist. He had Carol.

The Black Bat staggered to his feet. He had to get to the car and follow after her.

He glanced down at the unconscious form of Butch O'Leary, a man who would gladly lay down his life for the Black Bat and his cause. Butch's body was shattered and was possibly near death.

The police sirens drew closer.

The Black Bat heard a moan.

On the other side of the downed monster, Silk Kirby was slowly standing up.

The Black Bat rushed to his side. The small man appeared to be in one piece.

"I'm okay. Just got the breath knocked out of me." When he saw Butch, Silk swore and raced to the fallen giant.

"We have to get him to a hospital," the Black Bat said.

"Wait," Silk said, still shaking the cobwebs from his head. "Where's Carol?"

"Later."

"And what about that thing?" Silk said, pointing to the Nazi monster.

Just then, the creature began to stir, shaking its head and trying to push up from the pavement.

The powerful gas, the Black Bat's best hope against the monster, had only stunned it for a few minutes.

The black-clad warrior felt the felt twinge of despair as it tried to settle in his mind. He pushed it away with a mighty effort. He couldn't give in to it, not while his friends and colleagues depended on him. Not while lives were at stake.

"Can you drive?" he asked Silk.

"I think so," his aide answered, though he still appeared woozy from the monster's attack. "Yes sir, I can."

The police sirens were only a few blocks away. Carol was a hostage, but if the Black Bat didn't take immediate action, Butch O'Leary might not survive.

"Help me get Butch to the car," he said. Together, the Black Bat and Silk carried the big man to the Black Bat's powerful sedan, aware of Butch's shallow breaths and his skin's sallow pallor.

Silk got the car moving, just ahead of the arrival of the cops. He took the quickest, most efficient route to a nearby hospital, racing at break-neck speed. Silk and Butch were closer than brothers, and the Black Bat knew that one would happily give his life for the other. He just hoped that wasn't the case tonight.

As they approached the emergency entrance to the hospital, Silk said, "Sir, what happened to Carol?"

The Black Bat gave him the details, through teeth clenched in anger.

The Black Bat removed his mask, revealing the scarred features of Tony Quinn. He pulled a trench coat on over his uniform and a low-brimmed hat to shade his face. He couldn't deliver Butch to the hospital as the Black Bat. Instead, he would claim he found the big man battered by the side of the road, then depart before any questions could be asked.

Silk didn't speak. The Black Bat knew his aide shared his own thoughts.

They would get medical treatment for Butch O'Leary, then they would find Carol.

He had a good idea where to start.

Chapter Six
QUESTIONS AND ANSWERS

Vic Castellini sat in the quiet bullpen area of the radio station as he waited for the phone to ring. He frequently wiped his wet palms on his trouser legs. He had done his part, as instructed. He had prepared the messages according to the instructions given to him by von Kleist. Now he awaited his final payment, which he would receive as soon as the night's activity had been successfully completed, money that he desperately needed.

But Castellini was nervous. The Cavendish fool had almost wrecked everything with his feeble blackmail attempt. Castellini was forced to reveal the problem to von Kleist, who dealt with the matter in a way promptly and efficiently. Catellini could never have handled a violent situation himself, so, in a way, he was happy to turn the situation over to someone who had no such reservations.

Now, though, he worried that his weakness and inability to handle Cavendish had affected his agreement with the Nazi ringleader.

Castellini was so tightly wound he jumped when the telephone on his desk rang.

He scooped up the receiver with a damp hand. "Hello?"

"Castellini?" The voice was whispered, without a discernible accent, just like a radio announcer.

"Yes?"

"A mutual friend sent me."

"Who?"

"Are you really going to make me say his name over the telephone?"

"I'm afraid so," Castellini said.

"Von Kleist."

A cold knot of tension in Castellini's gut dissolved away. "You have my money?"

"Uh-huh," the voice whispered.

"Where are you?"

"Down the block. We need to meet."

"I get off at midnight," Castellini said.

"That won't work. We're leaving immediately."

"Then the job went well?"

The voice on the phone did not reply.

"Okay," Castellini said. "Meet me downstairs. I'll unlock the door."

The man on the other end of the phone hung up. Castellini loathed dealing with von Kleist and his ilk. If he'd had a choice in the matter, he would have run the other way. But it would all be over soon. Castellini would get his money and the Nazis would be gone.

He took the stairs to avoid any of his coworkers, even though there was only a skeleton staff this late at night. There were no big shows in the studios. In fact, other than the band remotes from that downtown club, WNWY didn't originate any programming of its own. Everything came from the network. That was another reason he was happy to get his payoff from von Kleist, since he had a feeling that the station wouldn't need a copywriter for much longer.

Castellini reached the small lobby of the building and stood by the double glass doors. There was no one in sight, but he'd learned that von Kleist preferred to operate under cover of darkness.

Castellini unlocked the door and shoved it open.

"Hello?" he called.

"Over here." The voice was so soft that Castellini couldn't be sure it was the same man who had been on the phone. A figure stood at the corner of the building, just out of the arc from the streetlamp. The silhouette was slight, a man who was even smaller than Castellini.

The copywriter took a step outside, holding the door open. In an exaggerated whisper, he said, "Do you have the money?"

The shadowy figure didn't respond.

Instead, a voice on the other side of Castellini said, "I have your payoff."

Castellini whirled in time to see the fist, encased in black leather crash into his face.

He fell back into the lobby, and was aware of the breath rushing from his lungs, before the light in the lobby wavered and went dark.

Castellini didn't know how much time had passed. He knew a cold breeze stirred across his face. He opened his eyes and witnessed a world gone mad.

Skyscrapers sprouted from the night sky. The headlights from automobiles soared in place of clouds.

And an apparition in black floated before him.

Vic Castellini bellowed in fear and twisted and writhed until he came to his senses. He was tied up and he was upside down. Castellini blinked. The cityscape came into focus. He was outside, perhaps even on the roof of the WNWY building. The air smelled like lightning. There was a rather large flagpole on the radio station roof, seldom used these days. He had a very good idea it was in use now.

And the man with the black mask was still there.

His face was entirely covered by a tight-fitting hood. Only his eyes could be seen. Castellini thought they burned with a terrible anger, anger directed at him.

When the masked man spoke, his voice was low and even. Yet each word felt to Castellini like the tip of a sharp blade jabbing into him.

"I'm going to ask you some questions. If you lie to me, I will know and your death will be very slow. Do you understand?"

Castellini nodded quite vigorously.

"Where is von Kleist?"

"I don't know."

The man in black nodded and Castellini fell down the side of the building. He screamed, until his descent was halted after ten feet or so. It seemed farther. He was slowly raised to his original position. The man must have an unseen accomplice on the roof to work the rope.

Now the masked man held a large automatic to Castellini's face. The opening in the end of the barrel – inches from Castellini's forehead – looked as big as the new Lincoln Tunnel.

"You're lucky, Castellini. Frank Cavendish didn't have a rope to keep him from falling." The masked man laughed. "I know I said I would kill you slowly, but I'm in a hurry."

Castellini started to cry.

"Don't," he blubbered. "Please don't kill me."

"Where is von Kleist?"

"I – I don't know for sure." The barrel of the big gun touched a spot between Castellini's eyes. "Wait! Let me finish! I don't know absolutely, but I think he's at the estate of a man named Graham Carter out on Long Island."

"Carter the banker? Why would he be there?"

"Carter loves this Hitler guy. Thinks he's the next great leader or something. He donates a ton of money to the Nazi party."

The gun moved a fraction of an inch away from the copywriter's head.

"How do you know this?" the masked man said.

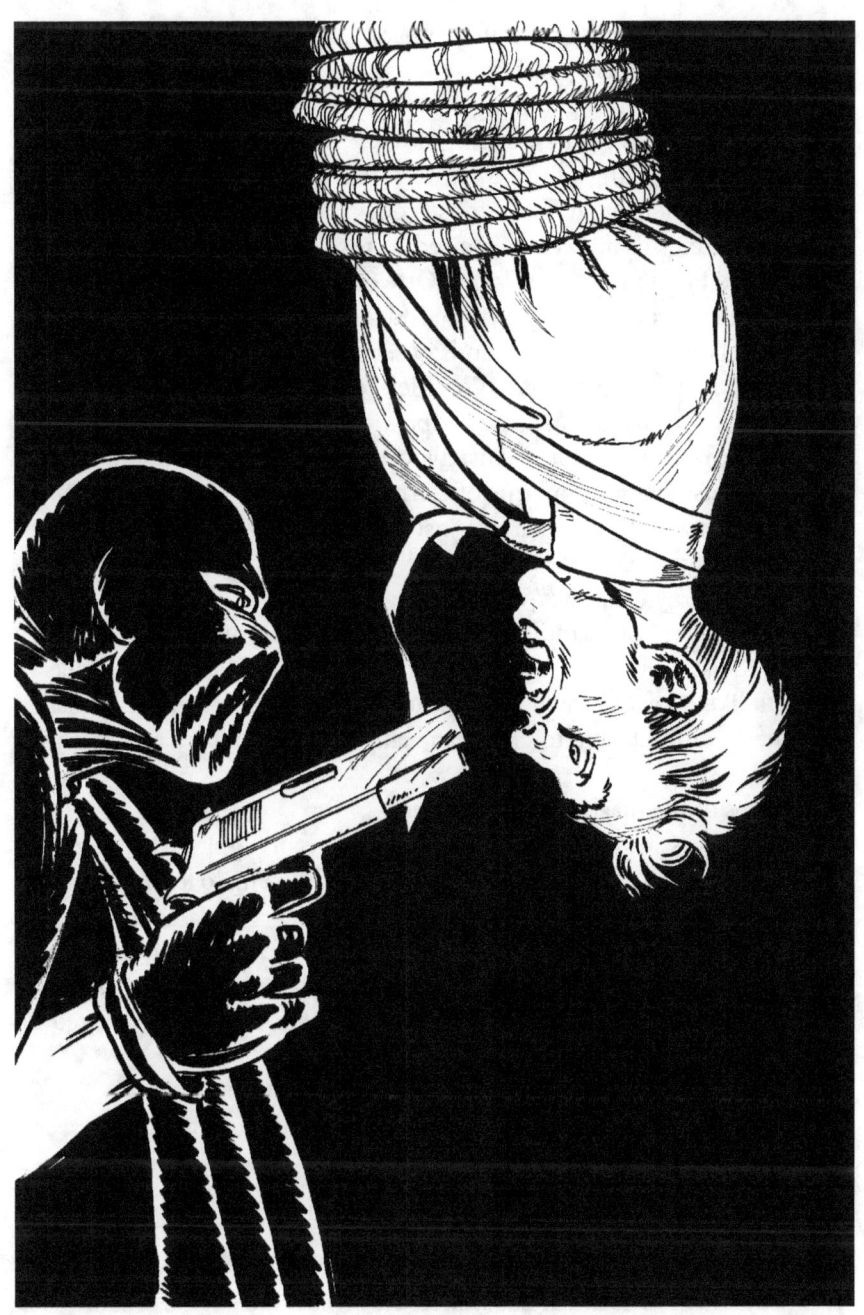

"If you lie to me, I will know and your death will be very slow."

"I did some digging after…after one of Carter's men approached me." Castellini squeezed his eyes shut.

"Was this about your gambling debts? Is that how you got in this mess?"

The copywriter's eyes flew open. "How…"

"I did some digging of my own. You owe money to a lot of unsavory people. Did Carter threaten to expose you?"

"No," Castellini said. "He promised to give me the cash to pay off my debts before I had my knees broken. Or worse."

"In return, you had to script coded messages into the evening commercials, revealing the locations of secret military laboratories."

"How did…yeah, that's right. Von Kleist would call me with the location and I'd work the address into the script with other code words that would tell his men where to meet. He used local guys, at first, to keep his profile low. But he also has a submarine of Germans in the river. The sub's how he got here. Every night they surface just enough to extend a radio aerial to check for a message."

"Do you know what they were looking for?"

"It's some kind of formula or treatment, I think. You've seen that huge guy von Kleist drags around with him? Well, von Kelist sometimes talks to the freak like it was his own kid. I heard him say that when they finished here, they would be able to create an army of *uber*-soldiers like that ugly monster."

The eyes of the masked man widened.

The gun was lowered out of Castellini's line of sight. A black-gloved hand was raised to the copywriter's face. "Are you going to let me go? I told you everything I know. I swear…"

The masked man snapped his fingers together. Castellini heard a faint pop. In a few seconds he became so relaxed he no longer cared that he was dangling upside down in front of a masked man. He was so relaxed he decided to take a nap.

Silk lowered the slumbering man to the rooftop.

"Sir, how do you think this Nazi creep found out about this secret whatsis anyway?"

"A leak in the military," the Black Bat said. "I'll have to let someone know about it as soon as this is over."

"Sir, do you think Carol is at this fella Carter's place?"

"I pray she is." The Black Bat stuffed the broken anesthetic capsule back into his equipment belt. Castellini would be out for at least an hour.

"Do you know where he lives?"

"Yes. I was there once. He donated to my first campaign for district attorney." The words tasted foul in the Black Bat's mouth. Rage blazed through his bloodstream like molten lava. Carol *had* to be alive. If she weren't...

No. That was a possibility too bleak for his consideration. If anything had happened to her, the Black Bat would ignite a crusade of vengeance that would make his enemies beg for Armageddon. Thank God Butch would heal from his broken bones and concussion. The Black Bat had gleaned that much from the emergency room physicians before he slipped away from the hospital.

"Shall we leave him here, sir?" Silk said.

The Black Bat looked at the unconscious traitor trussed up on the rooftop. It would be so easy to end him with a single shot. Or his bare hands.

He drew in a deep breath. He had to focus his wrath where it would do the most good.

"We'll call McGrath along the way," he said.

Silk started to the door that led downstairs. When he realized his employer hadn't flowed, he stopped. "Sir?"

The Black Bat knelt next to Castellini. He had the bat brand in his good hand.

"Silk," he said grimly, "give me your cigarette lighter."

Chapter Seven
BLACK VENGEANCE

Graham Carter's luxurious home sat on several acres of carefully cultivated grounds, surrounded by a tall fence of imported stone. The Black Bat and Silk had slipped across the fence near the back of the property an hour earlier, slowly making their way to the main house.

Now they crouched in a copse of trees thirty yards from the rear entrance to Carter's home. They had observed the grounds for some time and had detected no guards.

Despite the hour, several lights were on in the house, though they hadn't seen anyone through the windows.

The Black Bat checked the clips in his automatics, a slow process, thanks to his shoulder injury. Following that he removed another vial of the purple anesthetic from a padded compartment in his equipment belt, checked to make sure it was intact, then replaced it.

"Sir," Silk whispered. "I hate to bring this up, but if that monster's in there…"

"I know, Silk," the Black Bat replied in hushed tones. "We know this will slow him down for a minute. Maybe we can do something with that time."

"Do you know what this is all about?"

"I think so." The Black Bat was silent for a moment as he gathered his thoughts. Images of Carol, tortured or dead, continually played in his mind like a horrible motion picture. He forced away the disturbing visions. "I remember hearing talk a few years ago about research the Army was conducting into creating the perfect soldier, a man who would be extremely strong, tireless and impervious to pain. There were rumors that the scientist who was developing the treatment had been kidnapped by a foreign power, but that was the last I heard."

"Sir, do you think Germany could have been behind the kidnapping, and that this Nazi beast was produced by that process?"

"If so, the treatment was flawed."

"But that thing can stop bullets," Silk said with awe.

"True," the Black Bat replied. "But it's mindless, little more than a super-strong child. It's not the result the Army was hoping for."

"Imagine if they get that formula," Silk said. "An intelligent army of those creatures could conquer the world."

"It will never happen, Silk."

"Excuse me, sir, but how can you be certain?"

"Because," the Black Bat said, "this ends tonight."

He stood from concealment and ran toward the house, his black cape fluttering behind him like the ebony wings of his namesake. He carried automatics in both hands. To hell with his pain. He was going to bring matters to a conclusion now, no matter the cost.

The Black Bat reached the one of the back doors of the big house and kicked it open with the heel of his boot. The lock shattered and he was in the house. He didn't care about the noise, not now.

He and Silk found themselves in a laundry room. He pushed through a door, fully expecting to have to search the house. Instead, he found himself in a large room, filled with expensive furniture and several people.

He recognized Graham Carter. The wealthy banker sat in an overstuffed chair with a brandy snifter in his hand. His mouth opened in shock. Two younger men sat near him, probably bodyguards.

The Nazi monster, too large for any of the chairs, sat with its back against the wall.

But it was the center of the room that drew the Black Bat's rapt attention.

Carol Baldwin was tied down to a table. Perspiration dotted her forehead and her features were contorted in pain.

Herr von Kleist stood next to her, a hypodermic needle in his hand, suspended above Carol's neck.

For an instant everyone in the room was frozen in a strange tableau.

Until the Black Bat extended his left arm and shot von Kleist through the center of his forehead. The back of the Nazi's skull exploded into crimson vapor. He fell against the wall and slid to a sitting position, blood dripping like a scarlet halo on the wall above him.

The monster – the failed *uber*-soldier – leapt to its feet and howled, a cry of grief and fury.

At the same instant, Graham Carter's bodyguards pulled revolvers from their jackets. The Black Bat started to call for Silk, but the bark of Kirby's own weapon told him his aide had seen the threat. The two men crumpled to the floor.

The Black Bat took a step toward Carol, who struggled against her bonds. Before he could reach her, the misshapen beast slammed into him with a tortured roar.

The Black Bat's guns were knocked from his hands. He had a spilt second to react before the *uber*-soldier crushed him against the floor. As he fell, the masked avenger drew his knees to his chest between his body and the creature. Grasping the collar of the monster's parody of a uniform, the Black Bat tugged, while pushing up with his legs. The creature's own momentum carried him past the Black Bat and sent the beast sliding over the floor.

The Black Bat jumped to his feet. His guns were too far away.

Silk's weapon coughed again and Graham Carter grabbed his neck, a small revolver falling from the banker's hand.

The Nazi beast had also climbed to his feet. It shook its head, confused by the Black Bat's Jiu-jitsu trick.

"Silk," the masked man shouted, "Free Carol and get her out of here."

Silk rushed to obey.

The Black Bat reached into his equipment belt for the vial of purple liquid.

"Tony! Look out!" Carol screamed.

The beast rushed the Black Bat, just as the vial of gas hit the floor.

The purple cloud bloomed to life, as before, but the monster's flight carried it through the cloud. It tackled the Black Bat and the pair slid across the floor, far from the gas cloud's effect.

The creature grabbed the Black Bat's head in two gargantuan hands. Those hands began to squeeze, and the masked man's skull erupted in white-hot agony. He remembered the crushed skull of Frank Cavendish and that gave a boost of adrenaline to his struggle, but it was futile. The brute was too strong.

A great roaring filled the Black Bat's ears, still he was able to hear the sound of smashing glass, followed by a *whoosh*. The monster howled and released the masked avenger.

Brightly colored flashes danced in the Black Bat's vision. No, it was flames, covering the back of the Nazi beast. Carol had thrown an oil lamp against the creature and Silk had used his lighter to set it ablaze.

Now the deformed *uber*-soldier advanced on the pair. The flames on its back were already burning out and the creature seemed undamaged.

The Black Bat had to draw it away from Silk and Carol. He saw his guns only a few feet away. He stood, ignoring the pain in his shoulder, and recovered his weapons.

He fired two shots. Both struck the monster in the head, barely causing the beast to flinch.

The man-monster roared its outrage. It spun and lumbered toward the Black Bat.

For the masked man, everything in the room faded away, save for the beast and himself. Carol's screams and Silk's shouts were a distant buzzing. He stood his ground and watched the monster approach, calculating his last chance for survival. The treatment the Nazis had used to transform a man into this freak of nature had made the *uber*-soldier nearly invulnerable, with hardened skin that could deflect bullets and survive fire.

But the Black Bat believed everything had one weakness. He was gambling everything on his hope that he had discovered the monster's Achilles Heel.

His timing had to be perfect.

The monster grabbed for him. The Black Bat ducked under the beast's arms. As the creature stepped back to see where the masked man had gone, the Black Bat stood up and pressed the barrels of his automatics against the *uber*-soldier's eyes.

He squeezed the triggers.

The powerful handguns sent their deadly loads through the gelatinous material of the monster's eyes and shredded the brain of the behemoth.

The beast of the Third Reich was dead before it collapsed on the floor.

The Black Bat backed up until he found a chair. He sat down hard, the two guns still in his hands.

He closed his eyes for only a second. When he opened them, Carol and Silk were standing over him, looking concerned.

Carol leaned forward and kissed him. He pulled her against his neck and hugged her tightly. "He tried to make me talk, Tony, to tell him about you. But I wouldn't."

"I know," the Black Bat said. He held her tighter.

Silk, gentleman that he was, looked away.

Finally, the masked man stood. He holstered his weapons and surveyed the room and its dead occupants.

"Will you be needing the brand, sir?" Silk said.

"Yes, but I'll be quick about it."

"Make sure you are, Tony," Carol said. "Because our next stop is the hospital."

"Butch is in good hands," the Black Bat said.

"I'm not talking about Butch," the feisty young woman said. "You're going to see someone about that shoulder."

Silk chuckled. When he saw the look on his employer's face he swiftly handed his cigarette lighter to Carol and left to fetch the sedan.

The End

Mark Justice lives with his wife Norma Kay and their cats in Kentucky, where he hosts a morning radio program. In his rare free time he writes fiction. He also hosts the podcast Pod of Horror and edits the Story Station children's fiction site at http://www.viatouch.com/. You can read his blog "Department of Justice" at: http://markjustice.blogspot.com/

Claws of the Crimson Commissar

A Black Bat Adventure

by
Frank Schildiner

Prologue:

The most dangerous men in the Soviet Union sat around a long rectangular table, a battered piece of furniture that was supposedly moved in this room by order of Lenin himself. It was a hideous item, but sturdy and provided just enough room for the assembly.

They were summoned to this location by the terrifying Party Leader himself, a man they all feared openly, especially during this time of show trials and mass executions. The men represented the many facets of the Soviet State, military, intelligence and the party, all were feared by their underlings and the masses. Yet they huddled in this room like a pack of naughty schoolboys waiting for punishment from the principal.

The Party Leader himself was not present, he never appeared at meetings of this sort. The men were here to learn of his latest plan, not to voice their assent or disagreement. They could be here to learn of a new production cycle or that several present would be the next victims of the purges. That was a power the Party Leader held over them all.

Instead, standing at the foot of the battered table, was one of the Party Leader's functionaries, a colorless, humorless man with absolutely no imagination or desire for power of his own. Standing medium height, he had wispy blonde hair, pale skin and dark eyes that seemed unfocused and disinterested. He gave his name as Yegor and even his voice possessed no tones or inclinations.

"We will begin," Yegor intoned, behaving as if the silent room needed to be brought to attention. All had been watching him with a feral fear you could sense from outside the room.

"The Party Leader believes you are becoming lazy and weak, failing the revolution. The capitalist Americans flourish and yet you do nothing more than attempt to discover their unimportant secrets. You all swore that you would bring about the end of the West, yet none of you have attempted to destroy them in any way." Yegor stated, his voice flat and robotic. If they didn't know better, the men present would believe they were listening to a recording device rather than a human being.

The men in the room shifted uncomfortably, many wishing they could reach for a cigarette or a drink. But they knew any display of weakness would be observed and reported exactly to the Party Leader!

"In response to your failures, the Party Leader is turning the destruction of the Americans over to the most trusted man in the State besides himself… the Crimson Commissar." Yegor said, a slight hush entering his voice.

All of the men visibly started at the title pronounced before their unbelieving ears. The Crimson Commissar, the legendary unknown mastermind who even Lenin himself treated with complete respect! It was said that every move of the Soviet state was known to him and any man who did not meet his approval disappeared without a trace! Even the terrible Party Leader himself rarely invoked the name of the Crimson Commissar, and then in the hushed voice of one filled with fear!

The first one to enter was a giant, stooping to enter the room with his head nearly touching the ceiling. The man was built like a wrestler, with enormous hands that seemed capable of rending anyone present limb from limb. A heavy beard, so black it almost seemed blue in the hazy light, covered his face and made the man resemble a bear rather than a human.

The second walking into the room was shorter, rapier thin with an eaglelike nose and a thin pencil mustache. He was dressed in the outlawed uniform of one of the late Czar's Cossacks and a curved sword was strapped to his hip. His long face was aristocratic and morose as he stared unblinkingly at the leaders of the Soviet state.

The final one to enter was the most startling for many present. Though the Revolution promoted equality for all, women were not granted access to the centers of power such as this one. A woman walking into this room was a startling sight, especially one more beautiful than any had ever seen in their lives! Long red hair framed a heart shaped face and her military styled uniform was cut to accentuate her perfect figure. She glanced at the powerful men with large green eyes that made everyone think of emeralds.

"What is that…that…enemy of the state doing here?" the tiny intelligence commissar snarled, pointing at the man in the Cossack uniform. The tiny man's name was Nikolai Yehzov and he was the feared master of the secret police. An unpleasant, horrific man who barely stood five feet tall, he delighted in the arrest and execution of anyone he considered an enemy. His nickname was "the Poisonous Dwarf" and it was known that thousands, possibly even millions, were murdered by his word alone.

"He serves me," said a voice from the front of the room. All three of the Crimson Commissar's assistants were standing still and no other person was visible. The giant stepped forward and placed a grey metal box on the table. "All three of my aides have assisted me for many years. I, the Crimson Commissar place all my trust in them!"

The men slowly realized the voice was emerging from the box the giant placed on the table! The stared at the gun metal gray case as if it was alive, but slowly realized this must be some advanced form of radio. The Crimson Commissar seemed to guard his identity even from the most powerful men of the Soviet state!

"But an enemy of the state?" Yehzov spluttered, his horrific face twisting with conflicting emotions. He, like everyone present, was terrified of the legendary power of the Crimson Commissar. It was said by some, in hushed whispers, that Lenin and his inner circle were merely puppets of the unseen master of secrets…a possibility that frightened Yehzov. But he also hoped to find out the infamous Crimson Commissar's identity! Then he could destroy the man as he had so many others since becoming head of the secret police!

"You have no say here, little Nikolai the poisonous," The Crimson Commissar's voice purred, "You are about to begin your fall from power… you will die soon enough…and quite poorly I believe…" The Crimson Commissar's voice trailed off, but the irony in his voice was apparent. Yehzov, the terror of the Soviet State, a man who killed untold numbers of innocent people, was tossed aside like a stripling by the true master of secrets, the Crimson Commissar!

"Now comrades, I, the Crimson Commissar, will explain what I shall do to assist the state. The Americans are quite dependant on men who operate secretly and fight what they consider injustice. They reveal their identity to few, but remain separate from the state. These so-called heroic men are considered heroes by the populace, are a source of strength to the foolish underclass of the American people. What I shall do is destroy one of these so-called heroes completely, before the eyes of his people! This will weaken the morale of the American people, enabling the revolution to begin in the United States!" The Crimson Commissar stated, his voice rising over the metal communication box.

"Do you have a target in mind?" The Marshal of the Soviet Armies asked, knowing better than to conflict with the terrible man on the other end of this device.

"Yes…a man who has destroyed our operations several times. He is called…the Black Bat!"

Chapter 1:

The Metropolitan Opera of New York was the place to be seen in Manhattan on a cold, blustery night in mid-December. All the luminaries of the city were present, the Governor and Mayor being the least important figures in the eyes of those who paid attention to such happenings. The performance of Mozart's "*le nozze di Figaro*" was flawless and being broadcast over the radio for the world to hear.

Act Two was completed and a short intermission followed, with all present moving to the halls outside for a brief visit to the bar or the powder room. The real interest to most was examining those in attendance, their dress and seat placement in the opera company. Two individuals were of particular interest, a man, tall and impeccably dressed and his lovely platinum blonde companion.

"Is that Tony Quinn, the poor soul?" a well-fed matron whispered loudly to her equally bountiful sister. Her snow white hair was held back by a white gold tiara and several diamond bands covered her pudgy fingers. She remembered the sad story of the young, handsome District Attorney, blinded by a gangster who threw acid into his eyes!

"Yes, dear." The sister intoned, touching the blue diamond pendant that nestled across her ample bosom. "But dear sister, who is that rather lovely young lady on his arm?"

"Carol Baldwin, I don't know her family but no doubt they're quite well-bred. Mayflower I would be willing to wager." The large matron responded as she accepted a flute of champagne from her escort of the evening, an Astor relative of the finest breeding.

Tony Quinn overheard the entire exchange, despite being across the room, and fought to keep himself from smiling. His story was known to most of New York, a young DA fighting for justice, falling victim to a terrible attack by having acid thrown into his eyes. What few knew was the rest of the tale, the most important facts in the story of Tony Quinn!

After he was blinded by the acid, the beautiful Carol Baldwin granted Tony a chance at a new start. Donating the eyes of her recently murdered policeman father, Tony Quinn received a graft that gave him sight again! The returned ability to see enabled Tony Quinn to see in the dark and lead him to make a new start. Still wishing to fight for justice, he chose a new path in his battle against evil. Instead of returning to the DA's office, Tony

Quinn created the secret identity of a midnight avenger, a warrior against the monsters that wish to harm the innocent…the Black Bat!

To help his fight, Tony maintained the illusion of remaining blind, hiding the eye graft from the world. Carol remained at his side, joining his two aides in the struggle against evil, loyal hulking giant Butch O'Leary and former confidence man, the whipcord thin but clever Silk Kirby. Their assistance caused the destruction of many an evil-doer, making the fight of the Black Bat all the more powerful!

"What's got you ready to start laughing?" Carol Baldwin whispered, touching her platinum blonde hair without affectation. She was clearly the most beautiful woman in the room, dressed in a simple blue evening gown, she stood out among the many luminaries present at this social occasion.

"Just listening to people discuss us. Apparently I'm a poor soul and you're a Mayflower descendant." Tony replied with a slight smile crossing his lips.

Carol suppressed a giggle of laughter at the thought. The daughter of a small town police officer, she was disinterested in the limelight that many at this evening's events appeared to crave. Her main focus was the amazing man whose arm she held, a man who risked his life regularly to protect the innocent from harm. Though she was afraid of losing Tony Quinn, she would aid his other self, the Black Bat, through any danger or horror that came their way!

"I need to go powder my Mayflower descendant nose. I shan't be long," Carol stated, her voice in the false tones of society matron.

Tony smiled but did not look her way, knowing behaving as a sighted person would be remarked upon by anyone witnessing such an act. Carol did have a wonderfully clear-sighted view of the world, one that did make it easier to continue his fight as the Black Bat. That she was remarkably brave and willing to risk her life for others only added to her beauty in his eyes.

A commotion at the far end of the room caught Tony's attention, though he refrained from turning to investigate. Fortunately his time as a blind man enabled him to possess far more acute senses, enabling him to hear what they were discussing at a distance most would find impossible.

"…to what the Post is reporting this evening! Apparently a Communist Agent is in the area and challenging some vigilante known as the Black Bat to a battle," stated an excited male voice.

"It would do us well if they killed each other." Replied and older, grumpier sounding man. "Unionist, vigilantes…all deserve each other!"

Turning slightly, Tony focused on the group discussing the recent events. The cover of the paper held a reproduction of a letter sent by this Soviet monster to challenge the Black Bat!

An Open Letter to the Black Bat from the Crimson Commissar:

Black Bat, you are called the protector of your country's largest city, New York, yet can you truly fulfill your mission? I believe not, you are merely another costumed fool attempting to prop up a failing people. I, the Party Leader's representative, do hearby challenge you to a battle of body, mind and skill! Should you fail, those you hold nearest and dearest will die a terrible death! Yes, the Crimson Commissar knows your true identity! Await my further instructions and prepare to meet your end, Black Bat!

The Crimson Commissar

Tony fought to remain in control of his features, hoping the message was a mere bluff. Others claimed to know his identity in the past, but so far the Black Bat was only known to three people…the very people threatened in that terrible message in the newspaper.

Just as Tony was about to turn to collect Carol from the powder room, the return to seats chime sound. Jostled by several, he felt a hand press a piece of paper into his hand, but before he could discover the source, the crowd parted. The note was a quick scrawl that read, "Miss Baldwin is in my hands. Fear the future! The Crimson Commissar knows all!"

Crumpling the paper in his hands, Tony Quinn swore that the Crimson Commissar would fall by the guns of the Black Bat!

Chapter 2:

Carol Baldwin came to consciousness slowly, her head fuzzy and slow. Her mouth felt dry and cottony and she soon realized someone had drugged her as she was heading to the powder room! Her hands were tied tight and she could feel that her feet were also restrained.

A man stepped before her, his face thin with sharp features and a pencil mustache. His eyes were sad as he studied Carol and finally he spoke, his voice soft and lightly accented, "You are well, Miss Baldwin?"

"Why have you taken me against my will? Who are you people?" Carol snapped, her eyes flashing with uncontrolled fury and fright.

"Why do you talk to this skinny American woman? She is hostage, not guest!" A giant of a man boomed, stepping into her field of vision. He stared at her with undisguised contempt and loathing.

"Until the Crimson Commissar says otherwise, she is to be treated with decency." The thin man replied with a total lack of fear of the giant before him. Carol noticed a long sword strapped to the man's hip and recognized his accent as Russian.

"Bah!" The giant snarled and raised an enormous hand to strike Carol across the face. The thin man's hand moved like a blur to his sword, drawing it out and stepping into a dueling crouch. They were going to fight over her!

Suddenly there was the boom of pistol fire and the wooden floor between the two men exploded with splinters! They both leapt back and spun in the direction the bullet was fired, causing Carol to swivel her head to the right. A woman stood there, a beautiful woman with long red hair dressed in the uniform of a Soviet military officer! She was clutching a smoking pistol that she trained between the two men.

"Stop this right this minute!" Her voice was a low, sensual growl and she looked at the two men the way a mother would stare at a pair of naughty children. "What would the Crimson Commissar say of your actions?"

Both men looked abashed, stepping away from each other and the thin man sheathed his sword. "I will go look in on our other guests." He replied and quickly left the room.

"Go make yourself useful, Alexei. Bring our final guest in from the automobile and make sure he is secure." The woman said to the giant, "Go!"

The giant nodded slowly and left without a word, his shoulders hunched and his head hanging low. The beautiful woman stepped forward and holstered her pistol while checking Carol's bonds.

"Who are you people? Why have you kidnapped me?" Carol repeated, trying to keep herself from sounding hysterical.

"I am Kara Gogol, I am a Colonel of the Soviet Red Guard. The large man is Alexei Petkus though we simply call him Ursa the Bear. The gentleman with the sword is Count Felix Romanov, Maestro of the once famous Moscow Fencing Academy. We are the aides of a man known as the Crimson Commissar. He is here to destroy your beloved, Tony Quinn, the Black Bat." Kara replied stepping away and pulling up a nearby chair.

Carol frowned, surprised to have been told so much information. Since helping Tony Quinn's war against the evils of crime, she had been prisoner to many an evil man. None had ever revealed so much!

"I am Kara Gogol, I am a Colonel of the Soviet Red Guard."

Kara smiled, recognizing the concern in Carol's eyes, "You're wondering why I tell you so much? Not to brag, but because it does not matter. Your beloved Black Bat knows that is what we have planned. He will learn soon that he must fight against us alone, no assistance of any kind. Then when he falls, all will know none can defeat the Communist Revolution!"

Carol knew she should feel terrified for Tony, but all she could feel at the moment was anger. "You'll never defeat the Black Bat!"

Kara laughed, long, loud and contemptuously, "You are brave, but bravery will not help the Black Bat! You see we are not merely the aides of the Crimson Commissar, we are his chief executioners! None can stand before our might!"

Chapter 3:

Tony Quinn strode out of the opera house, his stride carefully controlled to prevent panic. He knew the Crimson Commissar had people watching him, therefore each step he took from now on would be watched. First was to get back to his car and consult Butch Leary. Butch, a hulking man who loved nothing more than a fight, was acting as his driver tonight on his date with Carol Baldwin

The roadster was parked a short block away and Tony took his time, using his cane and playing the part of a blind man. It was tempting to run the whole way, jump into the car and drive off into the night, but his mission as the Black Bat required greater self-control. This trained response was second nature to Tony Quinn, made easier by his miraculous ability to see perfectly in complete darkness. As he slowly moved through the night, Tony Quinn was more aware of his surroundings than anyone in the City.

Turning the corner he spotted his roadster immediately, the driver's seat–empty! The driver's side door was still open and there was no sign of a struggle in or around the car. Tony Quinn stood still and observed the area for clues, a skill he learned years ago. There was the faint smell of gunpowder in the area and some barely visible tire marks at the side of his roadster. He couldn't smell or spot any blood, so there was a chance Butch was not shot!

"Hey Mister!" a voice called out from across the street. "You named Quinn?"

Tony didn't turn, but caught sight of the source of the voice, a young boy, a sack of newspapers slung over his shoulder. There were always a few children who moved into the area of the opera house on a busy night.

They could sell all their papers fairly easily and make some money for their family. Tony hated child labor, seeing it as a failure of their society. But for now the Black Bat was unable to combat that evil!

"Yes, I'm named Quinn. How may I help you, young man?" Tony asked, playing the part perfectly. Anyone watching would think he was merely a lost blind man speaking to a young newspaper boy.

"I was told to give you this," The boy managed to say as he crossed the street and pressed an envelope against Tony's hand. The child was clearly embarrassed and wished to get away.

"Thank you," Tony replied, took the letter and handed the boy a dollar. That would represent more than a day's profit to the child, a small gesture overall but a well-intentioned one.

"Thanks Mister!" The boy nearly shouted and ran away before the blind man changed his mind. What did a blind man need with a letter anyway?

Tony, suspecting he was being watched, hailed a cab and gave his address. Fortunately the driver was a grumpy, older sort with no interest in conversation. Covering the ripping sound under a cough, Tony hunched over and read the brief note.

Do not doubt the Crimson Commissar, Black Bat! Your underling Kirby is in my grasp as well! Proceed to your home, you will be contacted soon!

The Crimson Commissar

Tony Quinn crumpled the paper and sat in the darkness. It was rare that he felt vulnerable against an enemy, but the Crimson Commissar came close to making him feel this weakness. But Tony Quinn didn't have the luxury of vulnerability, not while the Black Bat was needed to protect the city!

Chapter 4

"**C**an you bust these bonds, Butch?" Silk Kirby whispered to his compatriot who was chained up behind him. When he came to he'd found that he'd been chained back to back with Butch Leary, with Carol Baldwin on her own nearby. But if anything she was trussed up tighter than they were now!

"No," Butch grunted, his voice strained and a little shaky. "I've been trying since I woke up and nothing doing. These ropes ain't normal."

"No, they're not." Felix Romanov seemed to glide in the room, a glass of tea in hand. "Those ropes were constructed by a new substance created by one of the Crimson Commissar's scientists. He protects them from the State and they provide him with wonderful toys."

Carol shot Butch and Silk a quick look that prevented them from making any clever rejoinders that might annoy the Count. She wanted to find out some information and this man seemed the one most willing to provide it. Kara Gogol appeared entirely loyal to the Crimson Commissar and the one called The Bear was a monster!

"Count Ramanova, may I ask you a question?" Carol asked, trying to look hopeful.

"You just did, my dear Miss Baldwin. But you may ask more if you please call me Felix. My land was taken away when the Czar fell and I am little more than a beggar since that time." Felix Romanov replied with a sketch of a bow.

"Alright…Felix…why do you work for the Crimson Commissar? He would, if I'm understanding him right, represent everything you'd hate! I mean he's a Communist!" Carol tried not to shout at the man before her, but seemed unable to do so by the end of her thought.

Felix Romanov lit a terrible smelling cigar and nodded, "Oh he is that and more, Miss Baldwin. He is the man who ordered the deaths of my cousin the Czar and his family. He has destroyed millions to achieve his goals and even Lenin was said to fear and obey the Crimson Commissar."

"Then why, why would you help him? He seems to be a monster from what you say!" Carol wished she could shake the man as he stood before her, placidly smoking and drinking a glass of tea.

"What choice did I have, Miss Baldwin? Serve in a labor battalion until one of the Security Commissars decided to have me shot? Flee to the West and become a beggar like so many of my countrymen? No, not for Felix Romanov. I was a Maestro of the Sword, a teacher to many and a duelist with honor. The Crimson Commissar is, as you say, a monster, but what man in power is not? The Czar was not an evil man, yet millions died because of his neglect. Lenin and the current Party Leader are more open in their evil and their underlings are far worse. But I do what I must to survive under the monsters. With the Czar I was untouchable because I was the Maestro of the Sword. The Crimson Commissar keeps me as his pet for just such a reason," Felix Romanov intoned, his voice solemn and sounding a little melancholy.

Carol Baldwin looked at the man with pity, seeing through the dashing façade he projected to the world. A sad man who's life was always under the control of men he did not respect. "I'm sorry, that sounds sad."

"An American writer once said, 'sadness is but a wall between two gardens'. I think he was correct. But there is an old Russian saying that follows that statement well…'only the living may feel sad.'" Felix stated, sipping his tea. "I live, so I am sad. But I am alive and retain my honor. It is all I have left."

With that, he gave her a bow and left. Butch Leary looked over at Carol, confusion written across his huge face. "What was that all about?"

"He's different from the other two that work for the Crimson Commissar. I wanted to know why he would serve so horrible a man. Now I know." Carol replied, a small smile across her face. She had an idea for a way to help the Black Bat defeat this terrible enemy!

Chapter 5:

Tony Quinn was surprised to find his home was exactly as he left it, not one thing out of place, not even the subtle bits of hair he placed on strategic door and window jambs to discover if someone entered. No, the Crimson Commissar appeared to have left his dwelling alone.

But there was always his sanctum, the secret base of the Black Bat! It was a distance from the house, hidden within a ruined and crumbling façade. Using a secret passage from his home to the sanctum, Tony pulled out a silver .45 automatic he kept hidden by in the passage. He doubted anyone was in the base, but it was never wise to walk into a potentially deadly location without a weapon!

Stepping into his base, Tony immediately knew something was wrong. The lights were on, the air felt unsettled, something was definitely wrong here. Pulling a switch near the door, he flooded the room in darkness, knowing any intruder would be blind where he, as the Black Bat, would see as easily as if it was full daylight.

Scanning the base slowly, Tony soon realized he was alone; the room was completely devoid of any life. The intruder must have left a very short time earlier. He could almost feel a retreating presence from this secret location. Leaving the lights off in case someone was trying to follow his movements, Tony searched the base to see if anything was stolen or damaged or worse yet, a bomb or some other dangerous surprise left behind!

But again, nothing was visible, nothing changed or moved about…or was it...? It was then that Tony spotted one small change in the base, an easily overlooked one in the search for sabotage or a bomb...the telephone receiver was moved! The intruder appeared to have lifted the receiver from its cradle, dialed a number or answered the telephone, and left. That was odd behavior to say the least!

Approaching the telephone, Tony prodded the receiver carefully with the barrel of his pistol. In past as the Black Bat he had encountered twisted geniuses, ones able to transform even the simplest item into a dangerous weapon of death!

"The telephone was not tampered with, Black Bat." A voice emerged from the receiver a moment later. The voice was a mere whisper, yet it carried clearly to Tony's ears. "I hear your breathing, so listen carefully because I will not repeat your instructions. I am the Crimson Commissar and I have captured your aides. Killing them or you would be child's play, but I have other plans in store for you! Are you listening, Black Bat?"

"Yes," Tony replied, hating that he was forced to be subject to the whims of the madman on the other end of this line!

"You're a controlled man, Black Bat. A quality few possess. Most would be cursing my name or crying and begging me for mercy by this time. You are to be admired, for the short time you have left!" A harsh, grating laugh emerged from the receiver, ending with a choking gasp.

"And you're a patient man, Black Bat. Good, I prefer to face an enemy I respect than a fool I will simply crush. Your instructions are simple...you will face the Claws of the Crimson Commissar. Lenin once told me the way to win the revolution was through Strength, Determination and Patience. My followers will face you in that manner, showing the world how simple it will be to destroy the West's greatest champion! First we will test your strength!"

"Where?" Tony asked, unwilling to give this madman more than a word at a time. People like the Crimson Commissar loved to twist your words and use them as weapons to throw you off balance.

There was a pause on the other end of the telephone, at least a full minute passed before the Crimson Commissar's voice intoned, "Washington Square Park in one hour. Prepare to meet the first of my claws!"

Tony listened to the grating laugh again before he reached out and hung up the telephone. He'd been tempted to shoot the instrument or yank the cord out of the wall, but a display of temper such as that would only benefit his enemies.

Instead Tony Quinn crossed the room and pulled off his jacket and tie. It was time for the Black Bat to emerge and destroy the evildoers who threatened Carol Baldwin, Silk Kirby and Butch Leary!

Chapter 6:

Washington Square Park was a beautiful small park in the heart of Greenwich Village, located in one of the most quaint areas of Manhattan. Surrounded by New York University and some of the nicest brownstones in the city, it was a popular spot for tourists and residents alike. A giant stone arch was situated at one entrance and monuments for George Washington and Italian revolutionary Garibaldi added to the uniqueness of the location.

The Black Bat wasn't interested in the lovely sights that made up this park tonight, not at all! A challenge had been thrown down by the infamous and monstrous Crimson Commissar and he was determined to rise to the challenge! His associates, all three of whom were far more than that to the Black Bat, were in danger and he had to triumph!

The park was surprisingly quiet and deserted, odd for Washington Square Park where people often gathered and debated late into the evening. But tonight the chess boards were abandoned; the common gathering areas were free of all life. The only sound was the gurgle of the fountain in the tiny park's center.

"This is not good," the Black Bat thought as he slid silently through the park's many shadows. Crouching behind the statue to Garibaldi, he was darkness come to life, impossible to see unless one was very perceptive or extremely lucky!

The Black Bat was in his standard action rig, black pants, jacket, gloves and boots with the symbol of a bat in flight on the belt buckle. His face and eyes were covered by a black cowl and a black cape further hid his features and gave the impression of a bat come to life! Tony Quinn created this impression intentionally, knowing that his costume would make it all the harder to discover his identity for both the criminals and the police!

Moving with the silence of his namesake, the Black Bat stepped out from behind the statue and began to move through the park. Staying in the shadows, he was nearly invisible to even the keenest of eyes. Since the horrible attack upon his eyes, Tony Quinn used the lessons of his brief period of blindness to learn to move with the silence of a night creature. This skill made the Black Bat a terror to all who committed evil in New York City.

Searching the park with the slow and careful eye of a detective examining a location for clues, the Black Bat discovered an empty park. Nobody was hidden behind the trees or benches, nor in any of the grassy areas that filled the park. He was about to leave, thinking this was a feint by the Crimson Commissar to unbalance him, when a sound filled his ears.

The sound was that of a man singing, the song an old Russian drinking song usually sung by older men from that country. The sound was distant, yet somehow very clear! The Black Bat moved slowly, but steadily towards the singing, sensing this was meant to lure him towards the Crimson Commissar's trap!

The singing grew louder as he approached the center of the park, but the location was still hard to determine. Crouching near the fountain at the tiny park's center, the Black Bat listened and tried vainly to discover the source. He was about to become angry when he realized this might be the intent of his opponent, make him angry and therefore the Black Bat would fight recklessly a short time later.

Calming his spirit, the Black Bat waited and did not move. The song ended a moment later and silence filled the park. The silence grew heavier by the moment, yet the Black Bat did not move from his hidden location. Finally a voice broke through the quiet, the same powerful one that sung the Russian drinking song a short time ago.

"I know you are out there, Black Bat. I cannot see you in the darkness, but I know you are there. You are warrior, like me! You would not fail to come to save your comrades," the voice intoned. The speaker had the heavy inflection of a native Russian speaker, and the powerful tones and volume only a large man could produce.

"You are cautious, Black Bat! This is wise of you! Look up to top of the stone arch, there you will see me!" the voice continued, amusement now evident in his statement.

As instructed, the Black Bat looked up to the top of the Washington Arch, a huge marble arch standing over seventy feet high! He knew it was built by the infamous womanizing architect Sanford White, a man whose sex-scandals out-lived most of the amazing structures he designed over the years. As Tony Quinn he'd learned long ago that notoriety often lasted longer than one's good work.

But now as the Black Bat he looked up and was astonished by the sight of a man standing on the top of the arch. The man, even from this distance, was easily the largest human being he'd ever seen in his life! Despite himself, the Black Bat tensed for a moment, but quickly brought himself under control.

"Come up and we will begin! I promise you safe conduct, Black Bat!" The giant intoned, crossing his enormous arms across his chest.

The Black Bat weighed his options. He could demand the giant come down to face him, but that might also risk the lives of Carol, Butch and Silk! But to go up there was guaranteed dangerous from the climb to the arrival at the top! The Black Bat would be helpless during the climb and even more so when he arrived on the top of the arch!

But the needs of his friends out-weighed the danger! Therefore a moment later the Black Bat crossed the park and began climbing the Washington Square Park Arch! Using the many indentations and designs built into the marble, he was able to scramble up with some ease. Still, the Black Bat was patient and careful, using the teachings he learned from a former circus aerialist.

"Having secure hands and feet and never hurrying, that's the way to climb and stay alive, kiddo!" The aerialist had yelled to him over and over throughout their lessons. "Climb in a rush and you'll fall in a faster one!"

That lesson taken to heart, the Black Bat took a full fifteen minutes climbing the arch. He could sense the giant's growing impatience, but continued to climb at the same careful pace. And finally he reached the top, his right hand grasping the edge of the structure. The climb was about to end safely.

Just then a hand the size of milk jug appeared and encircled the Black Bat's wrist! The fist was like a band of steel as it lifted the hero up in one quick motion! The Black Bat dangled helplessly in the air, held effortlessly by the largest man he'd ever seen in his life!

"Oh ho ho! I've caught a bat by its wing! I could drop you off the edge with no effort, my friend! A simple opening of my hand and you would fall to the ground and die badly!" The giant roared and laughed. He was at least seven feet tall with a barrel chest and slab-like muscles that looked like carved granite! His body was covered with thick black hair that resembled the pelt of an animal and his beard was thick and wooly. A pair of dark eyes lay nearly hidden in the hairy face seemed alight with pleasure.

"What say you to that, Black Bat? Shall I just drop you to the ground and end this quickly?" The giant laughed and gave the Black Bat a bone-jarring shake. "I think I will do that!"

Chapter 7:

"**A**re you well, Miss Baldwin?" Kara Gogol asked from across the room. She had a gun trained on Carol and was watching as the Black Bat's closest companion ate a meal of potatoes and cabbage.

Carol looked angrily at the Russian woman, but soon realized the question was sincere. Kara Gogol did seem to be an odd woman, protective of the hostages yet completely willing to kill them for her unseen master. Carol Baldwin had met unusual characters in her time helping Tony Quinn's war against crime, but Kara was the first that might have been a friend under other circumstances.

"I'm fine, Kara. And please call me Carol. May I ask you a question?" Carol replied, hoping she was right in her reactions to Kara Gogol.

"Please do," Kara answered, leaning back against the wall but keeping her pistol trained on Carol.

"Why are you helping this Crimson Commissar? All I've heard about him is terrifying! They say he ordered the murders of the Czar's family… executed whole villages of people in the name of communism…his actions have been monstrous!" Carol explained, putting down her fork and focusing all her attention on the other woman.

Kara Gogol seemed to consider the question for several minutes before finally saying, "Women were not treated kindly by many during the Revolution. Although I was a believer in Comrade Lenin's dream, I questioned my lesser role in the State. I was the greatest shot in all of Russia, but was working as a filing clerk for the NKVD…the People's Commissariat for Internal Affairs. I expressed my disgust for the leadership and was to be arrested when the Crimson Commissar intervened. I was promoted from Corporal to Colonel and was finally allowed to use my skills for the good of the State!"

Carol was shocked by the answer and was momentarily at a loss for words, "You…you approve of his actions?"

Kara Gogol nodded quickly, "Indeed I do, Carol! And soon, so will you!"

Carol Baldwin recoiled at the words, but stopped moving as Kara raised her pistol again. She felt sick that she had ever thought well of this woman. Though Kara Gogol appeared decent and kind, she was secretly as terrible a person as the criminals the Black Bat fought against.

"I would never, NEVER, help someone like your murderous, monstrous master! The Crimson Commissar can't convince me his way of life is better than that of the United States!" Carol snapped, feeling very patriotic at that moment.

Kara Gogol merely chuckled and shook her beautiful red hair with open amusement, "You will have no choice, Carol. You see the Crimson Commissar invented a device for Comrade Lenin that enabled the revolution to defeat all of their enemies. Let me tell you about the Mass Mind Machine."

Chapter 8:

The giant Russian smiled and was about to release his hand, when the Black Bat raised a large black automatic. This weapon had brought about the deaths of many an evil-doer and was a familiar presence in his gloved hand.

"Let me go and we'll both die," the Black Bat whispered, training the weapon on his enemy's furry face.

The enormous Russian stared at the gun for a moment and suddenly roared with laughter! He pulled the Black Bat up and onto the arch and took several steps away once both feet were on solid marble. "Ho, ho, ho! You are very brave, Black Bat! I like that! You are a true warrior! Was a joke on my part, to see if you are brave or no!"

"Hysterical," the Black Bat said, not lowering his pistol. "Who are you and why are we up here?"

The giant continued to chuckle and finally replied, "Forgive me, I was being rude. I am Alexei Petkus, though my countrymen call me Ursa the Bear. I am a servant of the Crimson Commissar and we will fight to the death."

The Black Bat cocked his head, recognizing the name. He'd also heard that a person by that name was one of many executed in the terrible Show Trials that killed thousands of innocent people in the Soviet Union! "Alexei Petkus, the Greco-Roman wrestler and strong man? I heard you were executed in the purges. You never lost a fight if I remember right."

Alexei Petkus nodded, happy to be recognized, "Never had a point scored against me!" he said happily, "Yes, I was to be purged with many others. My father was friends with an enemy of the Party Leader. But the Crimson Commissar ordered my family to be pardoned in return for my loyalty. It is a different life, but my family is well!"

The Black Bat nodded, having expected that to be the story. Men like the Crimson Commissar wanted loyal servants that he could control, not comrades he could trust. The Black Bat had met victims like Alexei Petkus many times in the past and unfortunately they were often more dangerous than normal criminals. Because unlike regular criminals, these men and women often fought to save their friends or family!

"Understood. Now why are we fighting up here?" The Black Bat asked, using the time to regain his strength.

Alexei waved his arms wide, sweeping over the whole park in a gesture. "Where would be better? You could not run away and I cannot charge you like a bull. It will be strength, skill and luck in this contest! The rules are simple…you may not use any weapons but your skills. To do so would cause the death of your comrades. If you win, I have a note in my pocket from the Crimson Commissar. But you will not win, The Bear is never defeated by the Bat! You are ready?"

"Ready," The Black Bat replied, stepping into a fighting crouch.

"Then we begin, to the death!" Alexei Petkus roared and leapt forward seeking to kill the Black Bat instantly!

Chapter 9:

The Crimson Commissar adjusted the televisor set slightly, bringing the picture into greater focus. His giant was attacking the Black Bat and it would be a marvelous show! It didn't matter if Alexei the Bear won or not, the plan was too perfect to fail! The Black Bat would live or die at the hands of the Crimson Commissar's aides, it mattered not. Because even if the American hero defeated the giant, the gunwoman and the sword master, the Crimson Commissar had weapons that would destroy an army of Black Bats!

The Crimson Commissar smiled, only giving the fight a tiny bit of attention. Only Lenin knew the truth of the infamous hidden master of the Soviet State, and the legendary leader was long dead. They met before the foolish Romanoff rulers were about to push Russia into the Great War, a conflict the country was not prepared to fight. The Crimson Commissar was already wanted by the Russian Secret Police for being the true mastermind by the murder of the Czar's advisor, Gregori Rasputin.

Now Rasputin had been a true battle of wills! They had fought several times, with the evil monk coming out the winner in their conflicts. Then the Crimson Commissar perfected the Mass Mind Machine and was able to induce some Russian nobles to kill his hated enemy. Then and only then

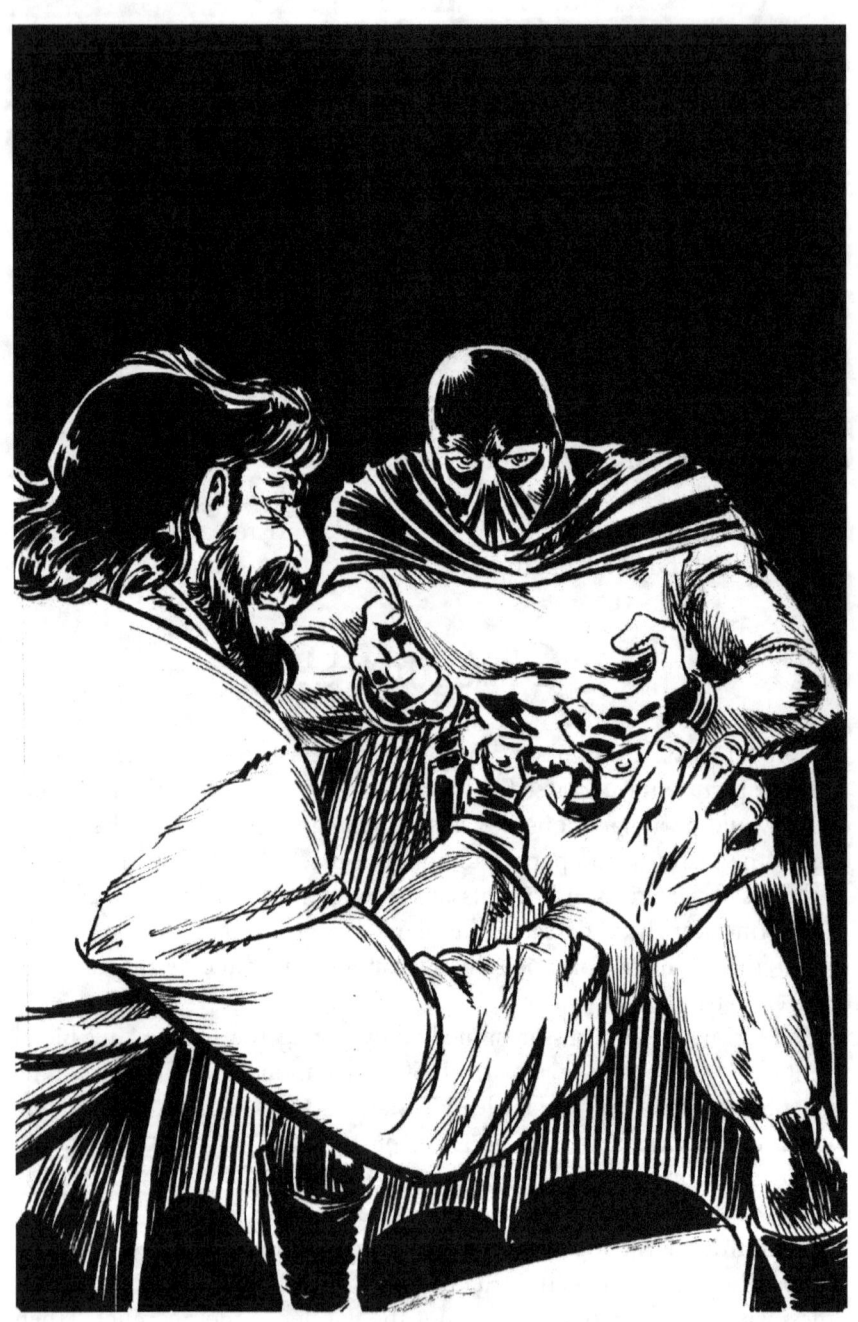

"Then we begin, to the death!" Alexei Petkus roared.

did Rasputin appear to have been destroyed…yet the Mad Monk may still be alive and waiting to enact some new evil plot!

The Mass Mind Machine made all of the plans of the Crimson Commissar come true in the end. Discovered by a scientist, long since executed at the Crimson Commissar's own hand, the device subjugated a person's will and made them a virtual slave for a short period of time. Repeated exposures led to paranoia and dangerously violent mood swings. Still, the device kept the Crimson Commissar as the virtual ruler of the Soviet State and soon the rest of the world!

Smiling slightly, the Crimson Commissar sat back to watch his giant battle the Black Bat. By destroying America's heroes, a loss of confidence would follow in the United States. Then, thanks to a series of sleeper agents placed in the highest reaches of power by Soviet Intelligence, the economy would fall into a depression worse than any witnessed in the world.

"Then the United States will be the second bastion of the Communist state!" the Crimson Commissar intoned, happily foreseeing the world united under one rule…that of the Crimson Commissar!

Chapter 10:

T he huge Russian known as Ursa the Bear was before the Black Bat in an instant, his enormous hands grabbing for the Black Bat's neck! This was his favorite tactic for winning, overwhelm your opponent with a quick and surprising attack and destroy them with maximum violence! Few men moved as fast as Alexei Petkus and fewer still could stand up to the sheer power of his assault!

But the Black Bat was far from the Bear's average opponent. Trained in the mixed fighting system known as Bartitsu by the style's founder as well as a form of fairground wrestling known as "catch wrestling," he knew that many fighters attempted to gain the advantage through a sudden attack when you weren't ready.

"The trick," his fairground wrestler teacher once said, "is to always imagine they're about to try and break your neck. A smart fighter knows the battle doesn't end until you're home and having your second beer."

Which is why when the Bear charged, the Black Bat waited until the giant was committed, stepped to side and kicked his enemy in the stomach! The shin struck the exposed gut hard and the Black Bat felt as if he had just hit a brick wall! Alexei Petkus was pure muscle, a man seemingly built of granite and iron! The Black Bat's kick usually knocked the wind out of his enemies, but this time it had no visible effect.

"Oh ho! So you know how to fight! This will be a pleasure!" Alexei the Bear roared as he spun towards the Black Bat. Raising his hands over his head, "Shall we test strength?"

"Why not?" The Black Bat replied, raising his hands. He knew what was coming next, Alexei was a dangerous fighter, but he had not proved to be a clever one!

Just as his hands raised to link with Alexei's, the giant raised his foot, intent on kicking the Black Bat off the arch! But the training of the hero took over and he parried the kick aside, slid to the side and kicked Alexei hard in his thigh! This was a move supposedly invented by the legendary gladiator Spartacus, a means of slowing your opponent down by destroying his legs!

Unfortunately Alexei Petkus aka Ursa the Bear was not your normal enemy! Taking the kick without a murmur or hint of pain, he stepped closer and backhanded the Black Bat with one arm the size of a tree! The Black Bat was thrown backwards off his feet, falling to the far end of the arch and causing him to nearly fly off the arch!

Alexei was on him in an instant, grabbing the fallen hero in one huge hand and lifting the Black Bat up in one enormous hand! With a roar the Bear slammed the Black Bat down on the top of the arch, lifted him up again and slammed the hero down a second time! The Black Bat felt as if he had been struck by a train…twice! The pain was enormous and Alexei was lifting him up again.

"You are not so strong, Black Bat! I could crush you with one hand, but what fun would that be for the Crimson Commissar and his warrior, Alexei the Bear? No, I will break you first!" Alexei roared and shook the Black Bat while spitting in his face with disgust.

That was all the time the Black Bat needed to respond! Stabbing out with his hands, he struck Alexei with spearhands in the most vulnerable spot in any human's body…the eyes! The hard fingertips struck home, lashing out and causing the giant wrestler to scream in shock and pain! Taking the opportunity, the Black Bat immediately clapped both hands against Alexei's ears, shattering the eardrums and destroying the giant's equilibrium!

With anyone else, the fight would be now over, but as already said, Alexei Petkus was no ordinary man. Despite being in agony and nearly blind, he lashed out with both arms, seeking the Black Bat. One gigantic arm struck the hero and Alexei pounced like a wounded bear! Grabbing the Black Bat with one enormous hand, Alexei threw an arm around the hero's neck and pulled into a vicious choke move! The air from the Black Bat's lungs rushed out of him in a loud "Whoosh!" and a second later was unable to breathe!

"You feel my arms around you, Black Bat? I will slowly bring you to the edge of death as many times as I like! Unless you beg me to kill you quickly...beg me and I will make the end fast, do not and I will prolong your agony!" Alexei hissed in the Black Bat's ear. His arms squeezed the Black Bat like a vice, causing the hero to gag and begin to black out.

Struggling in vain, the Black Bat did realize that Alexei the Bear did have a weakness that could be used now in this fight...his vanity! Alexei Petkus was so used to being the strongest and most unbeatable fighter on the planet, the idea that a person, any human on the planet, could injure him made Alexei Petkus insane with rage!

Using the international means of showing his surrender in a fight, the Black Bat tapped Alexei's arm three times. The giant visible relaxed and chuckled, his grip on the hero's neck relaxing. The Black Bat gulped some air and released a croaking sound as if he was trying to speak.

"Oh, ho ho, Alexei has injured your throat, Black Bat? Then whisper it to me and I will end your misery quickly!" Alexei laughed and leaned closer to the Black Bat's face.

At that moment the Black bat sprung into action! Firing a hard elbow into Alexei the Bear's nose, he hammered the giant's face three times, shattering the cartilage and breaking a cheekbone as well! Alexei screamed in shock and pain, his grip slackened for an instant! The Black Bat spun towards the giant, his other elbow striking the orbital bone on Alexei's face!

But the giant known as the Bear still had some fight left in him! Grabbing the Black Bat again, he lifted the hero over his head with a roar of triumph! He shook the Black Bat over his head several times and continued to snarl like a wounded animal in battle!

"Die, Black Bat! Now you die!" Alexei screamed and threw the hero off the Washington Square Park Arch!

But the Black Bat was ready for this attack! Despite the shaking, he grabbed his grapple gun and fired it the minute Alexei hurled him from the arch! The grapple hooked instantly onto a nearby tree and the Black Bat used the momentum of Alexei's throw to swing around the tree and back to the arch! His feet struck Alexei Petkus square in his wounded face and threw him back so hard, he fell off the far end of the structure!

The Russian giant hit the pavement with a dull thud, a pool of blood instantly forming around his giant body. Alexei Petkus, champion wrestler and killer for the infamous Crimson Commissar was dead and the Black Bat felt no pity as he looked down at his now deceased enemy.

A moment later the Black Bat was in his roadster, the slip of paper Alexei promised in hand. It was a simple message:

Central Park Great Lawn, bring your pistols. 1AM.

Chapter 11:

The Crimson Commissar chuckled as the Black Bat rushed off for his battle with Kara Gogol. That would be a short fight as Kara was the deadliest woman with a pistol in the world. But the Crimson Commissar would never underestimate the Black Bat! His adversary was certainly the most challenging he'd faced since Rasputin!

The next test would be quite interesting to watch, Kara Gogol's beauty caused her to be even more lethal! Men and women often were struck by her startlingly spectacular figure, face and bright red hair, causing them to be tense or slow when they were forced to battle against her. The Crimson Commissar enjoyed observing such conflicts. They demonstrated why mankind needed to remove all non-communist ideals from their lives!

Once again the Crimson Commissar sat back and dreamed of the day, the day when all mankind lived in the ideal communist state. There would be no war, because nobody would disobey the Crimson Commissar's commands. All worries would be lost and then mankind would look to the stars.

"Those living on the Moon, Mars and the other planets will join the Earth Communist League or they too will die!" The Crimson Commissar thought happily. The dream of the future was always the best means of relaxing before another battle was to begin!

Pressing a button, the Crimson Commissar said, "Has Count Romanov moved to his assigned location?"

"Yes, sir!" Silk Kirby replied with a quick salute to the camera. He was dressed in a Soviet military uniform with the insignia of a Corporal.

"Tell the other two, we are changing locations. Have the female bring my car around. You and the other one follow with my equipment in the truck." The Crimson Commissar ordered and watched as all three of the Black Bat's former aides scrambled to fulfill their duty. There was a true pleasure in watching the Mass Mind Machine convert enemies into fanatical allies.

Chapter 12:

The Great Lawn of Central Park was a site that always gave the Black Bat mixed emotions. During the height of the Great Depression this was the location of one of the largest "Hoovervilles", those shanty homes created by people unable to find work or a place to live. As Tony Quinn, young lawyer intent on helping the world, he'd come to this location many times, trying to relieve the suffering in some small way.

Now the Great Lawn was just that, a huge expanse of grass and trees meant to be beautiful and admired. The suffering formerly in this location was erased for most, but for Tony Quinn aka the Black Bat, this was a site filled with sad ghosts. He doubted the Crimson Commissar chose this location for that reason, but the emotions were there none-the-less.

The Black Bat pushed the sadness aside as he slinked silently through the park, heading for the next test from the Crimson Commissar. He assumed the battle would be one using guns and the expanse of grass was meant to prevent him from using his ability to hide in the shadows. It was a good plan on the part of the Crimson Commissar, taking away the Black Bat's greatest weapon against his enemies!

The Great Lawn was deserted, nobody visible on any of the expanse as far as the eye could see. For most people that expanse would look eerie, with patches of moonlight bathing stretches of lawn and making the grass look rather unearthly. The Black Bat stood in the darkness, everything clear as day to his eyes. Nobody appeared to be hiding, looking to shoot him from the shadows in ambush.

Deciding to take a chance, the Black Bat exhaled and stepped from his hiding spot and walked briskly to the center of the grassy expanse. He was completely exposed here. A child could sight and shoot him down at this moment! But the hero knew his enemy, the Crimson Commissar did not want him merely dead, he wanted to defeat the Black Bat and prove his evil philosophy was greater than any in the world!

Gathering his cape about his shoulders, the Black Bat waited and then caught a movement out of the corner of his eye. A woman walked in a leisurely pace down the path next to the Great Lawn, turning off the walking area and stepping onto the grass. This was definitely his opponent, though she was truly nothing like Alexei the Bear! Tall, shapely with flaming red hair and sensual lips, the woman approaching him resembled a Broadway actress! But that illusion was broken by the Soviet Union military uniform she was wearing with open pride not to mention the well-used pistol strapped to her hip!

"Black Bat I presume. I am Colonel Kara Gogol of the Soviet Red Guard, seconded to the Crimson Commissar. It is a pleasure to meet you! I presume, based on your presence here, you executed the foolish Alexei Petkus." Kara Gogol's voice was a throaty growl, meant to entice anyone listening to her. A seductress who used her beauty to place her enemies off-balance.

"Um...yes..." The Black Bat replied. While Kara Gogol was quite a beautiful woman, he had immediately caught a terrible aspect in her emerald eyes. She was death, a seductress like the mythological sirens who tempted men to their deaths!

Kara smiled widely, catching the stammer. The Black Bat would be easy to defeat, but she wished him even more off-balance. "You are strong and brave then, Black Bat. You must be strong to defeat Alexei the Bear! And I know you are brave because you waited for me here, open to all attack! I wish we did not have to fight...perhaps...no, I am being foolish!"

"I don't understand. What do you mean?" The Black Bat asked, his face creasing with concern.

Kara Gogol leaned closer, looking around as she moved up against the Black Bat. "If we pretend to shoot at each other and miss, you can rescue me from the Crimson Commissar! I will declare you dead and then we will meet and you can act as my protector, da?"

"I understand," The Black Bat replied in a whisper and gulped noisily. Speaking louder in case someone was listening, he asked, "How shall we conduct this duel, Miss...excuse me, Colonel Gogol?"

Kara Gogol moved back a few inches and gave the Black Bat a dazzling smile, "We will stand back to back and walk ten paces. We will then turn and count aloud to three at the same time. We will then draw and fire... acceptable, no?"

"It's acceptable," The Black Bat replied and studied her as he asked, "We shoot to miss?"

"Da, we shoot to miss." Kara agreed, nodding quickly and turned her back. "We begin, Black Bat!"

The Black Bat moved against Kara Gogol's back, her hair brushing against his cape. Touching the pistol at his side he stepped and began to count with each step, "1, 2, 3.." he said, hearing Kara's voice echoing his own.

At ten he turned and threw back his cape and placed a hand near his pistol. "Ready!" He called out, "One!"

"Two!" Kara yelled back, her hand poised above her well-used gun.

"Three!" both yelled and their hands flashed for their guns. One gun was a heartbeat faster than the other and fired, a tongue of flame arcing out like a dragon in the darkness. A body fell to the ground, blood immediately staining the moonlit grass.

The Black Bat looked down at the body of Kara Gogol, pausing only to kick aside her gun. His eyes held no emotion or judgment; they merely looked down upon her and watched as she bled from a bullet hole in her chest.

"How…how…did you…know..?" Kara Gogol gasped, vainly struggling to get up or find her weapon.

"That you intended to shoot me all along? That your request was just a ploy to put me off-balance?" The Black Bat asked, his voice cold and harsh.

"Yes!" Kara gasped, trying again to rise but finding she had no strength.

"It was in your eyes, Kara Gogol, Colonel of the Red Guard. I could see death there, waiting for anyone who fell for your charms. You are an expert with a gun, but you know there is always someone faster in the world. Rather than lose, you use your charms to weaken your opponent's resolve. Then you gun them down without mercy. Correct?"

"Da…" Kara mumbled, her eyes closing, "The…note…Crimson Commissar…in my…pocket…"

"Thank you," The Black Bat said, reaching for Kara Gogol's jacket. But she never heard his response, Colonel Kara Gogol of the Red Guard, aide to the Crimson Commissar, was already dead.

The Black Bat unfolded the note, sighing aloud. He shook his head and read the words, "The Empire State Building 86th floor, one hour."

The Black Bat holstered his pistol and ran into the night. The Crimson Commissar had a strange sense of humor, sending him to fight at New York City's major landmarks!

Chapter 13:

The Crimson Commissar studied the televisor image of Kara Gogol's dying body before turning the device off. An unfortunate loss, Kara was totally loyal and exceptionally gifted with a gun. Had she killed the Black Bat, the Crimson Commissar had planned on promoting her two ranks to Major General and placing her in charge of security in the Kremlin.

"Poor Kara," The Crimson Commissar mused, switching on the third televisor. "You had potential for so much more…possibly the first female leader of the Communist Party! But you will be avenged! The Black Bat will die!"

Standing, the Crimson Commissar barked out a series of orders and began to pace. The Black Bat was a dangerous enemy, but he was about to meet the most dangerous of the Claws! Count Felix Romanov was a true artist with a blade, respected worldwide as a dueling master!

"And if you defeat my swordsman, Black Bat, you will die at my hand! All who oppose the Crimson Commissar die!" The Crimson Commissar screamed.

Chapter 14:

The 86th floor of the Empire State Building is one of the most famous spots in all of New York City. A huge 360 degree observation deck on the tallest building in the world, the location was a popular attraction since it opened less than a decade earlier. Marriage proposals were commonplace at all hours and the guards in the late hours of the morning were often only on the lookout for trouble like potential suicide attempts.

Therefore, a tall thin man in white carrying a large long case attracted no attention from the few employees present in the late hours of the evening. Felix Romanov sat calmly on a bench, unmoved by the twinkling lights of New York City. In truth he was unmoved by most scenery in this world. His life was always the sword, the study of the weapon, the training, teaching and most importantly, the dueling.

Glancing down at the sword-case by his side, Felix remembered the days of the Czar, his cousin, and their many attempts to involve him in politics. He had refused without hiding his contempt for the whole process, little games of little men. Ultimately, to Count Felix Romanov Maestro of the Moscow Fencing Academy, life came down to the point of the sword. The warrior with skill and control would win. The one with the weak spirit would fall and die gloriously at the hand of their better.

This hadn't changed when Felix was forced to work for the Crimson Commissar. He was not allowed to train men and women at the sword anymore, but all of his duels were real and to the death. Forty-four members of the Communist party had fallen by Felix Romanov's blade, including three sword champions of the Red Guard. Few proved a worthy adversary, but that was the way of the world. The old ways, such as life by the sword, were falling away in this new and modern world.

Felix pushed away the wave of sadness that always filled him when he thought of the future. He needed to be calm and focus. The Crimson Commissar's latest enemy would be arriving soon if he defeated Kara Gogol. Defeating her would be difficult, but not impossible for a resource-ful warrior such as the Black Bat.

"I know you," A voice intoned solemnly from the shadows near Felix. "Count Felix Romanov, Maestro of the Moscow Fencing School."

Felix slowly turned around, facing the Black Bat and impressed by the man's skills at stealthy movement. "Moscow Fencing Academy." He corrected, "How do you know me?"

"We met in Paris when I was young. You were present to defend your championship against Andre LeCarre. You defeated him without being touched once. My teacher declared you were the greatest swordsman that ever lived." The Black Bat explained stepping up to the older swordmaster. "I was surprised you were so young."

Felix Romanov clicked his heels and gave the Black Bat a small bow, "You do me honor, Black Bat. It will be a pleasure to cross swords with you now."

The Black Bat tilted his head to indicate his surprise, "No declaration that you will kill me? You are the master of the sword after all."

Felix Romanov threw back his head and roared with laughter, his whole taut body shaking with open mirth. There was no mockery in the amusement, but open and honest pleasure. "You thought I would be like Alexei the Bear and swagger about my skill? No, my friend in black, I do not behave that way. It would not be proper manners nor would it be true. To be a true warrior one must walk into every battle as if it is your last. I believe you will fall by my sword, but it is not assured."

The Black Bat chuckled and shook his head, "You're a unique man, Maestro Felix Romanov. Is there any way we can avoid this duel?"

Felix Romanov chuckled and shook his head, "I wish that were so, but challenge has been offered and accepted. To refuse would cause your associates to suffer and would violate my code of conduct. No, Black Bat, we will duel and if you win you will face the Crimson Commissar. You will find a file in my case should you win, it will aid you in this last struggle should you defeat me. But please understand this, when we fight, I will treat you as I do all opponents. And the battle will be to the death!"

"I understand," The Black Bat replied sadly, regretting his need to fight such an amazing human being as Count Felix Romanov. The Crimson

Commissar had much to answer for, his enslavement of an artiste of the sword being another of the terrible Communist's crimes!

Felix Romanov placed the long case on the bench he was sitting on and opened it with the infinite care of one handling their child. Within the box was a pair of matching sabers, their razor like edges glinting in the light. "These were made for me by hand by one of the last great sword makers in the world. They are sharp enough to slice a silk handkerchief out of the air. The tip is quite sharp as well in case you prefer to use a stabbing form of attack. Please examine both swords at your leisure, you will find they are exactly alike and quite exquisitely made."

The Black Bat picked up the two weapons and examined them carefully. They were heavier than sport fencing sabers and perfectly balanced in his hands. As the swordmaster said, they were identical, well made and incredibly dangerous to handle. The Black Bat suspected that if you dropped one of these blades, it would slice off your foot!

Handing one of the weapons over to Felix with a bow, the Black Bat removed his cape and stepped back several feet. Tossing his cape over another bench, he assumed a ready stance and saluted Felix Romanov in the traditional manner. The Black Bat held the salute, acknowledging his opponent as the superior in the traditional manner.

Felix Romanov was surprised by the salute, momentarily nonplussed, not having been acknowledged in that manner since before the fall of the Czar! But as a professional swordmaster, he regained his composure and returned the salute as he once did to his students and friendly opponents. "You do me honor, Black Bat. Thank you; it has been a long time." He whispered, his eyes watering slightly at the memory of better days.

"I'm honored to face you, Maestro. Even if it is a battle to the death." The Black Bat answered sadly.

Felix nodded his head and his face suddenly turned blank, the picture of calm readiness. "En Garde, Black Bat!" he cried and leapt forward, his blade flashing!

The Black Bat did not reply but raised his sword and blocked Felix's slash at his neck. The swordmaster's attack was lightning fast, a blur of steel that would bring instant death! The Black Bat's block stopped the attack and he immediately sliced at Felix's legs, which was blocked with a simple flick of the swordmaster's wrist.

"Well done, my young friend!" Felix cried, his face creasing briefly with a smile, "My last three opponents fell for that attack and the match ended immediately!"

"En Garde, Black Bat!"

"Always assume your opponent's opening attack will be their strongest, an act of surprise to shock you into wariness." The Black Bat recited, smiling briefly under his mask.

Felix nodded and pressed the attack, "I said that once I believe. I'm not sure at which venue."

The Black Bat nodded and backed up, all defense at the moment, "You did, after winning your third Olympic gold medal. I never forgot it."

Felix continued to press the attack, his saber flicking out like a serpent's tongue and forcing the Black Bat to only defend himself. After a few moments, the Russian swordmaster feinted and sliced across the Black Bat's stomach. A line of blood immediately appeared and the hero was surprised that the cut did not hurt.

Reading the surprise, Felix Romanov chuckled and replied to the unasked question, "Your body was shocked by the assault; it will be numb for a time. But soon it will ache badly. First blood to me!"

The Black Bat nodded in acknowledgement and blocked another slice to his leg. First Blood, under the old dueling rules was simply the first hit that scored blood. Second Blood was severe injury in which a person could not continue and Third Blood was a duel to the death! Most duels with swords were First Blood, so that only accident would cause death. But this battle was Third Blood, the most dangerous allowed under the old code of combat!

Seeing an opening, the Black Bat lunged towards Felix, seeking to stab him through the stomach. Just as the point of the blade was about to hit, the swordmaster smiled and stepped aside, allowing the weapon to pass by him and placing the Black Bat at a disadvantage! With a quick upward pivot of his hips and sword hand, Felix knocked the sword from the hero's hand and sent the weapon skittering across the stone floor of the observation deck. He placed his sword against the Black Bat's neck, but chuckled, withdrew it and stepped away.

"Go ahead, pick it up and we will resume." Feliix Romanov stated happily, waving towards the fallen blade.

"Why would you do that?" The Black Bat asked, walking unsteadily over to the saber and picking it up. "You'd won the fight!"

Felix shook his head and continued to chuckle, "You demonstrated respect and decency towards me earlier. I can do no less towards you in this duel, Black Bat! You are recovered? Good! We resume!"

With that statement, Felix Romanov leapt forward again, his sword slashing out fiercely but with uncanny control. The Black Bat was blocking for all his worth, but still a few nicks and cuts got through! The hero was forced back until he could move no further, the thick stone wall that separated the Empire State Building's observation deck from the open air!

Back against the wall, the Black Bat desperately attacked the Russian swordmaster, knowing he was out-classed. The man was just too good, his skill was just too great and it would take an act of desperation to win this duel!

Then the Black Bat had an idea! Slashing furiously and recklessly at Felix Romanov's face, he backed the swordmaster away a few inches. This was just what the hero needed and with a quick leap, he vaulted onto the top of the stone wall. Running backwards a few feet, the Black Bat bowed and stood waiting for his opponent's reaction.

"I could merely attack your legs and watch you fall, but that would be an unfortunate end to an enjoyable duel." Felix Romanov mused and with a bark of laughter, leapt up onto the wall.

The duel continued, but now the movements were tighter, more controlled and careful. Even the great swordmaster needed to be wary about his attacks, to overextend his slashes or lunges could result in a fall of eighty-six stories! This suited the Black Bat better, giving him a greater chance of surviving!

But a few moments later, the Black Bat realized the location was only making Felix Romanov more cautious and controlled! Yes, the hero could attack now, but the swordmaster was an expert at defense too! The Black Bat attacked with hard slashes, lunges and cuts, but Felix's sword always seemed to move just in time to stop the blow from landing!

Finally the inevitable happened, the Black Bat slashed at Felix's arm, only to have his sword struck from his grasp! The Russian swordmaster caught the fallen weapon in his free hand and shrugged elaborately.

"It has been an enjoyable battle, Black Bat. You were a worthy opponent and I will remember you fondly. Do not worry, I will make this fast." Felix Romanov intoned with obvious sadness. His shoulders slumped and he shook his head once, as if he was wishing to avoid the death blow he was about to deliver. But the swordmaster's face returned to the customary look of calm control and he stepped forward, a sword in each hand.

The Black Bat could read what Felix planned next! By swinging a sword from each side, the swordmaster would behead him with next to no effort! But the Black Bat had an idea, a risky one and his last chance. Slumping his shoulders down as if he was accepting his forthcoming death, the hero waited until the swords were close to each side of his neck.

Then with an explosive backward leap, the Black Bat bent his body backwards and threw his hands over his head! Grabbing the stone wall with both hands, the hero spun his body into the air and hit Felix Romanov with both extended legs! With a yell of shock and surprise, the Russian swordmaster pitched sideways off the observation deck of the tallest building on the planet.

Landing on his back, the Black Bat pushed himself to his feet and dove after the falling Russian swordmaster. Felix was cartwheeling in the air, grasping desperately for a ladder or means to stop his fall that wasn't there! The Black Bat, pointing himself like a dart, reached and grabbed the swordmaster. Pulling his grapple gun from his belt, the Black Bat fired it at the observation deck and held it tight.

A second later they stopped falling with a harsh jolt, the impact almost ripping the Black Bat's arm out of joint! Swinging towards the building, they crashed through an office's closed window and landed hard on the top of the desk of a working secretary!

"You…you…you…" the secretary spluttered, with shock. Her blonde hair was in disarray and she shrieked as the desk collapsed under the collective weight of the Black Bat and Count Felix Romanov.

"We are window washers, madam. You have our apologies." Felix Romanov stated with a bow as he helped the Black Bat to his feet. Tucking both swords under his arm, he added, "We will leave you now. Das vedanya!"

A moment later they were out of the office, the woman's screams muffled behind them. Felix Romanov studied the Black Bat for a moment and stated, "You saved my life, why?"

The Black Bat rubbed his arm painfully, "You won the duel, but I couldn't let you kill me. My friends are prisoners of the Crimson Commissar!"

"I understand. But why did you then risk your life to save me?" Felix asked, studying him closely. The swords were still in his hands, but he did not seem inclined to raise them and try to kill the hero again.

"I didn't want you to die, Maestro." The Black Bat replied, using Felix's swordmaster title. "Your death would mean a loss of a great body of knowledge to the world. As far as I know, you're one of the only true masters of the sword left in the world!"

Felix Romanov clicked his heels and bowed to the Black Bat, "You honor me, my friend. I will assist you in defeating the Crimson Commissar. No, do not object, you will require my aid. You see the Crimson Commissar has a terrible weapon he will use to destroy you…the Mass Mind Machine!"

"That doesn't sound good." The Black Bat mused, moving towards the elevators.

"Worse than you know! I will explain as we travel!" Felix replied, falling into step besides the hero.

"Where are we heading?" The Black Bat asked, heading for the observation deck to retrieve Felix's files and the Black Bat's cape!

"Where else, my friend? The symbol of liberty that guards your country! The Statue of Liberty!" Felix Romanov stated with amusement.

Chapter 15:

The Crimson Commissar laughed as the Black Bat appeared on the televisor screen. The foolish American hero attempted to save Felix Romanov from falling from the top of the ridiculous symbol of capitalism, the Empire State Building! Obviously he failed, but his bravery was interesting at least. The Crimson Commissar admired bravery, right up until the point that the brave person was killed.

The Crimson Commissar was brave. Anyone who took on the Czar and all the enemies to the Revolution had to be brave. But there was a mind behind the bravery, unlike the Black Bat and his like. One of the Crimson Commissar's greatest weapons was using the bravery of others against them. On the rare occasions an enemy defeated the three Claws, they were usually injured, exhausted and feeling the anguish most feel from killing another human being. Then they would either die or be beaten down by the hand of the Crimson Commissar!

Pushing a button, the Crimson Commissar chuckled and began the latest set of orders, "Set the explosive charges throughout the statue. When the Black Bat has been executed, we will leave his body within the rubble of this symbol of a weak culture. This will weaken the American resolve and our comrades can begin the next Communist Revolution!"

"We obey, Crimson Commissar!" Silk, Butch and Carol replied and began to unpack the demolition charges.

The Crimson Commissar watched his three minions work, knowing they would die at the hands of the Black Bat. And that would kill the American hero emotionally, causing the Black Bat to fall in battle when they finally met!

"The United States is doomed," The Crimson Commissar intoned and began to laugh.

Chapter 16:

Bedloe Island was the location of Statue of Liberty, though everyone called it Liberty Island. Located in between New York and New Jersey, the island was all but uninhabited before the assembly of the great statue. The statue towered above the island, majestic and beautiful, a sight that never failed to overwhelm people no matter how jaded.

Traveling to the island was easy enough, the Black Bat had a fast boat ready at all times for emergencies such as this one. A small quick one originally used as a Coast Guard cutter, the boat was one of the many tools the Black Bat used in his war against the evils of crime. It was a temptation to take a faster means such as his autogyro, but the time spent traveling could be used resting and preparing for the battle against the Crimson Commissar.

"Remember, the Crimson Commissar always has a means of placing you in a position of weakness. That is why the monster has ruled my country for so many years. Or should I say, my former country?" Felix Romanov asked, sadness filling his voice.

"It's still where you're from, Maestro. And maybe one day we can bring back freedom!" the Black Bat replied, hoping there would come a day when the communists were no longer able to try and take over the world.

"Too much for me, my friend. I dislike politics and merely love the country I lived in for its beauty. But mostly I live for the sword which has no place in this modern world I'm afraid." Felix explained, checking his swords again.

The Black Bat chuckled and shook his head, "More probably you'll be the most in demand teacher in the country. We'll discuss this when we're back in the city. Right now we need to keep our eyes on the job before us, the Crimson Commissar."

They tied off the boat and stepped out on the pier, the footsteps the only sound other than the lapping of the waves against the boat. The statue loomed up above them, magnificent and beautiful and standing atop a brick base that made it look even larger. Felix Romanov stared up at the Statue and smiled.

"Magnificent, no? I must visit her if we defeat the Crimson Commissar." Felix Romanov stated, and fell into step beside the Black Bat.

"Agreed, I'll..." The Black Bat began when he was suddenly tackled from the side! Silk Kirby, dressed in a Soviet military uniform held onto the Black Bat and was reaching for the hero's throat.

"I'll kill you! The Crimson Commissar orders you dead!" Silk Kirby screamed as he reached for the Black Bat's throat and began to choke the life from the hero. The Black Bat had his gun in hand, but he couldn't shoot his close friend and aide.

Suddenly Carol leapt on the Black Bat's fallen form grabbing the hand holding the gun and fighting to pull it free. She too was dressed in a Soviet military uniform and was screaming at the top of her lungs.

"Killyou-Killyou-Killyou-Killyou-Killyou-Killyou-Killyou-Killyou-Killyou!!!" Carol shrieked while pulling at the gun. The Black Bat could shoot her, but this was Carol Baldwin and he could never hurt her!

Suddenly two swords flashed across his vision and both attackers fell away. The Black Bat struggled to his feet, seeing Felix Romanov holding Butch Leary at bay with his flashing blades.

"Do not worry, my friend! I hit them with the flat of the blade, they will be bruised but fine. Go! Go and fight the Crimson Commissar! I will keep your friends busy."

The Black Bat was about to protest, but realized that the swordmaster was completely right. He could hold off Silk, Butch and Carol and allow the hero a chance to take on the evil Soviet mastermind.

"Don't hurt them!" The Black Bat called out and dashed for the statue's entry.

The Black Bat walked into the base of the statue a moment later, his gun in hand, his eyes seeking out every corner for his enemy. The large chamber in the statue's base was empty, a huge room cleared recently based on the dragging marks all along the floor. The Black Bat could not see any evidence of a trap, but with the Crimson Commissar, one could never be too careful.

"I see you, Black Bat!" A voice said from all around the chamber. "Are you sad, Black Bat? Sad that your friends were reduced to my servants by the Mass Mind Machine? Sad that you were forced to kill them?" The voice asked, laughing with open contempt in each word.

The Black Bat realized that the Crimson Commissar had made a mistake. He hadn't set up a means of observing the attack of Silk, Carol and Butch. Whether it was ego, pride or some other reason, it was a flaw in the mastermind's plan. Felix Romanov had indicated that few ever faced the Crimson Commissar, in fact not even the three aides known as the Claws had a clue as to the Crimson Commissar's identity.

Assuming he was being watched, the Black Bat limped slowly up the staircase, his gun in hand. His every movement looked slow and tired as he headed up, each step appearing slow and weak. "Where are you?" He screamed, sounding exhausted and enraged.

"Come upstairs, Black Bat! I am in the most decadent portion of this disgusting statue, the crown! It will be quite a walk, so to make it easier I suggest you leave your gun behind. You see the whole statue is wired to explode!" The Crimson Commissar crowed, his voice coming from everywhere.

The Black Bat paused and sighed, unbuckling his gun belt and leaving in on the steps along with the gun in his hand. He placed a hand on the rail and slowly began climbing up the pedestal and into the winding staircase within the statue.

"Very good, Black Bat! You will be a pleasure to defeat! When you are dead I will blow up this symbol of American and leave your body within the ruins! You will be blamed and the United States will fall to the Communist Revolution!" The Crimson Commissar laughed mockingly as his enemy continued to climb the steps.

What felt like an hour later, the Black Bat arrived in the crown of the Statue of the Liberty. A desk was hastily assembled there and televisor screens were placed in different locations on the desk, showing the interior of the statue. Behind the desk was a large person, covered head to toe in a Soviet military uniform, the face covered by a steel mask, the head under the peaked cap of a Commissar. In the extended hand was a huge pistol, pointed directly at the Black Bat's head!

"It is good to finally meet you, Black Bat." The Crimson Commissar intoned. "You have been an excellent foe, but the battle ends now!"

Suddenly the pistol fired, but instead of a bullet a beam of light emerged and hit the Black Bat in both eyes! The Black Bat stiffened, his limbs freezing in place as the Crimson Commissar began to speak again.

"You are in my power, Black Bat! All your will belongs to the Crimson Commissar. Do you understand me?" The Crimson Commissar snarled.

"Yes, I understand," The Black Bat mumbled, his body still stiff and unmoving.

The Crimson Commissar stood, towering above the Black Bat and handed the hero a small pistol. "Take this gun and place it against your head."

The Black Bat moved stiffly and took the gun placed the barrel against the side of his head. He waited, unmoving, his eyes unblinking.

"Shoot yourself in the head, Black Bat. Serve your master, the Crimson Commissar!" the Crimson Commissar screamed, hands raised in the air in triumph.

"Yes, Crimson Commissar," the Black Bat replied softly and began to squeeze the trigger.

Suddenly the Black Bat turned the pistol and fired, hitting the Crimson Commissar in the chest. He fired again and again, emptying the pistol into his enemy's torso. There was a loud metallic sound accompanying each shot and the Crimson Commissar was hurled backwards into the desk, knocking over the televisors.

"How? How...?" The Crimson Commissar gasped, struggling to stand again.

The Black Bat tossed the empty gun aside and chuckled, "Count Felix Romanov told me after I saved his life. He told me the Mass Mind Machine operates by a light beam to the eyes followed by hypnotic suggestion. Therefore he told me the way to defeat the evil weapon was to close your eyes. The rest was just simple acting."

"You have not defeated the Crimson Commissar yet! I am still able to fight and destroy you!" the Crimson Commissar rose and extended the large hands that had just held the Mass Mind Machine. Five wicked claws extended from the fingers, each glinting in the darkness. With a scream, the Crimson Commissar ran forward, the claws slicing the air and aiming for the Black Bat!

Though the attack was nasty, the Black Bat was calm as he stepped aside and swept the legs from under the Crimson Commissar. The Soviet mastermind crashed to the ground with a metallic SMASH and moaned in pain. The Crimson Commissar scrambled up and ran for the Black Bat again, claws swinging clumsily.

The American hero ducked the claws and struck with a hard kick, hearing the metal sound and feeling the steel covering. The Black Bat's boot protected his foot from breaking and he was happy to see the Crimson Commissar hurled back again.

"For a mastermind who declared I was going to be destroyed, you're not much of a fighter. Never took lessons I'm guessing. Got by making everyone fight for you. But now you have to survive on your own, which you can't do. But I won't kill you. Instead I think I'll hand you over to the Soviets. I'm sure they'll just love to put you on trial along with all the innocent people they're killing in their show trials." The Black Bat snarled, approaching the Crimson Commissar, fists raised.

"That will not be necessary, Black Bat," the Crimson Commissar replied and stepped over to the opening in the crown. With a quick pull, the Soviet mastermind was through the opening and vanished from sight without a sound.

It took some time to discover the body of the Crimson Commissar, the corpse was between the feet of the Statue and was twisted in an unnatural position. The Black Bat and Felix Romanov stared down at the now-dead mastermind behind the Soviet Union, face still covered by the crimson mask. Felix Romanov tore aside the face covering and shook his head.

"I am sorry, my friend. I do not recognize this person." Felix stated, dropping the mask to the ground.

The Black Bat stared at the dead face and shrugged, "Doesn't matter anymore. Let's go get Carol, Silk and Butch and let the military know the statue is wired to explode. Someone will recognize him I imagine."

The dead eyes of Yegor, the Party Leader's colorless assistant stared back at the Black Bat. The Crimson Commissar was dead, one less evil in the world...

The End

Finding a Good Enemy
by Frank Schildiner

Finding a good enemy is the biggest trick to writing a fun pulp yarn for me. If the villain is blah, the story goes nowhere. We all know it. Heck, most actors prefer to play the bad guy because they have more style! Think about it, what would Star Wars be without Darth Vader?! Life in fun fiction is all about an amazing hero fighting a terrible villain!

With this in mind, I took a little time to think of a proper enemy for the legendary Black Bat. Avoiding all similarities to a villains list owned by another Bat hero, I turned my attention to the period itself. Gangsters were too like…well, you know who's enemies, and as much as I love using Nazis as the bad guys, I'd just written a tale for Airship27 with Ratzis. Where to go?

Then I remembered a documentary I watched one night on cable during an insomnia attack about 20 years ago. This documentary told the true story of the first leaders of the Soviet Union's Secret Police that we know as the KGB but actually had a lot of names. The men in question were terrible–monstrous on a level equally as horrific as the Nazis but mostly unknown in the West.

The character that stuck out of a sea of evil men was Nikolai Yezhov, the head of the secret police and mastermind behind the show trials and purges that caused the deaths of at least a million people in a two year period. Yezhov, an evil, unpleasant man known as the "Poisonous Dwarf" for both his personality and five foot height, was a sadist who delighted in the pain of others and rose to great power. He was executed at Stalin's orders in the end and died after being brutally tortured by his former underlings. Oh and Stalin ordered all traces of his former underling scrubbed away. If you search for Yezhov online you'll find a picture of him walking with Stalin and then the same picture with the Poison Dwarf "miraculously" removed.

From there it was easy to assemble a villain! Take the worst characteristics of those horrible secret police leaders and the Crimson Commissar was born! The story was far easier from that moment on, the Crimson Commissar and his minions wrote themselves, so to speak.

The Crimson Commissar's underlings came straight from my brain, no clue how that process happens. If I could explain to you where most of my demented ideas come from, I'd probably never be able to write another book, ha! If you want to learn more about the mind of a writer, I'd suggest Stephen King's *ON WRITING*. The master of horror is far better than I am at attempting to explain the brain that churns out fictional fun!

As to the rest, the Black Bat's impressive fighting style, that comes from Shihan James Amorosi. Shihan is my martial arts instructor, mentor and one of the best men I've ever known. His lessons have changed my life for the better and I can't express what a pleasure it is to learn from such an accomplished individual.

The locations in the story are all, of course, very real. As a child in the NY/NJ area I was taken to each and instead of admiring their beauty, I'd be imagining pulp heroes fighting their enemies…yes, I've been this way my whole life…

In closing all I can say is that the Black Bat was truly a fun ride for me and I hope you felt the same way. I read many of his tales growing up, so this story, in a very real way, was a dream come true!

Frank Schildiner has been a pulp fan since a friend gave him a gift of Philip Jose Farmer's *TARZAN ALIVE*. Since that time he has published articles on Hellboy, the Frankenstein films, Dark Shadows and the television's Lovecraftian links. He is a contributor to the fictional series *TALES OF THE SHADOWMEN* and has been published in *Secret Agent X Volume 3*. Frank is currently working on a series of graphic novels with artist Jay Piscopo and works as a martial arts instructor at Amorosi's Mixed Martial Arts. He resides in New Jersey with his wife Gail who's his top supporter.

AFTERWORD

Where the Comics Came From

When I was a kid growing up, I discovered comics early and by the time I was entering my teen years I was hooked. I'd been reading mostly DC as Marvel wouldn't arrive until 1960. So I was obviously more familiar with DC's line up and, like all comic readers, was well aware of the Batman, that Dark Knight who, unlike his pal Superman, had no super powers but relied on his own physical prowess and intelligence to bring down bad guys.

He was intently creepy, using his Bat totem to frighten criminals because we were told they were a superstitious and cowardly lot. With his cowl, ribbed black cape and utility belt, Bruce Wayne became the scourge of the underworld.

Then along came Marvel and suddenly we were being handed dozens of other new costumed heroes. One of these was Matt Murdoch, a young man accidentally blinded in childhood, but thanks to a dip in a radioactive spill, his sense of hearing becomes super amplified so that using this hyped up sonar, he becomes Daredevil; the Man Without Fear. Now how cool was that, a blind crime-fighter! Who would have ever thought?

Actually others had, long before Stan Lee put pen to paper. Or for that matter, there was another "bat" hero long before Bob Kane and Bill Finger delivered Batman. You see, prior to comics, there were the pulps and by no small coincidences those men who would grow up to write and draw those colored graphics were products of their reading of those bygone publications. In fact one particular pulp avenger displayed both the look and characteristics of Batman and Daredevil. He was known as the Black Bat.

He was the star of Black Book Detective which ran for 62 issues from July 1939 to the winter of 1953 and his writer was G.Wayman Jones. Anthony Quinn was a crusading district attorney sworn to destroy organized crime. During a trial, one of the hoods he is questioning suddenly hurls acid into his face, totally reminiscent of the famous scene where lawyer Harvey Dent is similarly attacked and as a result becomes Batman's twisted nemesis, Two-Face. Whereas poor Tony Quinn is left blinded and horribly scarred around the eyes. It looked like his crime-fighting days were over as he began to adjust to a life without sight.

Enter the beautiful Carol Baldwin, daughter of a county sheriff gunned down in the line of duty. Having heard of Tony's plight in the newspapers, she comes to him with the offer of donating her father's eyes so that his sight might be restored. He agrees and the doctors proceed to perform a radically new procedure and give him Sheriff Baldwin's eyes. When his bandages are removed days later, Tony's new eyes work perfectly. But then he discovers his new eyes also possess a unique ability to see in the dark. He can actually see in pitch blackness as if it were high noon.

Tony realizes immediately this strange new gift is an advantage he can put to good use and proceeds to create a new identity for himself, that of the avenging Black Bat. Taking Carol into his confidence, they allow the world to believe the operation was a failure and that Tony Quinn, defense attorney, is still blind. From that point on Tony Quinn begins his second crusade to eradicate the criminal element, only this time as the mysterious, black garbed avenger.

He wears a full hood that covers all of his face but his eyes, contrary to the way artist would portray him on the covers, a scalloped black cape, black boots, clothes and two holstered .45 automatics with which to bring hot-lead justice to those he would battle.

Along with Carol, who quickly became the love of his life, Tony Quinn was aided by two ex-criminals he had helped reform during his days as District Attorney. One was Silk Kirby, a sophisticated con artist who become his valet. The other, Butch O'Leary, is an ex-boxer now Tony's loyal bodyguard. Quinn went on to build a secret laboratory under his house and here he and his three allies plotted their campaign against the underworld.

Tony did have a recurring headache in his old friend, Captain McGrath, a detective on the police force. After the arrival of the Black Bat, McGrath began to suspect the vigilante and the lawyer were one and the same and although he admired and respected Quinn, he was forever trying to expose him. To that end, McGrath believed Tony's blindness was a sham and was always trying to make Tony give himself away.

Considering the many similarities from costumes to origin and extra human abilities, the Black Bat was clearly the template from which both Batman and Daredevil were later cast. This is nothing unusual or improper as younger writers and artists have always taken inspirations from the heroes that have gone before. The adventures of the Black Bat were glorious, classic pulp yarns and that they should inspire the heroes of the future is as it should be.

Meanwhile, this black clad warrior seems to have found a whole resurgence in the past few years. Several new Black Bat adventures in prose have been released and recently Moonstone Books has brought the character to comics, somehow completing an ironic circle of inspirations. And now Airship 27 Productions is pleased to add to that canon with four brand new Black Bat action tales. We've had a blast putting this volume together and it won't be our last. Thanks always for your support and drop us a line, we'd love to hear your thoughts on this book. As always, all Airship 27 Productions are available at a discount price out our on-line store (http://www.gopulp.info/). We invite you to stop by and take a look around. *Airship 27 Productions, pulp fiction for a new generation.*

Ron Fortier
4/20/2010
Somersworth, NH
(Airship27@comcast.net)
(www.Airship27.com)

Crusading Attorney Anthony Quinn believed his career was over when a criminal threw acid into his face blinding him. Months later, desperate to regain his sight, Quinn underwent a unique transplant operation which gave him the eyes of a slain lawman. Not only did the procedure work, but it also gave Quinn the ability to see in the dark. Using this fantastic gift, he created the Black Bat, a justice seeking vigilante able to battle those villains beyond the reach of the law. Aided by his team of loyal crime-fighters, Carol Baldwin, Silk Kerby and Butch O'Leary, the Black Bat is once again on the prowl, his target, the depraved and evil denizens of his beloved city.

New pulp writers, Aaron Smith, Joshua Reynolds, Jim Beard and Frank Byrns offer up a deadly quartet of fast pace action thrills. Stories that pit the Black Bat against super human Nazis monsters, corrupt politicians involved with Major League Baseball and even team him with another classic pulp legend, Jim Anthony the Super Detective.

Featuring a stunning cover by Ingrid Hardy and Rob Davis with interior illustrations by Andres Labrada, BLACK BAT MYSTERY Vol. Two is another great pulp collection from the high flying Airship 27 Productions you won't want to miss.

PULP FICTION FOR A NEW GENERATION!

www.ingramcontent.com/pod-product-compliance
Lightning Source LLC
Chambersburg PA
CBHW071239250626
47163CB00001B/242